Rhythm Man

A
RED DOOR
NOVEL

DYAN LAYNE

Human Authored™, Reg #: 3627550,
https://authorsguild.org/human

ISBN: 979-8-9923243-2-7
ASIN: B0DXJC1D3J

Cover photography: Michelle Lancaster, @lanefotograf
Cover model: David Bodas
Cover designer: Lori Jackson, Lori Jackson Design
Editor: Zee, The Blue Couch Edits
Formatting: Stacey Blake, Champagne Book Design

Playlist

Stream the full playlist on Spotify here

Or on YouTube here:

Hidden Citizens, Tim Halperin | *Hungry Like the Wolf*
The Killers | *Glamorous Indie Rock & Roll*
MISSIO | *Wolves*
Styx | *Too Much Time On My Hands*
Marcy's Playground | *No One's Boy*
Rival Sons | *Open My Eyes*
Shirley Ellis | *The Name Game*
Adam Jensen | *The Hunter*
The Hoosiers | *Run Rabbit Run*
Red | *Mystery of You*
The Black Keys | *Wild Child*
Alexisonfire | *Side Walk When She Walks*
Matthew Mayfield | *The Wolf in Your Darkest Room*
Sleep Token | *Sugar*
Stone Temple Pilots | *Sex Type Thing*

Portishead | *Glory Box*
Falling In Reverse | *Sexy Drug*
Sam Tinnesz, Silverberg | *Wolves*
Ghost | *Hunter's Moon*
Twiztid | *Hungry Like the Wolf*
Klergy, Mindy Jones | *Hide and Seek*
Caspian Wulf | *Ecstasy*
Chase Holfelder | *Animal*
††† (Crosses) | *Bitches Brew*
I Prevail | *Bow Down*
Dorothy | *Dark Nights*
Nation Haven | *Bad Things*
Us in Motion | *Wolves*
Foo Fighters | *Shame*
Highly Suspect | *Wolf*
Motionless In White | *Werewolf*
Eels | *Fresh Blood*
Sleep Token | *Provider*
Imminence | *Heaven in Hiding*
Saving Abel | *Addicted*
Black Veil Brides | *Bleeders*
Steven Rodriguez | *Like You Mean It*
Florence + The Machine | *Howl*
Grayscale Season | *Pillow Grin*
Sleep Token | *Granite*
5 Seconds of Summer | *Teeth*
Meatloaf | *You Took The Words Right Out Of My Mouth*
Falling In Reverse, Marilyn Manson | *God Is A Weapon*
Thornhill | *Obsession*
Red | *Take It All Away*
Tommee Profitt, Stanaj | *Ave Maria*
Jaymes Young | *Infinity*

Author's Note

This book contains subject matter that may be sensitive or triggering to some readers and is intended for mature audiences.

While it isn't necessary to have read the previous books in the series, as this is a standalone novel featuring a unique romance, it is _highly_ recommended. *Red Door* is a series of interconnected standalone novels. All of the main characters reappear and some storylines connect from book to book. For the best experience, the series should be read in order.

If you are following the series, **Rhythm Man** overlaps with some events in **Drummer Boy**.

This one's for you, Jackie!

Because you're the only person I know who twerks to
"Hotel California",

and because I love ya!

P.S. Hold out for a wolf. He can see you better, hear you better,
and eat you better.

Run
Run fast
Start this chase
It will not last

Amongst the trees
Upon the ground
I'll take my prey
Without a sound

—Hydrus

Rhythm Man

Prologue

Matt, eighteen years old

He sat on a stool in a dank corner behind a dusty velvet drape, tuning his guitar. The neighborhood dive bar reeked of stale Pabst Blue Ribbon, tobacco smoke, well-worn leather, and sweat. He didn't mind it, though. Mickey's Place had been a fixture around here since the '40s. Matt remembered coming here with his grandpa and watching him shoot a game of pool with his buddies when he was only seven.

Mickey was still alive back then. He gave him a Shirley Temple, a pail of peanuts in the shells, and told him to be a good boy. Tightening his D string, Matt smiled at the memory. The old man had to have been in his seventies. His grandson ran the place now, but not much else had changed.

"Beer, mate?" Taylor handed him an ice-cold bottle.

He slammed it back with a nod of thanks, the lager bathing his parched throat. Maybe it was the stifling city air on a muggy

August night, or maybe it was just nerves, but he could've chugged down another right then. Mickey had booked local acts to play for the house on Friday and Saturday nights, and tonight was Venery's first official gig.

First one that counted, anyway.

They were getting paid.

Five hundred bucks for the weekend—that was a hundred for each of them.

Not too shabby.

Bo stood off to the side with Sloan, braiding beads into their lead singer's shaggy long mane so he'd look more like a younger version of the late Layne Staley than he already did. Normally, he'd think that was weird, but considering they covered a lot of AIC songs, it was all right, he supposed.

"Want me to do yours next, man?" Bo asked, grinning like the goofball he was when he caught Matt looking.

"Nah, I'm good, bro." Matt ran his fingers through wavy locks that went a few inches past his shoulders. Luckily for him, he'd been blessed with amazing hair. "I'll take another beer, though."

Never mind, none of them were old enough to legally drink it, but they were playing, and that was one of the perks. Drinks were on the house. They had a cooler here at their disposal.

The drummer passed him a beer. "Where's Kit? He should be here by now."

"What're you asking me for?" Tipping the bottle back, he took a swig. "He's got a wife. I'm not his fucking keeper."

Except for Taylor—who moved to the neighborhood from London when he was fourteen—the boys who formed the band, Venery, had known each other all of their lives. Living in the same three-flat apartment building, Matthew McCready and Christopher King, who'd gone by Kit for as long as he could remember, had always been inseparable. More like brothers than best friends. Where one went, the other followed.

Until Courtney got her hooks into him, that is.

The bitch had to have a magic pussy or something because after Kit took her to their eighth-grade dance, he didn't so much as look at another girl. The fool drove up to Wisconsin and married her the day after their high school graduation. He told them he was going to do it. They all warned him not to. Did the idiot listen?

Nope.

Now, they were living in the basement of his parents' bungalow while Kit bagged groceries at the Jewel to pay the bills. Courtney controlled every little thing he did. It was fucked up if you asked him, not that anyone did.

Was Matt bitter about it? Yeah, to be honest. Once fun to be around, his quirky best friend had been withdrawn ever since. Something was going on in the basement, but he wasn't confiding in him—or anyone else, either.

And speaking of the annoying little bitch, here she comes.

A walking advertisement for Hollister or Abercrombie & Fitch, Courtney was pretty enough, but then she had to be, considering she worked part-time selling their stupid T-shirts at the Michigan Avenue store downtown. Still, Matt would never understand what Kit saw in her. She was a cheerleader. With his long blond hair, he looked like a surfer dude. Throughout high school, she acted as if Kit—hell, all of them—were far beneath her.

"So glad you could make it."

"Fuck off, Sloan." Kit flicked him off and pulled his bass from its case.

Her nose in the air, Miss High-and-Mighty took a seat at the bar.

Brendan, CJ, and Bo's sister, Allie, poked their heads behind the curtain.

"You look so good, Bo-Bo." Face like an angel. Straight blond hair down to his waist. No shirt on. Tight pants. Bo *was* a pretty boy. "All of you do. Break a leg. Isn't that what you say for good luck?"

"Close enough." Brendan grabbed a couple of beers and slung his arm over her shoulder. "C'mon, I got us a table in front."

Matt waved them off and turned around to see Kit frantically fingering the frets on his bass. "You okay, man?"

"Yeah."

"If something's wrong, you can talk to me, ya know."

"I know," Kit said, gnawing on his lip. "Everything's fine."

But it wasn't.

Nine months later, he showed up, crying on his porch.

Cunt.

She told him he'd never amount to anything.

It took another eight years, but Kit proved her wrong.

Venery released their first studio album and made it big.

Shaking his head at the stoplight, Matt gazed at the building where Mickey's once was. Empty now, a "For Rent" sign was taped inside the grime-covered window. It was a boba tea shop for a while, but the place never took off. Gentrification hadn't spread this far east of Coventry Park when it was there. Now, the building looked rundown and out of place. Someone would have to throw a lot of money into rehabbing it to make it marketable again. He wondered if people still lived in the apartments above the storefront.

It wasn't often he came this way since the turnoff to Park Place was eight blocks west of here, but he missed his exit on the Kennedy. Some asswipe in a fucking Tesla wouldn't let him over.

The light turned green. The old building disappeared from his rearview mirror but not the memories.

Shit changes.

Back then, he couldn't get laid, no matter how hard he tried. And now? He didn't even have to. Chicks from fifteen to fifty threw themselves at him. Took all the fun out of it, though. He missed the hunt. The thrill of the chase. The only thing they wanted was bragging rights, anyway. To tell all their friends they got fucked by a rock star.

"Heh." Over that groupie shit, Matt patted his dick. "They can suck it, but they don't get to fuck it no more. Ain't that right?"

These days, he did most of his fucking at the Red Door. And

even that was getting old. At thirty-four, so was he. It was about time he found himself a nice girl to make babies with, wasn't it?

Taylor and Bo found one.

But that was a fluke.

Nice girls don't end up with rock stars.

Especially not someone like him.

One

Matt woke up feeling like utter shit.

Last night was one helluva night.

Chloe's twenty-fifth birthday *and* the Eros party at the Red Door—need he say more? It's not like he made fucking his bandmates or their girlfriends a habit, but Bo did ask him to. He couldn't blame it on the alcohol, either. Matt was only on his second drink when he followed them into that private alcove.

The truth? He wanted to.

The real question was, *why?*

Yes, Ava was a lovely girl, and yes, Matt was attracted to her. But she wasn't his. And while he fucked a dude now and then, he wasn't into Bo—or men in general—though he loved the guy. He couldn't explain it, but when Venery's drummer whispered the request in his ear, his dick got hard.

Bo didn't have to ask him twice.

Would he do it again? *Yeah, maybe.*

On the regular? *Hell, no.*

He understood that what Chloe, Jesse, and Taylor had together was a rare and beautiful thing, but it wasn't for him.

It could be that he was just ready to fuck when Bo asked if he'd play with him and Ava. And who better to play with than people you know and love, right?

Right.

So why did he feel like shit then?

Matt sat up in his bed, and while rubbing his eyes, he glanced around at the black furnishings, white walls, and the kitschy artwork he'd collected over the years. "Fucking Kit, that's why."

Not many understood how close all of them were and how much they all loved each other. Matt, his bandmates, and the Byrne cousins grew up together on the same block in this very neighborhood. It was no accident they turned Park Place into a family compound in the middle of the city because that was what they were. Family.

And there was no one in this world Matt cared about more dearly than Kit.

He didn't get it. They were at a sex club, for fuck's sake. Matt and Kit frequented the playpen downstairs, banged groupies, models, and starlets together. It wasn't like Bo didn't invite Kit to play with them when he walked in on their scene, so why did he look so butthurt to find them naked and covered in each other's cum?

Determined to understand it, Matt got out of bed. As soon as he showered and sufficiently caffeinated himself, he was going across the street to talk with Venery's bassist. At the very least, he owed Ava an apology. The girl did nothing wrong. As sweet as could be, she reached for Kit, and he rejected her. *Dick move, man.* Whatever was going on in that fucked up head of his, she didn't deserve that.

There wasn't nearly enough coffee circulating in his bloodstream for this. He opened the door of his three-level brownstone and stepped out into the cutting February air. *Fuck this shit.*

Matt spotted Bo and Emmy with their dog, so he went next door instead.

"Yo, Bo-Bo."

"Hey, man." He stopped on the sidewalk in front of his house. Emmy wiped her runny nose on her mitten, Chester dutifully positioning himself at her feet. "It feels colder than I thought it would. I need to get my ass back in the house. Wanna come in?"

"Sure, okay." Matt crouched on his haunches in front of Bo's little girl. "Is that all right with you?"

"Uh-huh." And her arms wound tightly around his neck.

"Hop on." He gestured to Emery to climb up on his back. "You're getting a piggyback ride."

She squealed all the way to the kitchen.

He set her down on the gleaming wood island. A clean freak, Bo's place was always immaculate. Matt looked on while the drummer unbundled his daughter, cleaned the snot running from her nose, and set her up with a cup of warm chocolate and *Frozen* on the big TV screen.

"That's a lucky little girl right there."

"Nah, man." Gazing across the room at his three-year-old mini-me, his lips turned up. "I'm the lucky one."

Truth.

"Coffee?"

"Yeah, I could use some." Maybe a third cup would do the trick.

"So, where were you going?" Bo asked, reaching into the cabinet for a mug. "I know it wasn't to see me unless you miss my dick already or something."

"Fuck you, man." He shook his head, chuckling, and climbed onto a stool. "You miss mine."

"It did feel rather nice." Bo shrugged, popping in a coffee pod to brew. He turned around and leaned back against the counter. "If Avie ever wanted to play again, I wouldn't say no."

"Why would she want to?"

And why did the thought of it make his dick hard?

"She enjoyed last night," he said and placed a cup of Sumatra roast in front of him. "It gets me off knowing she accepts that side of me, you know?"

"Yeah, I get that." Isn't that what everybody wants? To be loved for exactly who they are. "I'm happy for you, my dude. Ava's a special one."

"Thank you for making her feel so good." Bo set a cup for himself down next to his, and rubbing his ass, he winked. "And me, too. You know I love ya, man."

"Back at you." With a short nod, Matt raised the mug to his lips and glanced at Bo's cookie jar on the counter. *Life is short, eat the cookie. Ain't that the fucking truth?* Then, he turned to his bandmate and said, "I wouldn't make a habit of it, but if you two ever wanted to play again, I wouldn't say no, either. We had a good time."

"Yeah?"

That he could admit it surprised him. Hell, it even surprised Bo. Matt discovered he much preferred playing with people he cared about as opposed to random members at the Red Door. While there weren't expectations beyond having fun on anyone's part, it was more than just sex, and that made it feel even better.

He tugged on his friend's hair. "Yeah."

"Can I top?" Bo waggled his brows.

Matt nearly choked on his coffee. "Now, you're pushing it."

"Hard limit then, eh? I'd be gentle," he said with a straight face, then chortled. "Just fucking with ya, but don't knock it 'til you try it."

"Pass, thanks." Matt chewed on the corner of his lip. "I'm just glad Ava's good with last night, especially after that bullshit with Kit. I was going there to ream him out for it."

"Don't."

"Why not? What he did was really shitty."

"Kit didn't mean to hurt her feelings, Matt, and Avie knows it." Wetting his lips, Bo tipped his head. "I explained it to her."

"Explained what?"

"You know. He's never been the same since Courtney. She fucked him up good."

Yeah, he knew. "Still…"

"Not to mention, I think we freaked him out a little bit."

"How?" Matt asked, cocking his head.

"I'm pretty sure he knows what we did." Rocking on the stool, Bo glanced at his daughter, then lowered his voice to almost a whisper. "And in all the years we've known each other, toured in that tin can on wheels… partied together… we're the first ones to… you know."

"Fuck?"

"Yeah." He nodded, drinking his coffee.

"You and Tay never…?"

"Nah, man," Bo said, looking him right in the eye. "We shared plenty of chicks back in the day, but that's it."

Well, fuck me.

Venery lived up to their name. All of them were sexual deviants by mainstream standards, there weren't many experiences they hadn't shared, but come to think of it, Bo was right. He couldn't recall a time when the drummer and their lead guitarist so much as looked at each other, but then Taylor had loved Jesse for a long time now. Chloe sealed the deal. The three of them married, and two kids later, they were more in love than ever.

"It's been sixteen years, for fuck's sake. Kit needs to get over that cunt. He deserves to be happy."

Just like Taylor.

Just like Bo.

Hell, Sloan deserved some happiness, too. And maybe even him.

"I hate to hear any woman called that, but I've never met one who earned it like Courtney did. Oh, and we can't forget Salena." Bo wrinkled his nose with a shudder. "Does Kit ever talk about it?"

"Never." Matt put down his mug and loudly exhaled. "Thought I was hearing things when he said her name at Thanksgiving."

"Yeah, and he kept a picture of her, too." Rubbing at his lips,

Bo nodded. "Maybe you can get him to talk to Monica. He needs therapy or something, bro."

"Heh." Like he hadn't already tried?

"Yeah, okay, maybe not." Bo raised his hands. "I'm not sure who to worry about more—Kit or Sloan."

"I'm right there with ya, man." Matt drained his cup and stood. "I should get going. Thanks for the coffee and the talk."

"Anytime." With a squeeze to his forearm, Bo led him out of the kitchen. "You're coming for Emmy's birthday on Sunday, aren't you?"

"Wouldn't miss it." Matt nodded, and turning toward Emery, he ruffled her hair. "Hey, Buttercup, I gotta go. You gonna hug me goodbye?"

"Yesss." She made a running jump into his arms and pressed a messy smooch on his cheek. "I wuv you, Unkey."

She called all the Venery boys that. Kodiak, Brendan, and Dillon, too. The girls were her aunties. The other kids, her cousins. See, no one had to share blood to be considered family here. They just were.

What the fuck was he doing with his life? Well past noon on a Saturday, Matt plucked at his guitar, staring at the bedroom ceiling. Five months since Venery's summer tour ended, he had little to fill his days when he was used to burning through them at full throttle. Record an album. Release it. Go on tour. Wash, rinse, and repeat. He was lucky if he was home six weeks out of the year then. But then, the label controlled them.

Not anymore, you don't. Fuckers.

Taylor got married and put the media on blast. Venery sued the record label, won, and built their own studio. They put out a new record every year or two and cut their tour schedule down— drastically. Running on fumes, at the grueling pace they'd been going for over a decade, the boys agreed they needed a rest. If they didn't, they'd break.

It was the right move, but since then, Matt found he had a lot of leftover time on his hands. *Too much.* He loved his house, but he was tired of sitting here, wasting most of his days doing nothing. Should he find a hobby? He liked to build model cars when he was a kid. *Nah.* Volunteer? *Maybe.* A project? *Now, there's a thought. Something music-related would be cool.*

The bell rang. He hit the button to open it.

"About time."

After another late night at the club, he was fucking starving.

Wearing a pair of grungy old sweats, Matt went to the door. A girl stood on the other side. Long dark hair in a ponytail, her eyes a mix of sable and green, she cocked her hip, his pizza in her hand.

He licked his lips. "You're not Luca."

"Nope." Shifting her eyes, she scanned his bare torso and made a face.

"Who are you?"

"The pizza girl." She smirked, shoving the box into his hands. "It's gonna get cold."

Then she turned around and skipped down his porch steps.

An urge to chase after her came over him, but he refrained.

"Hey, you got a name, pizza girl?"

"Doesn't everyone?"

What the hell?

Her ponytail swinging, she glanced back at him from over her shoulder. Shaking his head, Matt took a step inside the house.

"It's Gina."

She'll be back.

And closing the door behind him, he grinned.

Two

Six children, all under the age of four, sat at a kiddie table in the middle of Bo's living room, having brunch to celebrate Emery's third birthday. Pretty in pink, complete with a tiara, she looked like a princess. With fresh flowers and linens, Ava and Katie had the place looking like an English tea party. Cute and whimsical, it made for some pretty pictures, but what made them think kids that small would sit still long enough to take any, Matt would never know.

Declan was only a toddler, for chrissakes. Ireland was just taking her first steps. And at two months old, Charlotte couldn't sit at all yet. Linnea had to hold her up for the photos. But this was the first birthday Bo got to have with his little girl, and the first one for Emery without her mother, so he got it. This party was as much for him as it was for his daughter.

Matt cut into pastel-colored pancakes, stuffed with Nutella and topped with candy pearls, edible flowers, and sprinkles. Talk about a morning sugar rush. Watching Bo and Ava fuss over the little ones from the sofa, he washed it down with champagne and orange juice.

Picking on grilled fruit salad, Kit sat to one side of him, while Sloan tucked into avocado toast and maple syrup-glazed balls of sausage on the other. Shocked that he came, since he rarely left his house, Matt nudged the voice of Venery. "Where'd you get that?"

"Miss Bo Peep has a spread for the grownups in the kitchen," he said, popping another sausage ball into his mouth. "These are damn good."

"I have to make a new plate." Matt stood. "I'm about to go into a diabetic coma here."

"Gimme the rest of your pancakes, then." Sloan snatched the plate out of his hand. "Heh, those kids are gonna be wired for days."

Now you can be, too.

But then, wasn't he always? The dude hardly ever slept. He stayed awake most nights penning lyrics or playing his stupid video games.

Kit tapped him on the shoulder. "I'll come with you."

Matt wasn't sure how he missed the bounty laid out on the kitchen island. Miniature quiches, chicken and waffles, bacon and eggs, pastries and breads. Coffee, juices, and bottles of champagne on ice. "Look at this. Ava was holding out on us."

"It's not her fault you went right for the kiddie buffet." Kit snickered, handing him a plate. "I saw her yesterday, you know. Told her I was sorry about the other night."

"You know, I don't get you sometimes," he said, loading the pink china with savory deliciousness. "How the fuck could you hurt sweet Ava like that?"

"She tried to, uh… never mind." Long hair hiding his face, Kit shook his head.

"You should've stayed and played with us."

"Nah, bro, I don't shit where I eat. That gets messy." He made himself a mimosa, gulped it, and poured another. "I'd rather not know their names. It's better that way."

"Safer, you mean."

He shrugged.

"That's so fucking sad, man." Matt took the glass from Kit and, staring into his puppy dog eyes, he drank it. "When are you gonna let her go?"

"Who?"

"You know who." There'd never been another, for fuck's sake. "After all these years, that bitch still has a hold on you."

"Is that what you think?" Kit turned away and reached for another glass. "Because you couldn't be more wrong, brother."

"If you say so." Matt blocked his way. "Keep on doing what you're doing, and you'll end up dying an old man in that big house of yours all alone."

He swiped his tongue across his lips, and the corners of his mouth ticked up. "Maybe, but the way your life is going, so will you."

Then, taking the bottle with him, he walked away.

Kit might be right. He'd never had a girlfriend. Not even in high school. He dated them, fucked them, but Matt couldn't say he ever had a true and meaningful relationship.

Ava followed Bo into the kitchen. "Hey, man, I'm glad you're alone. I want to ask you something."

"Shoot."

"Did you mean it when you said you wouldn't say no if we wanted to play again?"

His dick turned to stone. Refilling his glass with champagne, he grinned.

"Yeah, sure." Matt turned to the drummer's girlfriend. The pretty, young thing chewed on her lip as she put candles on Emery's pink-frosted birthday cake. "You want to, Ava?"

"I do. Bo and I talked about it, and I know I can trust you. I don't want to go to the club, though." She leaned back against the counter, wringing her hands. "I think I'd be more comfortable here at home."

"Avie wants to know what DP is like," Bo explained, tucking her beneath his arm.

Hell, fuck her with a toy in her ass, then. Though it likely didn't feel quite the same. Matt fondly recalled that time at the club when Brendan asked him to take his place. He walked into the alcove to find Gillian, one of the club's bartenders, impaled on Dillon's dick. There was no way Brendan's monster cock was getting in there, but he was happy enough to make it happen.

I wonder what ever became of her.

Gillian may have gotten her heart's desire, but she didn't get Dillon.

He called her Linnea by mistake and left her crying while Matt picked up the pieces.

Maybe he had a penchant for ferocious play, but he could be patient and gentle when it was called for.

"Well, I'm always up for that," Matt said and drained his glass. "When do you want to get together?"

Ava looked up at Bo and then at him. "Not on a school night… how about this Friday?"

"Works for me."

"We can order pizza," Bo said like they'd just picked a date to play poker.

The girl from Rossi's came to mind. Maybe he'd get to see her again.

"I'll bring some wine."

Lots of wine.

"We can watch a movie or two with Emmy." Bo slung an arm around his neck, and drawing him and Ava close, he lowered his voice. "Then, after she goes to bed, we will, too."

"God, I love watching the two of you fuck," Ava squealed. "It's so hot."

"Know what's gonna be even hotter, angel?"

"What?"

The drummer's lips ghosted across his girlfriend's jaw to her ear. "Me and Matt fucking *you*."

"Bo's right, Ava. We'll go slow and take real good care of you," he said, looking into her big blue eyes. "Thank you for trusting me."

"Course, I trust you. We're friends, right?"

Yeah, friends who fuck.

"More than that, Ava." He pressed a kiss to her cheek. "We're family."

Matt wiped the condensation off the glass, and studying his reflection in the mirror, he debated whether to shave the three-day growth of stubble on his face.

"It's not like this is a date."

He decided against it. Besides, girls liked it when his prickly chin rubbed against their swollen clits. And so, he pulled on a pair of army-green khakis. Well-worn, faded, and soft, they were comfortable. More importantly, they were easy to take off. He paired them with a thin, white, long-sleeved V-neck tee. It's not like he had anyone to impress next door.

With his dick raring to go and a case of Valpolicella Ripasso waiting on the kitchen counter, Matt took to the stairs two at a time. It was nice not having to deal with the bullshit of going out for a change. He noted the time. Half-past five. He had thirty minutes to kill. Bo and Ava weren't expecting him until six.

Kit came strolling through the door. He didn't bother knocking, but then he rarely ever did. Pushing his hair away from his eyes, the bassist plopped his ass down on Matt's overstuffed leather sofa. "I'm restless tonight. Let's go to the club."

Fuck.

Now, what was he supposed to say? He couldn't betray Ava's trust and tell him what his plans were.

"Not up for it, man." Feigning a tired sigh, Matt sat across from Kit and kicked his feet up. "How about tomorrow?"

"What are you gonna do, then?" His brows knitted, hazel eyes taking him in.

"I'm hitting the sack early." It wasn't a lie, right?

"Yeah, all right." He pursed his lips, nodding as he rose. "Tomorrow's good, I guess."

"See if you can convince Sloan to come." Matt grabbed onto Kit's forearm before he passed. "An evening drowning in pussy."

"Down in the pen?"

Tense muscles relaxed beneath his fingers. He squeezed Kit's arm and let him go. "Where else, brother?"

Why did he feel like a piece of shit sneaking over to the house next door? And why did he feel like he had to? Instead of going out his front door, he slunk through the backyard with a case of wine under his arm.

With a kiss on his cheek, Ava let him in through the door on Bo's terrace. She wore a lacy black bralette beneath an oversized tee, the sleeve sliding off of her shoulder. Yoga pants. Bare feet. She wasn't trying to impress him, either… still, she did.

I hope you know what a lucky sonofabitch you are, drummer boy.

Sometimes, nice girls *do* end up with rock stars.

"You trying to get us drunk, Matt?" she asked, following him and Bo into the kitchen.

"Why not?" He put the Valpolicella on the island and leaned against it. "Especially if we're gonna be up all night."

"Are we?"

"Guaranteed." His thumb skimmed along her jaw. "Ain't that right, Bo-Bo?"

"Absofuckinglutely." His arm around Ava's waist, he tugged on the ends of Matt's hair. "Now, where's my kiss?"

"Where's Emmy?" His gaze flicked around the room. Matt wondered why he hadn't seen her yet.

"Monica's." And he winked. "She, Elliott, and Chandan wanted to have a sleepover."

"How convenient," he said with a snigger. "That your idea?"

"Nope. Chloe's."

"Well, in that case…" Winding Bo's hair around his fist, Matt yanked, pulling the drummer's bare chest to his. "I know how much Ava gets off watching us."

In the past, he rarely kissed the men he fucked. At least, he didn't remember it if he had. Usually, he was pumped up and drunk. A beast when he fucked, Matt could pound into a dude without restraint, but he couldn't allow himself to tap into that base need with a woman, no matter how much she begged him for it.

A man touching a man is just… well, different. As much as Matt loved suffocating in a woman's cunt, it was easy for him to rationalize what they were doing. He didn't have any concerns about his sexuality. He didn't identify as gay or bi. His preference had always been pussy, but with his tongue down Bo's throat, his fingers pulling on his hair, their rock-hard dicks rubbing against each other, at that moment, the only thing he thought of was how good it would feel to fuck his friend.

And his friend's girl.

Ava's sweet lips joined theirs. Her hand slipping inside his pants, she stroked his cock. Judging by the drummer's groan, she was inside his, too. Gripping Bo's hair at the nape, Matt moved his lips from his mouth to hers. His fingers delved into her silky hair, and holding them both by the strands on their head, he kissed one and then the other.

The bell to the gate rang.

Bo panted, out of breath. "That'll be the pizza."

Gina.

"I'll get it."

But it was Luca who stood on the other side of the door, not his pizza girl.

"Hey there, dude."

"Oh, hi, Matt." Looking over at his house next door, the kid did a double-take. "Thought I was at the wrong address for a sec."

"Heh, no, you're at the right place."

"Yeah, I know." He passed him a pizza box and a white paper bag with Rossi's logo printed on it. "Well, here you go. An extra-large Chicago special and twenty hot wings."

"Thanks, Luca." Matt tipped him a twenty. "Hey, where's the new pizza girl?"

"Huh?"

"Gina." He liked the way her name rolled off his tongue. "She delivered to my house last weekend."

"Ohhh, her." The kid, who wasn't a kid by definition, he drove a car after all, slowly bobbed his head. "She just helps out once in a while. Why?"

I'd like to sink my teeth into her.

"Just, um… curious."

Tipping his head slightly, Luca grinned. "You wanna ask her out or something?"

"She single?" A snicker escaped. Matt licked his lips.

"As far as I know."

I just might, then.

"Be safe out there, dude." Matt waved as Luca went down the porch steps. "Have a good night."

Ava laid out a blanket on the living room floor in front of the fire. Their backs against the sofa, they ate pizza and wings from paper plates. They drank wine. Kissed. Touched one another.

Comfortable since he was among friends, Matt felt no shame jerking Bo's dick while he sucked on Ava's nipple. "I can't wait to fuck your tight little hole, sweets."

"I felt that." She bit into her lip.

"Good."

Then Bo pulled his pants down. "Wanna suck Matt with me, baby girl?"

"Yes, but I want to watch you for a while first."

"I think your girl's a voyeur, Bo-Bo." The drummer gripped his length, and he hissed. "If it's all right, I'll be playing with her while you swallow my dick."

"Would you like that, angel?"

"I would."

Bo lapped up the precum and groaned. His fingers sliding under Ava's waistband, Matt rubbed between her folds, and sinking inside her welcoming hot hole, he pressed his thumb into her clit. What a fucking high. His hand in a soft, warm cunt. A brother sucking his dick. Yeah, playing with people who cared about you made all the difference.

Close to coming in Bo's mouth, Matt kissed Ava. Maybe someday he'd find a girl as free as her. One as vulnerable as Linnea, as spirited as Chloe, and as submissive as Katie. God, if Katie's heart hadn't already belonged to Brendan, he could have loved her. It was a fucking good thing his friend wised up, because he would have loved her anyway if he hadn't.

There was no holding back, and Matt didn't want to. Bo was good at sucking dick. Fervently rubbing Ava's clit so she'd come with him, he came in the drummer's mouth.

Bo kissed him then, and he tasted himself on his tongue.

"God, I love you. Let me taste him." And Ava kissed her man. "I didn't know sex could be like this."

"It's never just sex, Ava," Matt said, licking her from his finger. "Even the fastest, dirtiest, filthiest fuck is more than that. It's the connection. It's looking at someone and seeing your own cravings, dreams, and neediness reflected back."

"You need this, too?"

"Right now, sweets, there's nothing I crave more."

And that was the truth.

"Are you good, baby?"

Bo wasn't. Poor guy hadn't come yet. There was a wet spot from his dick leaking in his sweats. He and Ava were going to have to take care of that.

"So good," she said, pinching her nipples. "Get these clothes off me."

"You have the most amazing tits, Ava." He sucked one into his mouth while Bo peeled her pants down her legs. Matt watched him finger her as he sucked on her other breast beside him. "Don't I always say that, Bo?"

"Mmhm." He released her nipple to kiss him.

"Naked. I want you both naked."

"Shall we take this upstairs, baby girl?"

"In a minute." She grabbed onto them both by their hair. "Please, I need to come again first."

"Whatever you want, Ava." Matt reached for the bottle. Pouring some wine on her perfect tits, he lapped it from her nipples. "This is for you, sweets. You're in control here. Understand?"

Whimpering, she nodded. If she was his, he'd fuck her with the bottle until she begged for his dick. But she wasn't. Her pussy was off-limits, so his fingers would have to do.

"We got you, baby."

They kissed her together. Their tongues in each other's mouths, Matt joined his fingers with Bo's in her cunt.

"Spread wide, Ava." He nudged her thighs farther apart. "Wider. That's a good girl."

With two fingers each in her pussy, Matt and Bo fucked her.

"It feels so good." She could barely get the words out. "I'm gonna die."

C'mon, sweetheart, I know you can do it.

Positioning his face near her pussy, Matt tapped on her swollen clit.

"Let it go, Av."

And she did. Ava exploded, drenching them in her sweet cum. He dove in, Bo's fingers still inside her, taking in his fill.

"Fuck." She held his head to her cunt.

"Oh, angel, we're just getting started." Bo pulled his fingers from her pussy and shoved them in Matt's throat. "Now, let's get you cleaned you up."

After they licked the cum from her thighs and sucked on her clit until she screamed again, Bo carried her up the stairs. The room was ready for them. Lube, condoms, toys, and a warmer filled with wet cloths were laid out on a bedside table.

Even though Bo had taken the edge off, fire licked at his spine. Matt had never been so ready to fuck in his life. He took a cloth from the warmer, and parting Ava's thighs, he washed between her legs.

"Are you two going to fuck, now?" she asked.

Bo got out of his sweats. "Is that what you want, angel?"

"I do."

Good, because that's what I want, too.

Grabbing Bo by the dick, Matt kissed him. They stroked each other until he needed air and pushed him down onto the bed.

"Suck him, Ava," he cooed in her ear. "I want his dick weeping for me."

She kneeled between Bo's thighs, then bent over, enthusiastically taking him in her mouth.

Matt lubed his fingers in her pussy before working one into her little hole. "Bo's fucked your ass before, hasn't he?"

Of course, with her mouth full of her boyfriend's cock, she couldn't answer.

"She loves it, brother. Except then her cunt feels so empty. That's why she wants this so bad, and I want to give it to her."

"Your man must really love you, Ava." Inserting a second finger into her hole, Matt hoped if the time ever came that he could be as selfless. "After I fuck Bo's ass, I'm going to fuck yours. Okay, beautiful?"

"Fuck, I'm gonna come," Bo groaned.

"Stop, Ava. Come here, now." He pulled her off the drummer's cock and brought her lips to his own. "That's it, sweetheart. Suck me. You too, Bo-Bo."

They sucked him together, Ava sneaking a finger into his ass. Finding he enjoyed the sensation, he grunted. Then Bo was there, wetting the finger that fucked his hole with his tongue, crawling up his torso, nipping at his skin along the way.

The beast at the surface, Matt grabbed Bo by the hair and kissed him. Then he rolled him over and spread his legs. "I'm gonna tear this ass up."

"Yeah? Do it, baby boy."

He tore open the foil packet with his teeth and passed it to Ava. She sheathed him, and he kissed her, lubing up his dick. "Keep doing what you were doing. I wanna fuck his brains out."

He entered Bo's ass as she penetrated his. And fucking hell, it felt good. Pulling on Bo's hair, Matt commanded her to put another finger in. Pounding his friend into oblivion, he growled, while Ava fucked his ass with her fingers.

The drummer's eyes rolled backward in his head.

And Ava moved out of the way to watch them. "Jesus."

"C'mon, Matt. Fuck me." Bo's nails scored down his chest. "Harder. You can't break me. I'm not a girl."

And he howled like the animal he was.

"See, baby. I know what gets him off," he said and bit into her nipple. "You're so fucking perfect."

Bo came all over his stomach.

Matt came inside Bo's ass.

Scooping her boyfriend's cum into her palm, Ava smeared it on his lips and fed it to him. Matt sucked her fingers into his mouth while she licked the cum from his lips. And lying on either side of him, Matt and Ava kissed Bo and each other, rubbing the cum left on his stomach into his skin, until his dick got hard again.

"Ready, Ava?"

"God, yes."

And God, he was dying to fuck her.

Matt kissed her clit, inhaling the salty-sweet musk. "Look at this pretty pussy, Bo."

"I love that pussy," he said, extending his arms to her. "C'mere, baby."

Matt helped her straddle Bo, and gripping his cock, he positioned him at her entrance.

He watched Bo thrust in deep, keeping his dick warm inside her.

"That's beautiful, man. Stay like that." Matt lapped at Bo's cock, tasting her sweetness, as it drifted in and out of her. "I'm going to get you ready for me now. Okay, sweets?"

"Please."

Christ, he loved it when they begged.

"You're so fucking tight, Ava." Sucking on the skin of her neck,

Matt fingered her asshole with lube. "I can't wait to get my dick inside you, baby."

"Hurry."

He notched the head into her little hole, and she hissed. "Tell me if you need me to stop, okay?"

"I will, but please don't."

Matt pushed his way in farther.

"Oh, fuck, fuck, fuck…"

Ava reached for him, tugging on his hair.

Matt's teeth sank into her skin.

"I can feel your dick, man." Bo pulled him down to his lips and kissed him.

"I love this. Oh, God," she cried out. "Fuck me the way you fucked him."

Christ, he wanted to. Bo's dick rubbed against his, and she was just so damn tight.

He glanced down. She must've torn a little because she was bleeding. Matt bit down on her shoulder, rubbing her clit instead.

I wish I could, sweet Ava, but see? I already hurt you.

"I love you, baby."

"I love you, angel."

God, he envied them. How freely they loved each other.

Maybe he didn't need just something to fill his days.

Maybe what he needed was someone to fill them with, too.

Three

f it had been a nicer day, she probably would've gone over to Stan's to grab a cup of coffee for the train ride home. Hell, if it weren't so damn cold, she'd probably walk. But since it was frigid on this February morning, Gina made do with shitty coffee from the hospital cafeteria and braced herself for the Arctic blast outside.

"Fuck." She pulled her scarf tighter.

It was a good thing the Wellington Station was just across the street.

Mindful of the ice, Gina crossed it while fumbling in her bag for her Ventra card. She tapped it, went through the turnstile, and headed up the stairs to the platform. If she timed it just right, and she was certain she had, the train would arrive at any moment. Because it would surely suck to stand in the icy wind, waiting for the next one.

No sooner had she taken a sip of the bitter sludge that passed for coffee, when the clickety-clack sound of the train on the elevated track signaled its approach from Belmont. Gina took a seat close to the doors. She wouldn't be on the train for long. It was only a couple of stops to Fullerton—three if she took it to Armitage.

The old Chicago townhouse where she lived was an equal distance from either. Most often, she got off at Armitage, for no other reason than to avoid getting caught in the university foot traffic, but this early on a Saturday morning, that shouldn't be an issue, so she'd get off at Fullerton instead. A five-minute ride. Walk four blocks. Another five minutes. *Okay, maybe ten.* Gina glanced at her watch. With any luck at all, she'd be curled up in her bed, shades drawn, and fast asleep by eight a.m.

What she wouldn't give for eight solid hours of uninterrupted sleep. Working twelve-hour night shifts was sucking the life right out of her. After nearly nine months of it, Gina felt like a cast member of *The Walking Dead* most of the time. If a spot didn't open up for her on the day shift soon, she might lose it.

Or lapse into an irreversible coma.

Night shift isn't for the weak.

She got off at Fullerton, thankful the students were still sleeping, and headed toward First Avenue where her family's pizzeria and bakery were located, but Gina wasn't going anywhere near Rossi's. Instead, she left Fullerton at Third and hurried to the house around the corner on Willow.

Her family wasn't rich even though it might look like it, but they weren't poor either. So what if they lived in a lovely home in a sought-after zip code? It wasn't always that way. Gina remembered when she was a kid, this neighborhood was shit. Nobody wanted to live here then. Her mom urged her father to move the family and the business out to the suburbs, but he wouldn't hear of it. His grandparents built this house in the 1920s when they were newlyweds, then his father opened the pizzeria in 1958.

"Things are changing, Rosemary," Anthony Rossi Sr. had said to his wife. "You'll see."

And sure as shit, her old man was right. By the time she graduated from high school, only a millionaire could afford to buy a condo around here, let alone a house. Real estate investors bought up everything, from six-flats to bungalows, then renovated them, or worse, tore them down to build these modern monstrosities that didn't quite fit the neighborhood's aesthetic to take their place.

They tried relentlessly to get her dad to sell, but Anthony Rossi was no dummy. With the rising value of his property, he took out a small mortgage, redid the house inside and out, and thumbed his nose at them. *Vaffanculo.* So now, they lived among the rich in a million-dollar house. Not to mention, with the influx of affluent people in the area, the pizza and bakery biz was booming.

She went around to the back and carefully opened the door. After hanging up her coat and taking off her shoes in the mudroom, Gina tiptoed toward the kitchen. Her parents had likely left for work already, but the last thing she wanted to do was wake up her brother, Matteo, who was no doubt sleeping off a Friday night bar-hopping binge downstairs.

"What in the hell?" Luca sat hunched over the kitchen table in the semi-darkness. "You scared me."

"Good morning to you, too, Gina Bobina," he said with a snicker, lifting a cup of coffee to his lips. The youngest of the Rossi brothers, and God help her, there were four, he'd been calling her that since he was little when they played "The Name Game". "How was work?"

"All right. Same shit, different day." She tossed her bag down on a chair and dumped the cafeteria sludge in the sink. "What are you doing up this early on a Saturday?"

Unless Luca had class or was working, he usually slept until noon.

"Think I wanna be?" He stretched his arms above his head with a yawn. "Couldn't sleep, so I thought, fuck it, and came downstairs."

"Sorry, little bro." Gina poured herself a fresh cup of coffee. "Sucks, doesn't it?"

"How the fuck can you drink that?" Luca lifted his chin at her. "Shouldn't you be going to bed?"

"I should, and I'm gonna." She inhaled the delicious brew, then took a sip. "Coffee won't keep me from sleeping. God knows I live off the stuff. I think I've become immune to the effects of caffeine."

"Jesus." He looked at her like she was an alien. "When are you off again?"

"Tonight's my last night."

And already exhausted, her shift tonight would be the hardest. Gina opted to work six twelves in a row. Then, she could have eight days off and regain some sense of normalcy before the cycle started all over again.

"You shoulda listened to Mom."

"And work in the bakery?" A shake of her head, and her ponytail swished. "No, thanks."

"The hours are better."

Is sweating in a kitchen from sunup to sundown seven days a week better? She didn't think so. Gina was well aware she'd disappointed *Nonna* and her parents when she went to nursing school. And how messed up was that? As the only daughter, it was their dream for her to follow in their footsteps, marry a nice Italian boy, and make babies.

Too bad it wasn't what she wanted anymore.

There was a time Gina might've settled for it, though.

"Baking is supposed to be a joy, not a job." Dunking a cookie in her coffee, she expelled a breath. "Besides, I always wanted to be a nurse, and so I am."

"You're good at it, though. Better than Mom is, but don't you dare tell her I said that."

"See? That's what makes all the difference. She's lost the joy in it. It's just work for her, now." With a shrug, Gina popped the cookie into her mouth before it fell apart. "And I'm an excellent nurse because I love what I do."

"So that's the trick, eh?" Holding back a smirk, Luca pushed his fingers through his shaggy, dark hair.

"What?"

"You gotta love what you do to be good at it?"

"Yeah, something like that." Her head tipping to the side, she smiled at him. Of all her brothers, she was closest to Luca. Maybe because, being three years younger, she always thought of him as hers. "Your life will be miserable if you don't."

"I don't know what I wanna do after I'm finished with school," he admitted.

"You're not gonna run Rossi's with Daddy?"

"Nah, don't think so." Luca stared into his cup. "He's got Tony and Nick. Doubt he needs me and Teo, too."

"Oh, I wouldn't be so sure about that." Gina took ahold of her brother's hand and squeezed it. "If Tony has his way, they're gonna open up a place in Wrigleyville."

"Let them," he said, his nostrils flaring. "Tony and Lina can run it, too."

Where the fuck was this anger coming from? Did their eldest brother piss him off somehow? Twelve years her senior, Tony could be bossy. Hell, he acted like *he* was their dad half the time. And his wife? Gina didn't pay her any mind. Nineteen and pregnant when she married her brother, Lina wasn't much older than she was.

"Lina's too busy popping out Tony's babies to do anything else. You've got time to figure out what you want, babes, and you will." She kissed his cheek. "Okay, Luca Bobuca, I gotta crash."

"I'll try to keep Teo quiet when he gets up."

"Knowing him, he won't wake up until after I do." Gina drained her cup and giggled.

"I'd say you're right, except he's on delivery duty at noon." Luca grabbed her hand. "Hey, that reminds me. Someone was asking about you last night."

"Who?" she asked, curious.

"Matt McCready."

Oh?

"Do I know him?"

"You're shittin' me, right?" His mouth hung open. "Tony's friend from high school. He's in Venery. You delivered a pizza to his house, for fuck's sake."

"You think I remember all of Tony's friends?" But she remembered him. "I was like six when he graduated."

"So? I know you know who he is."

Of course, she did. Gina knew who he was when she delivered his pizza, too. But everybody knew who he was. Even if they didn't grow up living a block away from him. She vaguely remembered Matt McCready, along with Taylor Kerrigan, Kit King, Bo Robertson, and Sloan Michaels hanging out at her house with Tony after school, but she was only four or five back then.

"What did he say?" She was more than curious now, because why the fuck would he ask about her?

"I think he likes you or something."

And she laughed. "I think you're delusional."

"He wanted to know if you were single." Lifting his hands, her brother shrugged. And then he grinned. "I told him you were."

The fuck?

"Jesus, Luca." She wanted to smack that smug look right off his face.

"You're welcome."

Gina wrenched her bag out of the chair, and cocking her hip, she pulled the hair on her brother's chest. "I wouldn't get involved with someone like him if he were the last guy on Earth."

"Ow." With a smack to her hand, Luca looked at her like she was crazy. "Someone like him? Matt's a good dude."

"Maybe so. Still, not interested."

His lip curling, he leaned in the chair and nodded. "Vinny fucked you up good, huh?"

Gina turned her back on him without an answer. The question didn't deserve one.

"Go out with him, Gina. Get yourself a little. You probably got cobwebs growing in there."

"God, you're disgusting." And she started down the hall.

He chuckled. "It's the truth and you know it."

Without breaking her stride, Gina flipped him off.

Luca hit the nail on the proverbial head, though, didn't he? Because she hadn't so much as kissed anyone since Vinny Passarelli, and that was three years ago. At first, Gina told herself she needed to focus on her classes and getting clinical hours at the hospital. Besides, as it turned out, he wasn't worth it, and sex was overrated, anyway. She'd never had an orgasm with him.

Gina was happy working in labor and delivery. She was going to take classes toward her master's degree in the fall. Her life was full. The last thing she needed was some guy fucking it all up—even if he was hot as hell. Not that she believed Matt McCready was interested in *her*, anyway. Because now, she knew better than to believe anything that came out of a guy's mouth.

Especially not someone like him.

Four

He pulled the zipper up on his slim-fitting black pants and snagged a tailored black blazer from its hanger. Should he even bother with a shirt? *Nah*. Matt didn't feel like wearing one, and he didn't feel like going to the club, either. Especially after last night. He was tapped out, but he promised.

There was no way for him to get out of it. Somehow, Kit talked Sloan into leaving his house, which was a good thing. The dude holed himself up in there night and day. And then, Brendan called him. When he found out they planned to go to the club tonight, he said he could have a drink or two with them after he met with Hans—like old times.

He missed those days. Before the wives. Before they lost Kyan. Like royal princes at court, the nine of them sat in that booth by the bar as if it were their throne, and in a way, it was. Their subjects would come and pay homage to them there. Once, as he sipped on his whiskey, a girl crawled under the table, took his dick out of his pants, and sucked him off right there.

He was younger then—in his twenties, still. None of them were married yet. Hell, none of them even had a girlfriend. Except for Sloan. Not that it worked out. It was a shame because the dude truly loved her. Matt was just thankful that she didn't drag him down into the gutter with her.

But he wasn't twenty-eight anymore. He'd be thirty-five in a matter of weeks. Half the guys were married now, or might as well be, and here he was going out on the hunt for pussy.

Fucking pathetic.

But Matt wasn't looking for any tonight. Changing his mind, he got a soft Bella + Canvas muscle tank out of his drawer and put it on. Bo, who had a thing about textures on his skin, turned him on to the brand.

Precisely at ten, the private car rolled up in front of his house. He and his bandmates slid into the back. It was ridiculous, having to hire a car to take them a few short blocks to the Red Door, but thanks to the relentless tabloid paps, they couldn't show up on foot, and taking one of their vehicles was simply out of the question.

Sloan tipped his head against the seat and closed his eyes. "Remind me why I let you talk me into this again."

"Because you need to get out."

"Do I?"

"You do." Glancing at the driver, Kit softened his voice and winked. "Female companionship, brother."

"Pussy?" Sloan said, loud and clear. Then he snickered. "Yeah, well, there's always that."

"Don't sound so enthused, man."

"How long have we been doing this shit, Matt?" He cocked his head, shaking it.

"What?"

"Parties. Clubbing. Fucking. All of it." Sloan rubbed at his temples. "Never mind. I'm just… I'm just tired."

But Matt got it. Hadn't he been wrestling with the same shit?

The town car stopped in front of the red double doors on Ash Street, and as he stood on the sidewalk waiting for Kit and Sloan to get out, his gaze traveled to the pizza joint on First Avenue. Gina came to mind.

"You wanna ask her out or something?"

Yeah, I think I do.

A heavy hand landed on his shoulder. "You coming or what?"

Matt half-turned, and looking into dull blue eyes, he nodded.

They bypassed the red velvet ropes, the doormen ushering them through. Inside the cavernous two-story lobby, with its immense crystal chandelier dangling above him, Axel tipped his chin in greeting. Easily as tall as Brendan, he was a silent, imposing figure in his custom black suit. Not a single tattoo was visible, but underneath those expensive clothes, the man's skin was covered in ink. Ex-military, the club's head of security used to be special forces, secret service, or some such shit—Matt wasn't sure. He couldn't even say if Axel was his real name.

I bet not.

"Hey, Axel." He slapped the towering man on the back. "Brendan here yet?"

"He's in the office with Hans," he answered with a curt nod. "He'll be out shortly."

"Let him know we're here, will ya?"

"Of course." Black eyes gazing down at him, the corner of Axel's mouth twitched. "Will you be upstairs?"

The lavish and private VIP spaces.

Before, they only went up for special club events, but once the girls came along, and more so since Kyan's death, they eschewed their throne on the main floor in favor of it.

"Not tonight, my friend."

It would be silly to go when it was only the three of them, so Matt led the way to their old spot by the bar that was always on reserve for them. The semi-circular booth, upholstered in tufted purple velvet, could easily hold a dozen people, and even as they took their seats, it still looked pitifully empty.

"It doesn't feel right sitting here—ain't the same, you know?" Sloan's gaze flitted around the mostly unoccupied booth, and pulling at the chain around his neck, his index finger slid back and forth. "We should've gone up to VIP."

"Why?" Matt pulled his phone out and tossed it onto the table. "So you can hide?"

"No, asshole, so I don't have to sit here with the memories of…"

"Kyan?"

"Yeah." His lips trembling, Sloan pushed his thumb into his wrist. "It fucking guts me to think about him. I loved the little shit."

Barely six months had passed since the tragic loss of the youngest of the nine princes.

"We all did."

"I still can't wrap my head around it… that he's…" *Dead. Gone.* But Sloan couldn't say it. "… not here. Linnea…"

His teeth raking over his bottom lip, Matt nodded. Only twenty-four, Linnea was a widow. Her two-month-old daughter would never know her father. Inseparable, Dillon was fucking lost without his brother, while Brendan and Jesse deeply grieved their cousin. But having grown up together, his loss affected every man among them. Irreplaceable, Kyan left a hole in their hearts that nothing could ever fill. They'd just have to learn how to live with it, he supposed.

"Why do they keep this booth empty all the time?" Kit asked, changing the subject.

"Hans keeps it that way for us." *As a sign of respect.*

Kit slumped against the purple velvet. "Well, it's fucking depressing."

"Stop with the sad shit—both of you," Matt said and slammed his fist onto the table. "That's the last thing Kyan would've wanted."

A girl he'd never seen before, wearing the club's signature

black thong uniform, approached their table. The fabric translucent, Matt could make out the shape of her supple breasts, their peaked, rosy nipples. Long, light brown, highlighted hair, curled into loose waves, framed her pretty face. She was likely a blondie when she was little.

"Gentlemen." The girl cleared her throat and took a breath. "Can I get you anything?"

Thirsty as all fuck, Kit stared at her chest like he'd never seen a pair of pretty tits in all of his life, before his gaze met hers. He chewed on his lip, but he didn't speak.

"Well, hello, pretty," Matt crooned on the bassist's behalf. "Glenlivet. Bring us the bottle."

"Yes, sir," she said with a nod and turned to leave.

His lip quirking up, Sloan stopped her. "And what's your name?"

"Savannah."

He stretched his arm out as if reaching for her. "I'm Sloan, and this is—"

"I know who y'all are." She didn't appear impressed.

And Sloan couldn't give two shits if she wasn't. He shrugged. "Have we seen you before, Savannah?"

"No, I don't think so." She tipped her head slightly and smiled. "I'll be right back with your drinks."

His eyes glued to her voluptuous ass, Sloan chuckled. "She's not from around here."

"No?" Kit asked with a roll of his eyes. "What gave it away?"

"*I know who y'all are,*" Sloan imitated her accent, raising his voice a few octaves. "Who in Chicago says *y'all,* huh?"

"Don't be a dick, Sloan."

"Isn't he always?" Matt asked with a snicker.

"Fuck off. Just making an observation." He lifted his chin at him from across the table. "She *is* a pretty little thing."

"Leave her alone, man." Kit nudged his shoulder.

"No worries, dude. Have at her." His palms up, Sloan leaned away from him. "She's not my type, anyway."

"You have a type?" Matt chuckled.

Kit snickered under his breath. "Redheads."

The look on Sloan's face was murderous. Once, his former fiancée had a crown of glorious auburn hair. But that was then. Before the dope. Matt hadn't seen her since Sloan broke it off, but he came across a photo of her in a supermarket rag a couple of years back. He almost didn't recognize her.

Before Sloan could jump across the table to throttle their bassist, and it looked like he was ready to, Brendan slid into the seat beside him. "Should I ask?"

"Probably not."

"Sloan starting shit again?"

"You could say that," Matt muttered. "And Kit finished it."

Which wasn't like him at all. Because he, out of all of them, understood the shit Sloan needlessly tortured himself with.

Savannah returned with bottle service for them, placing glasses, a bucket of ice, a decanter of water, and club soda, along with their favorite scotch whiskey on the table. "Will you be joining these gentlemen, Mr. Byrne? Shall I fetch another glass for you?"

"Yes, thank you." He glanced at her with a smile. "And call me Brendan."

"Who is she?" Kit asked.

"Savannah?" His smile building, Brendan tilted his head. "She's new. Has a class with Katelyn. Ava knows her too, I think. She just started working here about a week ago. Why?"

"No reason," Kit said, his cheeks flushing pink.

With a sly grin, Sloan's gaze turned from Kit to Brendan. "Where's she from?"

"Denver. She's here for college."

"Told you so." Chuckling, he plunked ice cubes into a glass.

"Where'd all this interest in my cocktail server come from?"

With a shake of his head, Matt sniggered. "She said y'all."

"I see." Looking from Kit to Sloan, Brendan sat back with a nod. "Don't even think about it. We don't allow Savannah to… um… engage with members of the Red Door. Club rules."

Engage? Fancy Schmancy. Don't you mean fuck?

"Are you forgetting about Gillian?"

"Why do you think I made it a rule, brother?" Chuckling, Brendan turned in his seat to see the girl standing there with his glass on a tray. "Thank you, Savannah."

It wasn't apparent if she'd overheard the conversation. She simply left the glass on the table and walked away.

"The meeting with Hans go okay?" Matt asked after they all poured themselves a drink.

"Yeah, we were tossing around some ideas for future events." Then, he proudly added, "Actually, they were Katelyn's."

Oh?

Intrigued, Matt encouraged him to say more. "Do tell."

"I can't. At least, not yet."

"Are you two planning to do more demos together?"

"Possibly." Brendan shrugged, but a faint grin curved his lips.

Sloan nodded. "She enjoyed being out there on the platform, huh?"

"She did."

"Sorry that I missed it," Matt said, and he wasn't ashamed to admit it, either.

His eyes narrowing, Kit stared down at the contents of his glass. He swirled it, then took a healthy sip.

"Where were you?" Brendan asked, his eyebrows raised.

He swallowed some scotch. "In the alcoves."

"He took off with Drummer Boy and Miss Bo Peep as soon as that big ole dick of yours flashed on the jumbo screen. Ain't that right, Rhythm Man?" Sloan shimmied his head. "And they were gone a helluva long time."

Fucker.

His lip curled. "Your point?"

Kit crooked his finger to call Hans over to the plum velvet booth. "Anyone down in the playroom yet?"

"Yes," he answered, his salacious grin wide. "And they'll be pleased to have you, gentlemen, join them."

"Go on." Matt lifted his chin toward Sloan. "I'll catch up with you. I'm gonna hang here with Brendan for a while."

"Suit yourself, man." He drained the whiskey from his glass and stood. "C'mon, Kit. You're the one who dragged me out."

After a moment of uneasy silence, Brendan finally spoke. "Something you wanna tell me?"

"No."

He cocked his head, a single eyebrow lifting. "Bo and Ava?"

"It's not like you're thinking."

His brow raised.

"Ava didn't want to scar herself for life, watching you and her BFF doing whatever it was you were doing out there. Bo asked me for a favor." Matt chuffed out a breath and picked up his glass. "It wasn't a big deal, so don't make it into one."

"Look, I'm not judging."

"I know." And he drank. "But I learned something. The sex is so much better with people you care about and who care about you, too."

"I can attest to that. Katelyn changed everything for me." With a nod, blue eyes bored into his. "Are there feelings involved here?"

"No, not like that." Emphatically, Matt shook his head. "And I don't see it happening again."

"But..."

"But nothing." He shrugged a shoulder. "Except maybe I wouldn't mind having a Katie or an Ava of my own, you know?"

Swallowing down the whiskey in his glass, Brendan stood, and clasping his shoulder, he winked. "I highly recommend it, brother."

Down in the playpen, at least twenty naked bodies tangled together on the cushion-covered floor, fucking in various configurations. More bodies lay sprawled on the chaise lounge chairs lining the perimeter of the room. Kit and Sloan shared a nubile beauty on one of them. A couple of weeks ago, he would've had a hard-on just watching the scene, but tonight, Matt felt nothing.

Nude, he leaned against the wall, holding onto the filmy drapery suspended from the ceiling that covered it. A warm, wet mouth swallowed him whole. He didn't look down at the blonde.

Matt closed his eyes, and tipping his head back, he imagined somebody else.

I'm coming for you, bunny.

And right then, the mere thought of her was enough.

Five

I t was tricky business, flip-flopping from working all night and sleeping all day to regaining some sense of normalcy when she was off. Night shift fucks with a person's natural circadian rhythm. And that was why Gina worked six twelve-hour shifts in a row every two weeks—to have those eight precious days for herself afterward. She learned early on that two or even three wasn't enough, considering the first one didn't count, since she was practically comatose for most of it.

Of course, it was this altered state of consciousness that explained why she was at the bakery on her first day off that counted. Yesterday evening, still coming out of a brain-fogged delirium, Gina's mother somehow convinced her to work this morning. They had a special order for two hundred and fifty cannoli.

Like, who in the fuck needs that many?

When Rossi's opened in the '50s, *Nonna* became somewhat of a local celebrity for the Sicilian confection. The torch was handed down to her mom when she and her dad took over the family business. As a young girl, there wasn't anything Gina loved more than spending afternoons in the kitchen with her grandmother, so naturally, everyone assumed she'd take the reins someday. But they were wrong.

She glanced over at her mother, hunched over a stainless steel table as she painstakingly piped buttercream onto the three-tier cake for the Campisi wedding on Saturday. It was on account of that stupid cake Gina had to get up before the sun to make the damn cannoli.

"But I'm exhausted, Ma."

"If you worked normal hours like everybody else, you wouldn't be," Rosemary said, reaching for the coffeepot. "When are you going to day shift?"

"I told you. As soon as there's an opening." Gina didn't bother telling her there were two nurses with seniority on the waiting list ahead of her. It could be years from now.

"Quit that job." Her mom handed her a mug filled to the brim. "You should be working in the bakery with me, anyway."

Not again.

"Let's not do this. Okay, Mom?" Gina curled her fingers around it and took a sip.

"Are you gonna help me?"

"With what?" she asked, taking the coffee and her sleep-deprived ass over to the kitchen table.

"Sara took a large cannoli order, and I already have a wedding cake to do on top of everything else."

Gina adjusted the clip holding her hair up and sighed. "Let Sara do the cannoli then."

"She can't make 'em like you do."

Bullshit.

Sara Malinowski Rossi, wife to her second eldest brother, Nick, had been working alongside her mother-in-law for nearly four years now. She was perfectly capable. Contrary to her mom's misguided and arrogant opinion, a person did not need to possess an Italian bloodline to make authentic Italian food. It was a learned skill, for chrissakes.

Not having nearly enough energy to argue with her, Gina caved, and here she was, folding mascarpone into Galbani whole-milk ricotta cheese. Since it wasn't the "traditional" recipe, Rosemary Rossi never used it in her cannoli cream filling, but Nonna had taught her that adding mascarpone, or even some heavy cream whipped thick, in with the ricotta made the dessert creamy and extra delicious.

"Sara said the flavors are up to us, but they asked for a variety, Gina."

"I know, Ma." Like she hadn't looked over the order form before she got started. "I'm gonna do chocolate chip, candied orange, and pistachio."

"That's my girl." Happy with her answer, her mother beamed. "Classic."

"And some in chocolate, vanilla, and lemon pastry cream." Shrugging off her mom's disapproving stare, she stifled a giggle. While not unheard of, they certainly weren't typical cannoli fillings. "I'll even make extra for the display case."

Which meant she'd have to whip up six different batches of filling versus three. She'd be stuck in here all day, but the small act of defiance was so worth it. With a satisfied smile, Gina sifted powdered sugar into the cheese mixture, humming Venery's latest single. She couldn't say why the song was in her head, except they played it on the radio all the damn time.

"Vinny's mother stopped in yesterday."

Was she supposed to give a shit?

"That's nice."

"His sister is getting married soon, and she's planning the bridal shower. I'm doing the cake, of course." Her lips twitching, Rosemary set the pastry bag down. "He's been asking after you."

"Who?" She knew exactly who *he* was, but Gina wasn't about to give her the satisfaction.

Ignoring the question, Rosemary went right on talking. "Vinny's a fine young man, Gina. He's a financial advisor now. Works for a big investment firm on Wabash, downtown."

Like I fucking care.

"Good for him."

"He's sorry, honey." Coming from behind, her mom hugged her. "At that age, boys think with their *cazzo*."

"Ma!" If she only knew. Vinny didn't just think with his dick, he was a dick.

"I know he regrets your misunderstanding." Rosemary turned her around, practically batting her heavily mascaraed lashes, her head tipped to the side. "You should give him another chance."

"Save your breath, because that's never gonna happen."

"Why not?" Her mom held her at arm's length, studying her. "You still have feelings for that boy. Think I'm blind? I haven't seen you go out with anyone else."

"Not interested." *At all.* "And I don't feel a goddamn thing for Vinny Passarelli."

"Grow up, Gina. You're twenty-three years old." Throwing her hands up in the air, she let her go. "You were just kids, then. Vinny has a bright future ahead of him. He can provide for you—"

"I don't need anyone to provide for me, Mom. I can take care of myself."

Maybe it was time to move out of her parents' house. Get her own place. She'd been tossing the idea around since she passed her nursing boards, but reasoned she'd wait until she finished grad school. Rent or tuition? She couldn't afford both, but her sanity was more important. A master's degree could wait.

"Just think of the beautiful babies you'd make together."

"*Basta!*" That's enough!

Naturally, Sara chose that moment to come in the back door. Her gaze flitting from mother to daughter, she hung her coat up on a hook. "Good morning."

"Morning, Sara." Taking a calming breath, Gina untied her

apron and plastered on a smile. "I was just gonna run across the street to get a coffee. Want anything?"

"Um…"

"You could make a pot right here, Gina." Her hip cocked, Rosemary folded her arms across her chest. "That's our competition, you know."

The hell?

"How do you figure?"

"Leo."

"Bakes muffins and cookies. Italian pastries and bread aren't his thing." Shaking her head, Gina couldn't help but laugh. "You're being ridiculous, Mama."

"Still…"

"I happen to know just how much he loves your cannoli." Appeasing her mother, she kissed her cheek. "I'll get you a cappuccino, okay?"

"All right."

"I'll take a coffee, too," Sara chimed in, pulling her long blonde hair into a pony. "Make mine a hazelnut latte with an extra shot."

"You got it."

Gina stepped outside. Leaning back against the brick wall, she inhaled a gulp of brisk March air and sighed. "*Madone.*"

Just before nine on a Thursday morning, Beanie's was a madhouse. She expected as much. It was a popular spot. Leo, Katie, and Kelly were busy behind the counter, serving customers. Taking her place in the back of the line, Gina contemplated getting some of Leo's buttery banana-nut muffins just to piss her mother off. She wouldn't. That would be childish. She was tempted to, though.

If only she would quit with the meddling and keep her opinions to herself. *At least where my love life is concerned.* Not that she had one, and that was the point, she supposed. Gina realized her mom just wanted to see her happy and settled with someone, but there was plenty of time for that. *Someday, in the faraway future.* Unlike most of the girls she knew, she wasn't in a hurry, and she wasn't desperate. And while she thought he might have been once, Vinny Passarelli was so *not* that guy.

"Gina, *ma belle.*" Wearing a green sweatshirt emblazoned with a sparkly silver shamrock, Leo leaned across the counter, kissing both of her cheeks. "Coming home from work?"

"No, uh, I'm helping Mom out in the bakery today."

"Oh?"

"Yeah. Two hundred and fifty cannoli." *More like three hundred, but who's counting?*

"You need a pick me up, *bébé.* What'll it be?"

She gave him her mom's and Sara's orders, then added her own. "And a quad-shot latte for me. A little sweet—"

"And a sprinkle of cinnamon." He winked. "Leo knows."

After Kelly swiped her card, she moved to the end of the bar to wait for the coffee.

Katie smiled. "Hey, Gina. Haven't seen you in a while. How've you been?"

"Okay. How about you?"

"Living the dream, babe." She placed a drink carrier in front of her and popped one of her drinks into it. "What do you need, Matt?"

"Can I get a refill, babe?" The guy handed Katie his empty cup, and leaning over the counter, he planted a kiss on her cheek. "Please?"

"Sure, gimme a sec."

Rude.

When Katie turned away to pour him some coffee, he turned to look at her. "Hello, pizza girl."

Her breath caught.

She took a good look at his face this time. Brown hair, streaked with blond, fell past his shoulders. His warm brown eyes appeared kind. Straight nose. Full Cupid's bow lips. He was a pretty boy—almost too pretty, not that she should think of a man that way. Matt McCready was the same age as Tony's, for fuck's sake.

"I have a name, you know."

"Gina." He smiled at her, and she almost forgot how to breathe. "I remember."

"You two know each other?" Katie handed him his refill.

"Yeah."

"No," Gina said at the same time.

Katie looked at them both, confused.

Matt cozied up to her. "You came to my house and brought me food, didn't you?"

"I delivered a pizza," she said with a roll of her eyes.

Nodding toward the espresso machine, Katie giggled. "I'll just be over here finishing up your lattes."

Sweat trickled down the back of Gina's neck. Her teeth raking over her lip, she glanced in every direction but his.

With a husky chuckle, warm breath ghosted past her ear. "Catch you later, bunny."

What?

She turned around, but he was gone.

Katie stood there, grinning. "He's got his sights set on you, girl."

"Yeah, sure." Grabbing the coffee, Gina shook her head. "I have to get back. Thanks, Katie. See you."

And hours later, after frying and filling three hundred and forty-two pastry shells, she was cleaning up the prep area with her mom when Sara poked her head in. "Some guy is out front asking for you."

"Who?"

"I don't know, but damn, Gina, he's cute," she said, nearly squealing.

He held a bottle of pop and a white Rossi's bag in his hand. Italian beef with sweet peppers and giardiniera. She could smell it.

"Just picked up my dinner." Swiping his tongue across his lip, Matt grinned. "Thought you could help me with dessert."

"Did you now?"

He sauntered closer to the glass case. And her. "Yeah, I did."

"How about the cannoli?" Sara gushed, her grin so wide it

looked like her lips might split open. "Gina made them. They're so good."

"Exactly what I had in mind." He spoke to Sara, but his gaze was on her. "Can't wait to taste it."

"Which kind would you like?"

"I'll take one of each."

Sara went to box up his cannoli.

Gina leaned across the counter. "Hope you're hungry. That's a lot, you know."

"Dessert's my favorite thing in the world, pizza girl." Matt winked. Then, leaning into her ear, he whispered, "And I'm starving."

Six

A stroke of luck put him inside Beanie's early on a Thursday morning. Most days, he didn't roll out of bed until ten, but Matt woke with the sun on that particular day, startled by a dream he couldn't remember. Unable to go back to sleep, and finding the coffee canister empty, he cut through the park to get his caffeine fix from Katie.

He saw her the moment she walked in.

Sipping on a cup of French pressed in an overstuffed chair in the corner, Matt took in every detail of her. His pizza girl waited in line, one arm dangling, the other draped across her front, fingers at her waist. She was thinking about something. Her features, beautiful and expressive, told him she was a feisty one. He liked that.

She tucked a strand of glossy dark hair that had escaped from its tie behind her pierced ear. Matt counted four. A diamond stud and two dainty hoops dangled from Gina's lobe, another from its helix. He wondered if she had piercings in places he couldn't yet see. His dick twitched at the thought.

The line moved. Leo kissed her cheeks. Kelly swiped her card. He had to get close to her. Smell her skin. Look into the depths of her eyes.

They weren't brown, nor green, but a combination of the two. The colors changed right in front of him while the warm scent of honey, vanilla, and cinnamon infused his lungs—a little sweet with a sprinkle of spice. The perfect blend.

He memorized it. Because now that he'd seen her, smelled her, and spoken to her, he was determined to have her. No one else would do.

She didn't blush, or simper, or fangirl. That Gina didn't melt into a puddle at his feet only heightened his desire. As did her apprehension. The telltale trickle of nervous sweat caught in the fine hairs at her nape had his mouth watering to taste the salt of her skin. Though tempted beyond reason, he held himself in check.

It wasn't the time.

And it wasn't the place.

But God help the girl once he had her where he wanted her.

Naked in my bed.

Lounging on a leather sofa in Taylor's family room, Matt absently strummed his fingers up and down his chest. It'd been two weeks since he'd seen Gina, and he was getting restless. "I need to see her again."

"So, call her then, my dude." Bo slapped his thigh, grinning goofily.

A strangled-sounding laugh escaped him. "Gee, now why didn't I think of that?"

"Idiot didn't bother getting her number, I bet," Sloan chimed in, tossing his hair back.

"Fuck off."

"Heh. Knew it." With a smirk, Sloan lifted his chin at their bassist. "Matt's way too cool for that shit, ain't he, Kit?"

He answered with a shrug.

"Has our boy ever asked a chick for her number?" Raising his eyebrows, Sloan leaned in. "C'mon, you should know."

"I don't think so," Kit said.

"Ever wonder why that is?"

It was the truth, but then Matt never had to. Ladies slipped him their number all the time, hoping he'd call them. He rarely did.

"Too easy."

Not to mention, he wasn't about to play his hand with Mrs. Rossi there, giving him the stank eye. The woman never did like him. Come to think of it, she didn't like Tony hanging out with Brendan or the other guys in the band, either.

"That's right. You crave the thrill of the chase." Turning his head, Sloan looked at Kit and smirked. "At least he admits it."

Does anything worth having come easily? No. It's fought for. Earned—just as Venery's success had been. And that's the only way Matt wanted it. He embraced a challenge.

"Who is this girl?" Taylor asked, bouncing baby Ireland on his knee.

"No one you'd know." He was sorry he'd even mentioned Gina to Bo with his bandmates around, but he didn't think they were paying them any attention.

Should've known better.

Ava, holding onto Chandan and Emery, came out from the kitchen. Chloe followed, a cake embellished with a guitar and alight with candles in her hands. "Happy birthday, babe."

He shook his head with a grin while they all sang, then blew out the candles.

Taylor passed him a beer. "You didn't think she'd forget, did you?"

No, but he had. Kind of. More so, he pushed the date out of his mind because he didn't care to remember the anniversary of the day he was born. The day Erin McCready sacrificed her life for his.

Kit draped an arm around his shoulders, his fingertips pressing in. "You're getting old, bro."

"Yeah, so are you." Funny, he didn't feel old yet, and as much living as he'd already done, he probably should.

"Happy Birthday, Matt." Ava gave him a piece of cake and pecked him on the lips. "Bo told me you love chocolate and peanut butter."

"Yeah, Reese's are my weakness." Smiling, he gazed at the chocolate candy on his cake. "You made this for me?"

"I did."

Even as a kid, no one had ever done that for him before.

"She loves you, man." Nodding, Bo squeezed his shoulder. "We all do."

He knew that, and he loved them all, too. Fiercely. Overcome by the depth of his feelings, Matt brought Ava in close and kissed her, slipping his tongue inside. It wasn't sexual per se, but a connection—an intimate expression of his affection for her. Except for the people here in this room, most people wouldn't understand that kind of love. They aren't even capable of it.

"Love you, sweet Ava." He breathed in her ear. "Thank you."

"You're welcome." She kissed him on the forehead. "I love you, too."

"Hey, what about me, Miss Bo Peep?"

Ava—Linnea, too—was one of the few women Sloan let his guard down with, but Chloe, not so much.

"And you, too, Sloan." Ava giggled and pressed a kiss to his lips.

"Cake." He cracked a grin. "Where's my cake?"

"Oh." She passed him a plate. "Here."

"I'll take another kiss, too."

Ava paused, pursing her lips in thought. "When's your birthday?"

"August."

She sat down by her man and quipped, "I guess you're just gonna have to wait until then."

Sloan stuck out his bottom lip like a child would and they all laughed.

"CJ called this morning," Taylor said, pouring whiskey into his glass. "Vanessa Parisi confirmed. She'll be here on the thirtieth to do the *Revolver* interview."

She'd done a piece on them for the magazine when they were on tour last summer. Now, she wanted to do a follow-up article, Venery at home, or some such shit. CJ arranged it and said they couldn't turn down *Revolver*, but none of them were keen to do it.

"I still don't get why she can't do it over the phone." Bo got funny vibes from the woman, especially after her photographer sold a photo of him kissing Ava to *TMZ*. The only reason he gave in and agreed to do the interview was because they had Danielle shoot the photos Vanessa wanted.

"It could be she needs to see where and how we live to write the article authentically," Jesse surmised. After what the press did to Chloe, Matt didn't know how he could give Vanessa Parisi the benefit of the doubt.

"Perhaps, but I don't like it, either." *Tell him, Tay.* "It's unnecessarily intrusive."

"I don't care anymore." Her auburn hair flying, Chloe whipped her head his way. "Let her come. I want the world to see how much I love you both."

"I do, too." Jesse kissed her. "God, I love you, baby."

With a roll of his eyes, Sloan snickered. "I can just imagine the shots Danielle got of you three."

"She got an eyeful," Taylor said, glancing at the ceiling.

"And it was beautiful." Chloe yanked on his beard and kissed him. "Poly is a real thing. The three of us love each other more than most couples do."

"We know that, Red." Bo reached over and squeezed her hand.

"The world needs to know it, too."

"Danielle took some lovely family shots as well." With a tender smile, Taylor rubbed his wife's thigh.

She giggled. "You should see the one we're having enlarged to hang above our bed."

"No one needs to see that, cherry cake." He put the baby in her lap. "It's just for us."

Matt chucked. *Nope, don't need to. I can just imagine.*

Ireland began fussing. Ava watched Chloe put the baby to her breast. She looked… sad. "You okay, sweetheart?"

"Yeah, I'm fine."

Every man knows when a woman says fine, it usually means anything but. Matt didn't believe her. "You don't look like it."

She sighed. "I just wish I could have that someday."

"Have what? A baby?"

With a nod, Ava wet her lips. "Yeah."

"You will," Matt said, putting his arm around her. "Bo would love to make a baby with you."

"I know." She smiled a little, but her voice was breaking. "He's such an amazing father."

"And you're a wonderful mom to Emery."

A tear slipped down her cheek.

"Ava, sweetheart, what's the matter?"

"I can't." She wiped her face. "It's nothing."

He should get out of bed. Vanessa was already making the rounds. Katie saw her arrive an hour ago when CJ brought her to Kit's door. She had to get through Sloan and Bo before she got to him.

Fuck her.

With thoughts of his elusive pizza girl, his dick was hard. He had yet to see her again, but as he flicked his fingernails over his nipples, Matt imagined what her tight, wet cunt would feel like riding his cock. Even better, riding his face. Breathing her in. Drowning in her sweetness.

He loved eating pussy as much as he loved fucking. Maybe even more. He envisioned tying her to the bed, fucking her with his tongue, sucking her swollen clit, and edging her for hours. One look in those chameleon-like eyes of hers, and he knew Gina could take it.

She'd cry and beg for him to let her come.

Then, when she couldn't take anymore, she'd cry and beg for him to stop.

And that was what he looked forward to most. The after. Caring for her. Bathing her. Holding her. Giving her whatever she needed to feel safe and loved. If given half a chance, he could be that man for her.

Was he crazy to be thinking of a girl he barely knew this way?

Yeah, man. You just need to get laid.

He hadn't been with anyone since Bo and Ava, unless he counted the chick who sucked him off at the Red Door the night after, which he didn't. Maybe he should call them and see if they wanted a replay, or ask Kit if he was up for hitting the club. Matt needed to sink his dick inside somebody. Too bad the only one he wanted was her.

His phone vibrated beside him. Sloan. *The pariah just left for Bo's. Good luck, fucker.*

Christ, he wasn't in the right frame of mind for this bullshit. Still, when CJ brought her in, Matt was ready and waiting, draped on his sofa in a pair of ripped-up black jeans, motorcycle boots, and a white button-up unbuttoned to his navel, as one would expect of a rock star.

Tight, short skirt. Thigh-high boots. Vanessa played her part to the hilt. Matt knew the type well. Fucked plenty just like her before he knew better, but now, he wasn't the least bit interested.

"I'll leave you to it," CJ said with a wink, and then he left.

He was sick and tired of his bullshit, too. The dude might be their manager, but ever since they left their old label, it seemed like he wasn't acting in the band's best interests—only his own. *Shame.* He'd been with them from the beginning, but perhaps it was time to part ways.

Vanessa tipped her head, indicating the leather wingback chair across from him. "May I?"

"Sorry." Matt nodded. "Yes, of course."

"You have a gorgeous home. The other guys, too. Magazine-worthy, all of them." She gazed around her, and crossing her legs, propped her iPad against her knee. "I've noticed each of you has your own flair—a unique style. What does your house say about you?"

What the fuck kind of question is that?

He glanced around his living room. Navy blue walls. Artwork he'd picked up on his travels with the band. Faux animal skins. Turkish rugs. Antiques. The silver disco ball Kit got him last Christmas sat on the hardwood floor by a fireplace filled with candles.

"I dunno." He leaned forward, shrugging. "I fill it with things I like to look at."

Glancing up from her iPad, Vanessa blushed.

No, sweetheart, I didn't mean you.

"I don't see any photos anywhere," she said, glancing at the white carved mantel. "How come?"

"I have some. Just not in here."

"Oh." And she uncrossed her legs. "Are you going to take me on a tour?"

"I think not." He sat back. "This is as far as you go. I prefer to keep where I shit and sleep private."

"I can respect that," she said, twisting her hair around her finger. "CJ tells me you just had a birthday."

Some journalist you are. A quick Google search and you'd have known that.

"Yeah, a week ago."

Bo was right. Vanessa could've done this interview over the phone. He was annoyed now that she didn't.

"Happy birthday."

Matt gave her a polite smile. "Thanks."

"Did you celebrate with your family? Your girlfriend, perhaps?"

For fuck's sake.

"My family." He'd throw her a bone. Maybe then she'd quit asking such lame questions. "Chloe made a fantastic dinner for all of us—seared scallops with lemon butter sauce. It's my favorite. And Bo's girl, Ava, she baked me a cake. Chocolate."

"Oh, I see." Biting into her lip, Vanessa tapped away on the iPad. "You've never spoken publicly about your family. Not that I could find, anyway."

"I haven't, and I'm not going to, either," he said, his tone sharper than he intended. Cocking his head, Matt shook it. "None of them are alive. The band is my family, and that's all anyone needs to know."

"I'm sorry."

"Don't be."

She placed her iPad on the table beside her. "No girlfriend then?"

"No."

"Why not?" she asked, leaning in.

He followed suit, the corner of his mouth quirking up. "Because I'm not worthy of her yet."

But I will be. Soon.

"So there's someone?"

"Potentially." And he moved away from her.

"That's all you're going to say?"

"Maybe I didn't make it clear." Tilting his head, Matt locked his eyes on hers. "But who I'm fucking is nobody's business."

"You're intense. You know that?"

He just chuckled.

Yeah, so I've been told.

Seven

t was a simply gorgeous afternoon. One of those rare spring days when the April sun was so warm, it almost felt like summer. The tulips in the park were opening, which meant the peonies would follow soon after. Her favorite flowers, Gina loved to see them blooming all over the city.

She was minding her own business. Truly. Winter in Chicago can feel like forever, and as nice as it was today, it could snow again tomorrow.

Gina sat on a blanket, resting against the trunk of a mighty oak, to read her book and take in the delightful spring air.

Sure, she could have accomplished the same thing in her own backyard, except she wouldn't have gotten any peace there—not with Teo and Luca at home, anyway. How was she supposed to know *he* would come prancing through the park?

And he wasn't alone.

Something made Gina glance away from her Kindle. A flash of movement in the periphery, perhaps. But there he was.

No man had the right to look that good in a pair of torn, faded jeans. She could make out the ridges of his abs beneath the tight, white Henley he wore. Sunlight glinted off the fine hairs on his muscled forearms.

Too busy talking with his shaggy-haired companion—Kit King, if she were to guess—Matt didn't appear to notice her. She lowered her gaze, pretending to be engrossed in her book, while discreetly watching him come closer as he walked along the trail. So much for peace. Gina was almost angry he'd disturbed it, which was stupid. It's not like he knew she'd even be here.

What was he doing in Coventry Park, anyway?

He lives here, Gina. Duh.

Still, shouldn't he be worried about encountering a mob of over-zealous fangirls or something? She glanced up again to see a pair of warm brown eyes looking right at her. Gina brought her knees up, balanced the Kindle on her thighs, and heard him chuckle, followed by a high-pitched shriek.

Four girls, bouncing on the balls of their feet, surrounded Matt and Kit. With their shiny, fresh faces, they couldn't have been older than fifteen. Taking advantage of the distraction, Gina gathered up her belongings and headed out of the park toward First Avenue.

Quickly, she glanced over her shoulder to see Matt staring after her while he signed an autograph. Gina hurried. Speed-walking, she broke into a run. For the past month, Matt had shown up at the bakery every Thursday morning to get cannoli. Sara said he probably came by to see if she was there. But the last thing on her agenda was to get involved with anyone, especially Matt McCready.

Once she made it out to the sidewalk, Gina easily blended into the throng of shoppers on the avenue. She paused at the corner. A latte for the walk home could salvage what remained of a perfectly good afternoon, but considering Beanie's was his likely destination, she thought better of it.

"Hey, Gina."

Fuck.

Should she stop, or just keep walking and pretend she didn't hear him? Her feet still moving, she went with the latter. She passed Charley's, maintaining a steady pace to Ash Street. Then, turning the corner, like a frightened little rabbit, Gina skirted past the red double doors and ran all the way home.

"Scaredy-cat."

"Am not."

Out of breath, after closing the door behind her, Luca caught her panting in the kitchen, so Gina had no choice but to tell him about her run-in with the rock star.

"Then why didn't you just talk to the guy?"

"Because…" She wasn't sure how to answer that.

Luca closed the fridge and chuckled. "You're afraid."

"I am *not* afraid of Matthew McCready."

"Yeah, you are," he said, tossing her a bottle of water. "Afraid of getting your heart broken."

With a shrug, Gina twisted off the cap.

"Get over it. We're not all assholes like that jag-off, Passarelli, you know."

"Let's leave him out of this, okay?" And giving her brother a meaningful glance, she slugged down the water.

Luca threw his hands up. "Fine, but I think you should at least talk to him."

"No, I shouldn't."

"Big mistake, *sorella*."

"Maybe." *Probably.* "But it's too late now, anyway."

Back in her room, Gina sat on the bed and switched her Kindle on. She didn't read the words on the screen, though. Instead, she gazed out the window, watching the sun's descent into the sky.

Gina hated Sundays.

It started with the eight o'clock Mass at St. Vincent's and usually ended with her brothers bickering at the dinner table.

In the name of the Father, the Son, and the Holy Spirit…

Under her mother's watchful glare, Gina made the sign of the cross and hastily exited their pew. She still hadn't forgiven her for her egregious sin this morning.

"You're not planning to wear that, are you?" Her brows knitted, Rosemary's gaze slowly traveled from her daughter's feet to the top of her head.

Glancing down at her buff ankle boots, Gina smoothed her fingers over her pants. "What's wrong with what I've got on?"

"You *cannot* wear jeans to church."

But I'm not…

They were black denim, not blue jeans, for chrissakes. Folks wore them all the time, but she wasn't about to argue with her.

"Go put on a nice dress, yeah?" Rosemary lifted her chin, urging Gina back upstairs. "That's what we wore to Mass when I was a girl."

Here we go.

"And be thankful you don't have to wear a hat anymore. *Nonna* used to pin a lace handkerchief to my head," she said for the hundredth time, her mouth twisting into a too-quick smile. "Besides, you might meet a nice boy, or Vinny could be there. Now, change."

He wasn't, thank God.

Outside on the church steps, wearing a dress her mother also disapproved of, Gina inhaled a cleansing breath of air. With the clouds covering the sun, it wasn't nearly as warm as it had been yesterday. She rubbed her arms, wishing she'd taken a sweater, and traipsed down the stairs to the sidewalk.

Matteo came up from behind her and, grabbing Gina by the shoulder, wrenched her around. "And just where do you think you're going?"

"Home."

Hazel-green eyes boring into hers, he cocked his head as his fingers raked through a dark forest of thick, wavy hair. "You're not riding with us?"

"No, I'm gonna walk," she said, glancing at the line of cars waiting to get out of the parking lot. "Wanna bet I make it to the house before you?"

"Yeah." Teo hooked his arm around her. "C'mon."

"What are you doing?"

"Walking with you."

Oh.

His fingertips pressed into her shoulder. "Don't let her get to you, Gina."

"Who?"

"Mom." He looked at the sky, shaking his head before his gaze landed back on her. "C'mon, I'm not stupid."

"Yeah, well, I can't seem to do anything right where she's concerned."

"Heh, and Tony can do no wrong," he said and kicked at a pebble on the sidewalk. "Fuck that. Keep on doing what you're doing, Gina, because you're doing just fine. Don't let her tell you different."

"I've been thinking it might be time to get my own place, but if I do, then I can't afford grad school."

A certification in midwifery had been her goal from the start. Was it still? Forty hours a week in an office besides taking call, Gina wasn't as sure as she'd been before. She loved obstetrics. The mamas. The babies. But she wanted a life outside of work, too, not that she had much of one now.

Teo's hand dropped from her shoulder to her waist. He stopped walking. "Want a roommate?"

"And leave your cushy apartment in the basement?" Her brother had everything a guy could want down there. "You can't be serious."

"Maybe," Teo said with a shrug. "If we don't open up that location in Wrigleyville, I'm leaving."

"You don't mean that."

Did he? No, he couldn't.

"Yeah, I do." Nodding, he wet his lips, then taking her by the hand, they resumed walking. "I can't work with him anymore, Gina. I can't stand to even look at him."

"I understand how you feel, but…"

"No one does."

She squeezed his hand. "He's your brother, Matteo."

"And he betrayed me." The venom in his voice was unmistakable. Teo unlocked the front door and ushered her inside. "C'mon, I'll help you get the sauce going."

By noon, she and Teo had a pan of ziti baking in the oven and beef *braciole* simmering in a pot of marinara on the stove. Stuffed with bread crumbs, parsley, onions, garlic, and fresh-grated parmesan cheese, the kitchen smelled heavenly. Gina had just put down the last layer of bananas, chocolate pudding, and graham crackers on an icebox cake for dessert, when Nick and Sara, followed by Tony, his wife, and their four kids, came in through the front door.

"Gimme that baby," their mother shrieked, and dashing out of the kitchen, she took the pink-wrapped bundle out of her daughter-in-law's arms.

Teo's features hardened. He took the icebox cake from her hands and put it in the fridge. "I'll be downstairs. Let me know when it's time to eat."

"Teo, don't…"

"Let him go, Gi." Nick stepped in between her and their brother. "He'll be all right. He just needs some time by himself."

"I hate this," she said, hugging herself.

"I know, babe." Two solid arms wrapped around her. "I do, too."

"Are they ever going to be okay again?" Gina asked, glancing up at her second eldest sibling.

The corner of his mouth ticked up, and tipping his chin, Nick shrugged at the same time. "Miracles can happen, yeah?"

They can, but after eight years, Gina had her doubts that the rift between her brothers would ever mend.

Teo never came up for dinner. When Gina went downstairs to get him, he pretended to be asleep. He wasn't snoring, and typically, he rumbled like a freight train when he slept, so she knew he wasn't.

Combing the hair from his face, she kissed his temple. "I'll bring a plate down for you, okay?"

"Thanks," he said, his strained voice so soft it was barely audible. "I love you."

No one mentioned Teo's absence at the dinner table as if it didn't matter, which only made her angry for him. Maybe if her parents had acknowledged Teo's feelings and addressed the issue between him and Tony head-on, they wouldn't all be walking on eggshells. But no, they swept everything under the rug. And now, all they had was a fractured, dysfunctional family to show for it.

While her mom served everyone squares of icebox cake, Gina watched her nephew, Anthony, chase his five-year-old sister around the table. Kids will be kids, but jeez, Tony and Lina didn't even attempt to correct him. She rescued Nina before the little girl face-planted on the hardwood floor and deposited the child in her father's lap.

"I'm gonna bring Matteo some dinner."

"Not now, Gina." Rosemary motioned for her to sit down. "We're having cake."

"Unbelievable." Appalled, she shook her head. "Do you even hear yourself?"

"Gina Marie Rossi, you will *not* speak to your mother like that!" Her dad's fist slammed onto the table, the impact knocking over the salt shaker. "Do you hear me?"

She nodded, then shooting daggers at her eldest brother, she turned and left the room.

"Hey." Gina found Teo sitting in the oversized leather bean-bag chair she got him last Christmas, staring vacantly at the TV. "You okay?"

"Yeah, why wouldn't I be?" He snickered, his gaze never leaving the screen. "I'm just a prisoner in my own fucking house."

"You could've come up." She put the food she brought him on the table, then made room for herself beside him. "I wish you would have."

"Better I didn't."

Gina picked up a magazine lying on the table next to his plate. "Since when do you read?"

"I don't, much." Clasping his hands behind his head, her brother chuckled. "Asshole's old pals are on the cover."

She flipped it over. The boys known as Venery stared back at her. "So, I see."

"Cool dudes," Teo said, and finally turned his head to look at her. "You probably don't remember, but they used to hang out here a lot."

"I remember."

"Yeah, maybe you do." Smiling, he tugged on her ponytail. "You pulled Bo's hair once. He pretended to cry, and you gave him your Furby so he'd feel better."

"I didn't give it to him. I let him borrow it," Gina said, correcting him. "Furby's tucked away somewhere in my closet."

"Jesus, you still have it?" Teo laughed.

"Yeah, I kept my Bratz and Monster High dolls, too." Gina punched his arm and stood. "Now, eat your dinner before it gets cold."

He reached for the plate, setting it on his lap. "I am. I am."

Tucking the magazine under her arm, she headed toward the stairs.

"Gina?"

She turned around. "Yeah?"

"I love you, too." Blowing her a kiss, Teo raised a forkful of ziti to his mouth. "Thanks."

After everyone had gone home, and she lay in her bed, Gina opened the copy of *Revolver*. Her fingers skimming over the glossy pages, she smiled at the images of the drummer whose hair she pulled as a child. Bo looked the same as he did back then. He had a daughter now. Taylor was married with two kids already. She vaguely remembered when Tony mentioned he was going to his wedding.

Gina gazed upon those warm brown eyes that looked for her

yesterday in the park, taking in every detail of him at her leisure. Music-driven. Protective of his privacy. Fiercely loyal to his family, who he said were his brothers in the band. The narrative painted him in a cold, harsh light. Funny, her perception of him was very much the opposite.

It's probably all bullshit, anyway.

She'd read it all later. There had to be more to the man than that. But as her gaze lingered on his image, Gina couldn't help but wonder if maybe, just maybe, Matt McCready might turn out to be worth the risk.

Eight

If he had to consume any more goddamn cannoli, he might vomit. It wasn't because Matt didn't like the rich Italian pastry, he did, but he'd been eating them on a weekly basis for how long—two months now? Every Thursday morning, he cut through the park, grabbed a coffee from Katie, then walked across the street to Rossi's bakery on the off chance he'd see her, but she was never there.

Where was she? And who was this girl who delivered pizza one day and tied on a baker's apron another? All Matt knew was her first name.

He should've gone after her that day he spotted her in the park, but Matt missed out on his opportunity, thanks to a gaggle of fangirls visiting the city on spring break. The Venery boys grew up in this neighborhood, so most folks who lived here had known them since they were kids and weren't fazed to see them. Sometimes, though, people came around to seek them out. Hence, the reason they gated Park Place.

By the time he finished signing autographs and taking selfies with the girls, Gina was gone. Matt tried to catch up with her out on First Avenue, but she was well ahead of him by then. Too late, he called out her name. He should've chased after her, and he would have if the sidewalk hadn't been so crowded with Saturday afternoon shoppers.

Catch you next time, bunny.

And there would be a next time.

It was Thursday, after all.

Matt watched the blonde chick stocking cookies in the display case through the storefront window. Thankful the bakery was empty and Mrs. Rossi wasn't in sight, he opened the door. At the tinkle of the little brass bells, the girl glanced up at him and giggled.

"Gina's not here, you know."

Of course, she isn't.

"How many cannoli would you like?" she asked, tongs at the ready. "We only have chocolate chip and pistachio today. My mother-in-law doesn't make the flavors Gina does."

"Mrs. Rossi's your mother-in-law?"

"Yeah, I'm Nick's wife."

How did I not know that?

"I'll take a dozen." Not that he planned on eating any of them. "I have a meeting this morning."

"You want to get something else, then?" And she moved to the other end of the glass case. "How about some *zeppole?* They're kind of like doughnuts filled with pastry cream, chocolate, or jam, but my favorite way to have them is when they're still warm, out of a paper bag, covered in powdered sugar."

"All right, you convinced me." Matt leaned against the counter and nodded. "Give me the doughnuts."

"They're so good."

"So… I'm sorry, I didn't catch your name…" He glanced up and gave her a flirty grin, the one that turned the ladies into goo.

She blushed. "Sara."

"Sara," he repeated. "Can you tell me when she *will* be here?"

"Sorry, I can't do that." Sara went to work, plucking Italian doughnuts out of the case with her tongs.

"Why not?"

"Because I don't know when that might be." She closed the lid of the bakery box, tying it with red and white string. "Gina only comes in to help sometimes—when Rosemary guilt-trips her into it. Like she doesn't already work her ass off at the hospital."

"Hospital?"

Her lips curving into a pretty smile, Sara took the box over to the register. "Yeah, she's a nurse over at Illinois Masonic—labor and delivery."

As in babies? And here he thought the only thing Gina delivered was pizza.

"You like her, don't you?"

Matt grinned. He didn't mean to. It just kind of happened all on its own.

"I knew it."

Nick came out of the back, wiping his hands on his white apron, staining it with splotches of red pizza sauce. He kissed his wife on the cheek, then greeted him, "Hey, Matt. How's it goin'?"

"Can't complain," he said, handing Sara his credit card. "Meeting up with the boys this morning, and I had a taste for something sweet."

"*Zeppole*—good choice." Nick nodded over his wife's shoulder.

She giggled. "He came to see Gina."

"My sister?" His head snapped in Matt's direction. "What for?"

"She's your sister?"

The Rossis had a lot of kids. Tony was the oldest. Nick was a couple of years younger. They had another brother, who might have been in fifth grade back then. Hell, Luca was toddling around in diapers. And yeah, a little sister.

No fucking way.

"C'mon, you don't remember the cute little pain in the ass?"

With a toss of his head, Nick chuckled. "Course, she was only six, maybe seven, the last time you saw her."

Christ…

He was an idiot. How had he not put two and two together? But fuck if it didn't all make sense now.

"Look, that was a long time ago, dude." Matt picked up the box of Italian doughnuts before Gina's brother came up with four and asked him any more questions. "I gotta run, Nick, but good seeing you."

"Yeah." He winked. "I'll let Gina know you came by."

The guys were waiting for him in the first-floor office when he got to the studio. They sat on eggplant-colored sofas with Brendan, Jesse, and Dillon, twiddling their thumbs while staring at Kyan's framed architectural drawings that hung on the exposed brick walls.

Taylor glanced at him with a heavy sigh. "You're late."

"Chill out, dude." And he tossed the bakery box onto the coffee table. "I went to Rossi's and got us some doughnuts."

Bo snorted.

"Sit."

"Can't I get a cup of coffee first?" Ignoring Taylor's command, he popped a pod into the machine. "What's this meeting for, anyway?"

"Plans."

Matt turned around, folding his arms across his chest. "Plans for what?"

"Our next record," Taylor said. "I'd like to have the demos down by September."

This wasn't news to him. It had been almost a year since they put out the last one. Their typical album cycle was eighteen months—two years, tops.

"Want to release it next spring?"

Though they could finish it in time for Christmas, he supposed.

"Perhaps sooner."

"Tour?"

Why was he even asking? They promoted every new album with

a tour, except these days, Taylor wasn't too keen on being away from his family for very long. Bo wasn't either now that he had one, but surely, he'd bring Ava and Emery along with them again.

"Most likely." Tipping his head onto the back of the sofa, the lead guitarist blew out a breath. "But that's what we're here to discuss."

"Okay." Matt grabbed his coffee and sat between Kit and Sloan. "In that case, where's CJ?"

If they were talking about release dates and tours, their manager should be here.

"I didn't invite him." Taylor lifted his head, scraping his hand through his hair. "CJ's contract is up, and after the shite he pulled with Vanessa Parisi, I think we need to re-evaluate keeping him on."

Matt picked up a doughnut, or whatever Sara called it, from the box and bit into it. He swallowed, licking the remains of vanilla cream from the corner of his lip. "Yeah, well, I've been thinking it's time we part ways with CJ for a while now."

"I'm with you, dude," Bo chimed in. "What he tried to do wasn't cool."

"Manipulative, meddling, greedy motherfucker taking twenty percent of our gross, and for what?" The voice of Venery had a way with words. It almost sounded like an angry ballad. "He doesn't give a shit about any of us and he isn't acting in the best interest of the band—only himself. We've done more for that ass-kissing dick than he's ever done for us."

Sloan wasn't lying. Fast cars. Plenty of women. Lots of money. The dude was rolling in dough, living the dream off of their sweat, their fame, their music.

"I don't know." Kit rubbed at the back of his neck. "He's been our manager for a long time, man."

Seventeen years.

Taylor nodded with a loud exhale. "I hate to say it, but he's changed since we left the label."

"Nah, man. He was a slimy motherfucker long before then. You just weren't paying attention."

Tell us how you really feel, Sloan.

"Perhaps, so." Conceding, Taylor shrugged. "Are we all in agreement, then?"

"Yeah," Kit said, pushing the hair from his eyes. "He's out."

"Think he'll start trouble?" Jesse asked.

Dillon answered, "I'd expect some backlash."

Yeah, count on it.

"I'll have Phil draw up a severance agreement." Taylor dismissed their concern. "We'll give him a nice bonus and send him on his way."

"We'll need to find a new manager," Matt reminded him. "Won't be easy."

"Brendan's offered to help us out until we do."

"Yeah?" He turned his head toward the club chair occupied by their tattooed giant of a friend.

"However I can." Brendan tipped his head as if the offer was nothing to speak of. "Finances, contract negotiations—that sort of thing. I don't know much when it comes to the rest of it."

And the rest of it was a lot.

A band manager wears many hats. Marketing and promotion, scheduling appearances, coordinating tours, and all the shit that goes with it. Brendan might not possess in-depth knowledge of the music industry, but he *was* a savvy businessman, and if there was anyone who had their interests at heart, it was him.

"CJ didn't know shit when we started out either, remember?" And that was the truth. "You got this, brother."

"I'll do my best."

"You're family, Bren." Matt slung an arm around Kit and the other around Sloan. "We trust you."

His guitar rested on his thighs as he looked over the notes Taylor sent over. Riffs. Chord progressions. Kit's bass, Bo's drums, and his guitar would create the rhythm section for each track. Lyrics, melodies, and harmonies come after. Then, they'd play it together, making numerous revisions along the way, until everyone was satisfied with the end result. Sometimes, everything came together on the first playthrough. Most often, it took many attempts and adjustments to get the sound just right.

He held down a series of chords with his fretting hand, alternately strumming and fingerpicking the strings with the other, composing the rhythm part in his head. The rudimentary beginnings of one, anyway. Because without Kit's bassline and Bo's groove, it fell flat.

His stomach grumbling, Matt set his guitar down on the sofa beside him. He'd been at this for hours, and after adding some notes of his own to Taylor's scribble, he picked up the phone to order himself dinner.

"Twenty minutes?" His fingers rubbed over his bare chest. "Sounds good, Nick. Thanks."

He knew Gina's last name now. Her kid brother could tell him what he wanted to know. Did she still live at the townhouse on Willow Street? What was her schedule like? Her phone number?

Restless, Matt got up, and walking past the clock on the wall and the photo of him and his grandmother that stared at him from the shelf, he cracked the blinds open to peek out the window. Nearly dark, the last remnants of what had likely been a magnificent sunset rapidly faded from view.

And the Fates shone down on him once again.

Pizza box in hand, he watched her come up the porch steps. Smirking, Matt opened the door. "You're not Luca."

"I thought we established that already."

Her stance casual, Gina cocked her hip, attempting to appear unaffected by him. He knew better, though. Dilated pupils. Rapid, shallow breaths. Her gaze fixated on his torso. She was nervous, but desire oozed from her pores.

"Filling in tonight?" Matt asked, and taking the pizza from her, he placed it on an entryway table.

Biting at her lips, she shrugged. "Something like that."

"Wanna know what I think?" He rested his elbow against the doorframe.

"What?"

The muscles in her fingers twitching, she tucked her just-brushed hair behind her ear. No doubt it had been up in a messy bun not ten minutes ago. A touch of mascara. Gloss on those tempting lips of hers.

"I think you wanted to see me."

Closing her chameleon eyes, Gina shook her head.

He reached out, his fingertips brushing her arm. "It's okay. I wanted to—"

"This was a mistake," she whispered and fled down the steps to her car.

Matt watched her taillights until she made it to the gate and closed the door.

A mistake? Yeah, maybe so.

Stunned, he picked up the pizza box and tossed it onto the kitchen island. Intent on grabbing a slice, Matt opened the lid, but found he wasn't very hungry anymore. Then the doorbell rang.

She came back. He knew she would.

"Wanna fuck?"

"What?" Gina cocked her head, indignant.

But then, why else would she be here? That's all any of them ever wanted. It disappointed him in a way. He wanted her to be different.

"You heard me. Do you wanna fuck?"

"Wow!" She slowly shook her head. "You're bold."

He didn't have time for bullshit. "The answer to an unasked question is always no."

Taking a step closer, Matt saw she wasn't just pretty with her long, dark hair and those hazel eyes that changed colors. No, Gina was beautiful. And she didn't back away from him, even though he almost wished she would.

Run, rabbit, run.

"Why should I?"

"Because you want to." He smirked. "I've seen you looking at me the same way you are right now. You've been imagining this dick inside that pretty little cunt of yours for weeks, haven't you?"

Heh, months.

Nuzzling his nose in her neck, he smelled her skin and growled, "Know what, bunny? I've been thinking about it, too."

"I don't even like you."

"Yes, you do."

"No, I don't."

"It's what you came back for, isn't it?" Matt took her hand and placed it on the hard bulge in his jeans.

She whimpered.

"You like me."

"I don't."

Then he slid his hand inside her pants and felt the wet heat between her legs.

"See?" Matt held up his finger, coated in her sweetness.

He watched the muscles play in her throat.

"You like me." He licked his finger, then grinned. "I'd say you like me a helluva lot."

Nine

She should slap that stupid grin right off his pretty face.

And there was no doubt in her mind that if any other man had dared to do what he just did, she would have. But it was him, and his directness took her by surprise.

"Do you wanna fuck?"

Matthew McCready wasn't wrong. It pissed her off he got it right. She did come here to see him. And embarrassed he saw through her ruse, Gina tucked her tail and took off, only to turn around and come back again. God, how in the fuck did her brothers convince her to do this?

She didn't ask for their help. Truly. On a whim, Gina texted Sara, and they made plans to go see a movie. Rossi's Pizza stayed open until midnight on Saturdays, but the bakery closed at eight. Her sister-in-law would have something to do until Nick got off work, and Gina? She was just happy to be getting out of the house.

Brothers are evil creatures.

They pounced on her.

"Gina Bobina," Luca crooned. "I need you to do me a favor."

"What?"

"Take a delivery for me." While batting his long, thick lashes that no boy had a right to have, his lips quirked into a devious grin. "Please?"

Nick was with him, and that alone should have told her he was up to something. He stood there, an arm dangling over Luca's shoulder, his tongue tucked into his cheek.

"Sorry, Luca Bobuca. Me and Sara are about to head out."

"C'mon, *sorella*, please?" He pressed his hands together like he was praying. "Kev scored tickets to the Cubs game, but I gotta leave now if I'm gonna make it. It's one pizza, and it's only a few blocks away. You'll be back in ten minutes."

"Help the kid out, Gi." With a lift of his chin, Nick put his arm around his wife. "I'll help Sara close up."

"Okay, fine, but you owe me."

"You can thank me later." His grin triumphant, Luca dropped the pizza box in her hands and kissed her cheek. "Love you."

Then she glanced at the delivery ticket taped to the box.

McCready. Park Place.

"Luca," she screamed, running after him.

But he was already gone.

Her lips pressed together, Gina stomped her foot on the linoleum floor and glanced over at her brother. "There's no Cubs game tonight, is there?"

"Nope." Laughing, Nick shook his head. "Don't get all pissy now. Luca's doin' *you* a favor."

"Oh, yeah?" She glared at him, her vision narrowing. "How do you figure?"

"I saw Matt just the other day, babe." And stepping into her personal space, Nick bopped her on the nose with his finger. "He was here looking for you."

"Yeah, he's been a committed cannoli customer for months now,"

Sara said, bolstering her husband. "Every Thursday morning, like clockwork, though I talked him into *zeppole* the other day."

"So? It doesn't mean anything."

"Yes, it does." Excitedly, her sister-in-law nodded. "It means he's interested."

"You take the delivery, Nick." Gina tried to push the box into her brother's hands. "I can't go looking like this."

"Why not?" With a dismissive wave, he took a step back. "You were gonna go to the movies looking like that."

"Never mind him," Sara said, and giving Nick a stern look, she took out her purse. "You're gorgeous. Let's take your hair down, put a little gloss on those lips, and you'll be good to go."

"Yeah?" Gina looked at her older brother.

He nodded his approval.

"Yeah." And smiling, Sara fixed her hair. "Hurry now, before the pizza gets cold."

So, here she was, standing on the front porch of a rock star, watching him suck her bodily fluids from his finger.

"I'd say you like me a helluva lot."

Holy cannoli, what am I supposed to say to that?

"Do I now?" To appear non-committal, or maybe to protect herself, she wasn't sure which, Gina crossed her arms over her chest.

A faint smirk curved his mouth. Matt came closer, and running his nose alongside hers, he inhaled. "The attraction is definitely there, so yeah."

"Don't flatter yourself." Flipping her hair behind her shoulder, Gina shook her head and looked at the ornate light fixture on the porch ceiling.

He cupped her cheek, bringing her gaze back to him. "I'm not, and you know it."

His eyes held her there. She couldn't look away. What in the hell was he after?

"I know you're used to women worshipping you at your feet, but you're dead wrong if you think I'm ever going to be one of them."

"That's too bad. I'd love to see you on your knees," he said, and licked his lips. "It isn't what I want, though."

"What do you want, then?"

Matt leaned in, and warm breath tickled her ear. "To earn the privilege to worship you at yours."

She felt his words. Right where he meant for her to.

"Oh, yeah?"

"Yeah." His hands on her arms, Matt pulled her to his chest and smiled. "I like you, and all I want is the chance to get to know you better, so can we start over?"

Gina shrugged, because how could she say no to that smile of his?

She couldn't.

"What are you doing tonight, Gina Rossi?"

"Going to the movies with my sister-in-law."

"Change of plans, bunny." His palms ran down her skin, leaving goose bumps in their wake, to squeeze her forearms. "I've got a delicious pizza waiting in the kitchen. We're gonna talk and you're gonna watch a movie with me right here."

"Think so, do you?" She found it difficult to breathe when he was this close. Gina put a modicum of space between them.

"I know so." He hooked his arm around her waist and drew her toward the door. "C'mon."

"Fine," she said, and crossing the threshold, Gina looked at him. "But I won't be having sex with you."

"Why not?"

Good question.

She should want to, right? There were probably a million other girls who'd sell their souls to be in her shoes right now, but something told her to tread carefully with Matthew McCready.

"I'm kidding." He chuckled, fingers gripping into her hip. "No fucking, okay?"

"Okay."

"I won't take what hasn't been offered. But once you give it to me, fully, and with intention…"

Pausing at the threshold, she glanced at him.

Dark eyes gleaming in the lamplight, his mouth curved into a smirk so subtle she thought perhaps she'd imagined it.

"… you won't need to think at all."

Gina looked around his fancy house as Matt led her down the hall. To her right was a formal living room, judging by the look of it. She spied an oriental rug on the polished wood floors. Leather furniture draped with throws of fur. Avant-Garde artwork on dark-painted walls. An antique record player. A mirrored disco ball? It worked, though. She wasn't sure what she expected, but it wasn't this. His tastes were an eclectic mix.

After passing a couple of closed doors, the hallway opened into a great room with a chef's dream of a kitchen on one end and a more comfortable-looking TV room on the other. A row of glass doors opened up to an outdoor terrace and a tree-laden back garden beyond.

The pizza sat on a slab of quartz with cobalt and copper veining. "It's probably cold by now."

"That's all right. I can eat pizza right out of the fridge."

"Three seventy-five." Gina set the temperature on his high-end, pro-style gas oven. "Five minutes should do the trick."

"Wine?" Matt offered, glancing at her from over his shoulder after he popped the pizza in.

"Sure."

He opened a liquor cabinet, and fingering a bottle of Ripasso, Matt skipped it, opting for the Sangiovese instead. He poured them each a glass. "Cheers."

"*Salute.*" She clinked her glass with his and took a sip. "You must do a lot of cooking in here."

"Nope." His chin dipping, Matt shook his head. "I know it looks like I would, but I order out mostly. Every night, I open up Uber Eats and ask myself what country's cuisine I want for dinner."

"But…"

The delights she could create in here. What a waste of a glorious kitchen.

"A very close friend of mine designed the renovations on this place." A sheen appeared in his eyes. Then he blinked, and it was gone. "His wife and Tay's helped me choose what appliances to put in. Look, I'm a simple guy. I can grill a steak and shit, but why bother when it's just me, ya know? Still, the girls insisted I needed all this stuff, and said I'd thank them for talking me into it someday."

"I'd say they chose well."

"I'm glad you approve," he said, and took the pizza out of the oven, carrying it over to the coffee table, along with the bottle of wine. "Maybe one evening you can help me make use of it."

"Maybe," she said, sinking into his fluffy cloud sofa. There was no doubt in her mind that the piece was authentic Restoration Hardware.

Matt handed her a slice of pizza on a plate and cozied up beside her. "So, tell me all about you, Gina Rossi."

"What is it you want to know?"

The question was too broad, not that she knew how to answer it, anyway. He already knew her family, where she grew up—all the mundane facts people usually spout off when asked about themselves.

"Everything, pizza girl."

"That's not my actual job. I'm an RN—labor and delivery." Glancing over at him, Gina blew on her pizza before taking a bite, and the corner of his mouth ticked up. "You knew that already, didn't you?"

"Sara told me," he confirmed with a nod. "Do you love what you do?"

"I love it but hate it too." She washed her pizza down with the heady, dry red. "I'm sure that doesn't make any sense."

"Enlighten me." His palm settled on her arm, fingertips caressing her skin.

"I love my job; the hours not so much." Gina put her plate on the table, and turning toward him, she attempted to explain. "I work night shift. Every other weekend. Holidays. Overtime. I thought once nursing school was over, I'd get to have a life again, but I was wrong."

"What do you do when you're not working? Besides making cannoli and delivering pizza, that is."

"Catch up on sleep, mostly." She winced. *Good one, Gina.* "And sometimes, I pick out a book to read in the park."

"Pick out a movie and lay your head right here," he said, patting his sculpted bare chest.

"But I don't know what movies you like."

"Doesn't matter." Matt shifted his weight, and leaning against her, he pressed the remote into her palm. "I'll like whatever you choose."

That he could be so charming surprised her. Gina assumed a man in his position, with his looks, wouldn't even bother trying. Had she misjudged him?

Maybe, but then the wolf charmed Little Red Riding Hood, too, until he tried to eat her.

Sparing Matt the pain of a chick flick, Gina clicked on the first comedy she saw and noticed pages of handwritten sheet music scattered on the far end of the table. "What's that?"

"Songs for the new album," he said, like it was no big deal, and then straightened the mess of papers into a neat stack. "I was working on the rhythm parts before you got here."

"You write them?"

"Taylor and Bo come up with most of the music." His head tipped to the side and his gaze never leaving her, Matt refilled their glasses with wine. "We all have a hand in it, though."

She had no idea how a song was written. Was there a process? Gina thought there had to be, but musically, she was inept. What a spectacular thing it must be to pluck notes out of your brain and put them to words.

"Did you always want to be a musician?"

"I got my first guitar when I was eight." He chuckled, a slight flush appearing on his cheeks. "A cheap acoustic one. My grandma got it for me with the S&H Green Stamps she had saved. I loved that shitty guitar—still have it."

She glanced at the guitar propped against the sofa and over to a picture of a teenage Matt with an older woman on the shelf. "So, you did then."

"Nah." Matt bit into his pizza with a grin. "I wanted to be a fireman like my uncle."

Doesn't every little boy?

But looking at him now, she couldn't picture it. "Yeah?"

"Uncle Mark was a genuine hero." He nodded, his brown eyes glossing over again. "He was killed in a fire when I was twelve. Changed my mind after that."

Gina couldn't recall ever hearing anything about Matt's uncle from her brothers, but then why would she? The man must've died around the time she was born.

His hand in hers, she rubbed her thumb across his knuckles. "Oh, God, I'm sorry."

"My grandmother was pretty torn up." He brought her fingers to his lips and kissed them. "Anyway, it was a long time ago."

"How did the band get started?"

"We used to play to songs on the radio in Bo's basement. God, his poor mom. We were awful." Laughing at the memory of it, Matt shook his head. "But we got better. By the time high school started, Taylor had joined us. Then, we started writing our own stuff and knew we were on to something—figured we had a shot, at least."

"And look at you now." Sipping on her wine, Gina took in the expensively furnished room with gold records and band memorabilia on the walls. "I hear Venery playing on the radio all the time."

"We sacrificed a lot. Worked our asses off." He popped the last bite of pizza into his mouth. "Eight years of shitty gigs in sleazy bars, county fairs, and festivals, warming up the crowd for the opening band. Didn't see our name on the *Billboard* charts until we were twenty-six."

"But the struggles were worth it, right?"

"Yes and no."

What does that mean?

"See, everything in life's a trade-off. Anything you gain, something else is lost in return."

A tiny thread of melted cheese was stuck to the scruff on his face. Gina reached over and wiped it away with her thumb. He seized her hand, and with his fingers sliding into her hair, Matt brushed her lips with his. Gentle, slow, and deliberate, the subtle touch sent a thrilling rush all the way down to her toes.

Effortlessly, his tongue slipped inside, her lips yielding to his kiss. His eyelashes touching her skin, Gina shared his breath while she explored the texture and taste of him. Savory. Delicious. Intoxicating.

And she fell.

Slowly.

Drifting on a cloud, Matt took her to a place where gravity didn't exist and heavenly music was everywhere.

Her mind numb, he laid her head on his chest. His hand skimmed over the curve of her hip to rub up and down her thigh. The sensation of his kiss lingering, Gina didn't watch the movie. She closed her eyes, listening to the beat of his heart, inhaling the manly scent of him. Fingertips brushed close to her breast, and she gasped.

"Shh… relax, bunny. I won't touch you there."

"What if I want you to?"

Matt brought her face up to his, and intense, dark eyes staring deep into her soul, he lowered those full, perfectly bowed lips to hers. Warm hands caressed her all over. He squeezed her breasts, thumbs sweeping over her nipples, and the nub of flesh between her legs awakened. Its pulsing incessant, her empty pussy ached.

She must've forgotten what it felt like to have a man's hands on her because she heard herself squeak at the contact. Jesus, she was bursting out of her skin. Her limbs trembled. Her stomach turned flips. She couldn't catch her breath even though she was breathing.

"Your brother's gonna want my balls on a platter," he said, pulling her shirt over her head. Then he kissed the skin between the mounds of flesh held captive in peach silk and lace. "But I don't care."

"Nick?" She giggled. "Who do you think plotted with Luca to get me here?"

"No, Tony." Callused fingers traced along her collar bone and down her chest to free her breasts from their delicate prison. "Fuck me, you're beautiful."

She didn't have time to respond because, in the next breath, her nipple was in his mouth. Astride his lap, her fingers tangled in his long hair, Gina threw her head back, the tugging of his warm, wet tongue a most exquisite sensation. If her clit was pulsing before, it was screaming at her now.

Her body demanded… some kind of release. It felt strange and wonderful and foreign. Vinny had never elicited the feelings this man was stirring inside her. Hell, she'd never been able to do it herself, either. Not like this. Never like this. Urgent, and so powerful and raw, the will to lose control frightened her.

Gina felt his cock growing hard beneath her. Holding his head to her breast, she instinctively pressed down. God, how she wanted him.

Matt growled, pulling on her nipple, and she whimpered.

"You should run, bunny."

"Why do you keep calling me that?"

"The wolf is a hunter, the rabbit its prey." And he captured her lip in his teeth. "I will catch you."

"And what happens then?"

His pupils dilated, eyes burning black with desire.

"I get to keep you."

Ten

I t all began in Bo's basement.

The music.

Four prepubescent boys tinkering with their cheap instruments to tunes on a record player never dreamed they'd become a multi-platinum-selling band back then. Those dreams came later. While all the other kids were tossing footballs in the street, building snow forts, or riding their bikes down to the lake, Matt, Kit, Bo, and Sloan were content honing their musical skills, talking about girls, and growing their hair long.

The summer before high school.

That's when everything changed.

That's when Taylor Kerrigan and his parents moved from London into the three-flat apartment building across the street.

He played guitar, too, and soon, the new kid with a funny way of talking was writing riffs and jamming with them in Bo's basement. Still, they talked about girls—and boys—and their hair grew even longer, only now they shared a dream.

The music.

And now, two decades later, Matt sat in Bo's basement, along with Kit, working out their parts on the tracks for Venery's upcoming album. That they were doing it here only seemed fitting.

"Blast beats would fucking slap here, man," Kit said, looking at their drummer.

He was referring to the bridge before the outro. The song started softly, building its intensity all the way through, until it ended as it began. Unlike the rest of them, Bo had studied music professionally from the time he was a small child. Classical piano. R&B. Theory and composition. He had a deep understanding of it and developed syncopated drum parts using Sloan's vocal line as his guide.

"It would be unexpected. Greater impact." Bo nodded, wiping the sweat from his bare chest with a discarded T-shirt. "Hammer it?"

"Hells, yeah." Playing along to a blast beat would require extreme focus and precise timing on their part, but Matt was up for it. "Go big or go home, brother."

Bo pounded out sixteenth notes on the snare and cymbal while double-thumping on his kick drums at two hundred and eighty beats per minute. The sound aggressive, it was perfectly suited to the build-up on this track.

"How's that, my dude?" And with his sticks in his hands, the drummer crossed his arms in front of him and grinned. "Think you can keep up?"

"Now, that's a stupid question." Then Kit played the bass line in time with Bo's breakneck tempo.

"That sounded sick." Matt slapped Kit on the back, and hooking an arm around his neck, he planted a sloppy kiss on his cheek. "Your fingers are gonna end up bloody, but I'm digging it."

"Blast beats." His chest puffing out, a rare smile crossed Kit's face. "See? Told you so."

"I can already hear Sloan's death screams." Squeezing the bassist's shoulder, Matt shared a happy glance with him. "Tay's gonna lose his shit."

"Yeah, he's gonna love it," Bo agreed, rising from his padded stool. "Enough for today?"

Tossing his blond surfer waves, Kit rubbed his fingers on his shirt. "Yeah, I think so."

"I don't know about you all, but I could use a beer," Matt said, putting his guitar away. They'd been holed up in here all day, working up a sweat.

"Me, too." Bo looped an arm around each of them, and together they climbed the stairs. "Hey, with Tay and everybody up at the lake house for Memorial Day weekend, why don't we get Sloan over here and grill some steaks or something?"

He won't come.

Today would have been Kyan's thirty-first birthday, and that fact wasn't lost on him, or any of them, Sloan included. Growing up, they'd celebrated many of his birthdays at the Byrne's lake house, and that's why Taylor and the others were there now. To sing "Happy Birthday" to a ghost.

Matt said, "Good luck with that."

"I'll have Ava call him and put Emmy on the phone." Bo winked. "You'd have to be a heartless sonofabitch to turn down a three-year-old."

Bo's daughter was their frontman's weakness. With a soft spot for Emery in his cold, dead heart, he didn't have it in him to refuse the little girl.

"Unkey Sloan, will you sing with me?"

"Of course, precious." With a chuckle, Sloan got down on his haunches and grinned. "'Baby Shark'?"

Pale-blonde pigtails flying, Emmy shook her head. "Nooo, that's a baby song."

"You're right. Forgive me?"

She nodded.

"What shall we sing, then?"

"'Let It Go.'"

"Emmy's in her Elsa era, I'm afraid," Ava explained with a shrug, taking a seat next to Bo. "She'd watch *Frozen* on repeat if we let her."

"Disney is not in my repertoire, but if you help me out, I think I can do it."

Emery climbed onto his lap, and together, she and Sloan belted out the chorus. It amazed them all to hear such a clear, powerful voice coming out of the little girl's throat.

"She has a gift, Bo." Stroking her baby-fine hair, Sloan smiled down at the child. "You need to help her develop it."

"I am. She started piano lessons a few months ago."

"And Emery sings along with Miss Rachel every day, don't you, sweetie?" Ava added, proud mama that she was.

"But I like singing with you better, Unkey," Emery said, then wrapped her arms around his neck and hugged him.

"Awe." *So damn cute.* Then a thought occurred to him. "The two of you should cut an album of children's songs together. Metal versions, of course."

"You know, that's not a bad idea." Matt wasn't altogether serious when he made the suggestion, but Bo seemed to like it.

"Heh, maybe we could," Sloan said, sharing a high five with Emmy.

"You're gonna make such a cool dad someday."

"Don't think so, Bo Peep." He glanced down at his lap, and the smile he put on for Bo's daughter fell from his face. "That scene ain't for me."

"What do you mean?"

"I don't want to have any." Sloan raised his gaze, and expelling a breath, he shrugged. Then, with a kiss to the top of Emery's head, he moved her off his lap. "I'm happy enough playing uncle to this little princess here."

"It would be a shame not to pass on those genes of yours," Ava said, not letting the matter rest. "One day, you're going to meet someone and change your mind."

"I can assure you I won't." His tone indignant, Sloan leaned forward. "Don't want a wife, either."

"Why not?"

"Are you volunteering?" He curled his lip. "I just don't."

Kit elbowed him in the ribs. "You don't have to be a dick about it, Sloan."

"I'm not." He turned to Ava. "But unless I were to come across someone as lovely as yourself, which is doubtful, I won't be swayed."

"I'm flattered, but that's sad."

Sloan responded with a subtle shrug, the smirk remaining in place. "I don't care for people all that much, you know."

And the saddest thing of all? He did once. Until that selfish bitch he almost married bled him dry, and CJ fucked with his head.

They moved outside to the terrace after that. Reclining on a wicker lounger, Matt closed his eyes to the waning day and breathed in the smell of freshly cut grass and wood-smoke. Like Bo, he craved outdoor spaces, and Kyan made sure he had them. A balcony off his room with a built-in bed. The rooftop garden.

He opened his eyes, and taking a sip of beer, Matt gazed across Bo's backyard to his. It was an overgrown mess, crowded with shrubbery and trees, when he got the place. The landscape architect thought to rip it all out and start anew, but Kyan knew what he liked and wouldn't let the guy do it. Instead, they removed the weeds, trimmed the overgrowth, and added mulched wildflower beds. He loved looking out the window at his little forest. Sometimes, he would lie there, naked beneath the trees, to reflect on life and take a break from the world.

Matt smiled. One day, he'd run naked through those trees with Gina. He'd fuck her on the ground, clawing at the dirt. He'd make her come, howling at the moon, on the rooftop. And he'd love her slow and sweet, all through the night, on the balcony with the built-in bed.

He was going to keep her, all right.

Maybe he'd been preparing for this girl his entire life.

"Yo, Matt?"

He looked up to see Bo hovering over him with a plate.

"Medium-rare okay?"

"Perfect, thanks." He took it, his mouth watering at the sight of the seared ribeye.

"Sides are over here, hun." Ava waved him over to the table where Kit and Sloan were already digging in. "We've got baked potatoes with all the toppings, grilled sweet corn, sautéed mushrooms, and a tomato-feta salad."

A refreshing breeze washed over him, rifling through his hair. It felt good. Reluctant to move, Matt motivated himself to join his brothers at the table.

"Hey, let's hit the club tonight." Kit smacked him on the ass as he took his seat, but the bassist was looking at Sloan. "What do you say?"

As if weighing his options, the reclusive frontman cut into his steak, brought a piece to his mouth, and slowly chewed. He picked up a bottle of beer and, holding it poised at his lips, he finally spoke. "Yeah, all right. I'm in."

"Matt?"

"Sorry, no can do."

Likely as surprised by his answer as he was by Sloan's, Kit's eyebrow shot up. "Why not? You got something better to do?"

"Not exactly."

"What is it then?" Kit asked, pressing the matter.

"I'm, uh… seeing someone." *Kind of.* "It's new, and I don't think she'd like the idea of me at a sex club without her."

He hadn't planned on announcing Gina into existence. Not yet. Matt didn't want to jinx himself, but he still harbored guilt over the only other time he'd bailed on his closest friend and owed him an explanation.

Kit looked at him like he didn't believe him. "Who?"

"Gina Rossi." He couldn't hold back. His cheeks tugged at his lips.

"The pizza girl?" Bo asked, and he nodded. "Well, all right."

"Tony's baby sister?" Kit cocked his head.

"Younger sister," Matt corrected him. "And she's all grown up."

It was difficult for him to reconcile that Gina and the little rugrat who took delight in annoying her older brother and his friends all those years ago were the same person.

Matt never paid much attention to her then. He couldn't stop thinking about her now.

"Remember that time she pulled my hair?"

He didn't.

Bo smiled, buttering his corn-on-the-cob. "Junior year. I think she was like five."

"You looking for trouble, rock star?" Sloan tilted his head.

Matt shot him a look. "What do you mean?"

"First, she's a helluva lot younger than you."

And?

It's not like Gina was some giggly, no-brained teenager he was planning to take advantage of. Inside, Matt was simmering, but on the outside, he kept his cool. "So? She's twenty-three. Gina's an adult, older than Ava—Katie, too, for that matter. So don't you dare twist this into something wrong, because it isn't."

"Age is just a number," Ava said, taking up his cause. "Ain't that right, baby?"

"Absofuckinglutely," Bo said, and kissed her.

"Second, and more important, Tony's our friend," Sloan went on, disregarding their drummer and his girlfriend. "Do you think he's going to be happy when he realizes you've got your dirty hands in his sister's virginal white cotton underpants?"

Probably not. He cracked a beer open.

Shaking his head, Sloan muttered, "Jesus, Matt, she's a goodie-two-shoes Catholic girl in a plaid, pleated skirt, and way too innocent for the likes of you, but maybe you're into that sort of thing…"

"Shut up. You know I'm not." Enraged, Matt tamped it down with a swallow of beer. "She went to Catholic school. So what? Gina's smart—she's a nurse. And she's sassy and beautiful."

"Do you like her?" Ava asked him. "I mean, *really* like her."

"Yeah, I really, really do."

"Babe, I'm so fucking happy for you," Ava gushed, clapping like a kid on Christmas morning. Following her lead, Emery clapped right along with her.

"I am, too, brother," Bo said with a reassuring squeeze to his shoulder. "You should call Gina over. I'd love to see her again."

Kit remained silent.

"She's working tonight, or I would," Matt explained, suddenly feeling lighter. "I want you all to meet her."

"Next weekend, then." Bo nodded, wearing his usual grin, as if it were already settled.

"I'm taking Gina out to see the Navy Pier fireworks from Lake Michigan next Saturday," he said, and smiling, drew in a deep breath. "Chartered a private boat."

Sloan snickered.

Matt glared at him. "What's wrong with that?"

Shaking her head, Ava sighed. "That's so romantic."

"I wanna go on a boat." Emmy tugged on her father's long hair. "Can we, Daddy?"

Bo kissed the top of her pretty little head. "Course we can, sunshine."

Still snickering under his breath, Sloan rubbed his upper lip. Blue eyes bored into his, and he said, "You're going to Hell, brother, and Tony's gonna be the one to send you there."

Maybe, but she's worth it.

"I'll talk to him." Matt tsked, dismissing his concern. "We've all been friends a long time. He loves me."

"Well, as I recall, Mrs. Rossi doesn't," Kit reminded him.

Bo bit into his corn with a shrug. "Tony's mom never liked any of us."

Truth.

"That's her problem then, isn't it?" Matt flicked his gaze from Bo to Kit and Sloan.

The man with all the words subtly inclined his head. "Yeah, but once she finds out you're involved with her daughter, that problem becomes yours."

"You sure you don't want to go to the club with us tonight?" Kit offered, suggesting he might like to change his mind.

Jesus, I'm fucked.

The thought of being inside anyone else held zero appeal.

"Yeah."

He tipped back the bottle of beer, draining it.

"I'm sure."

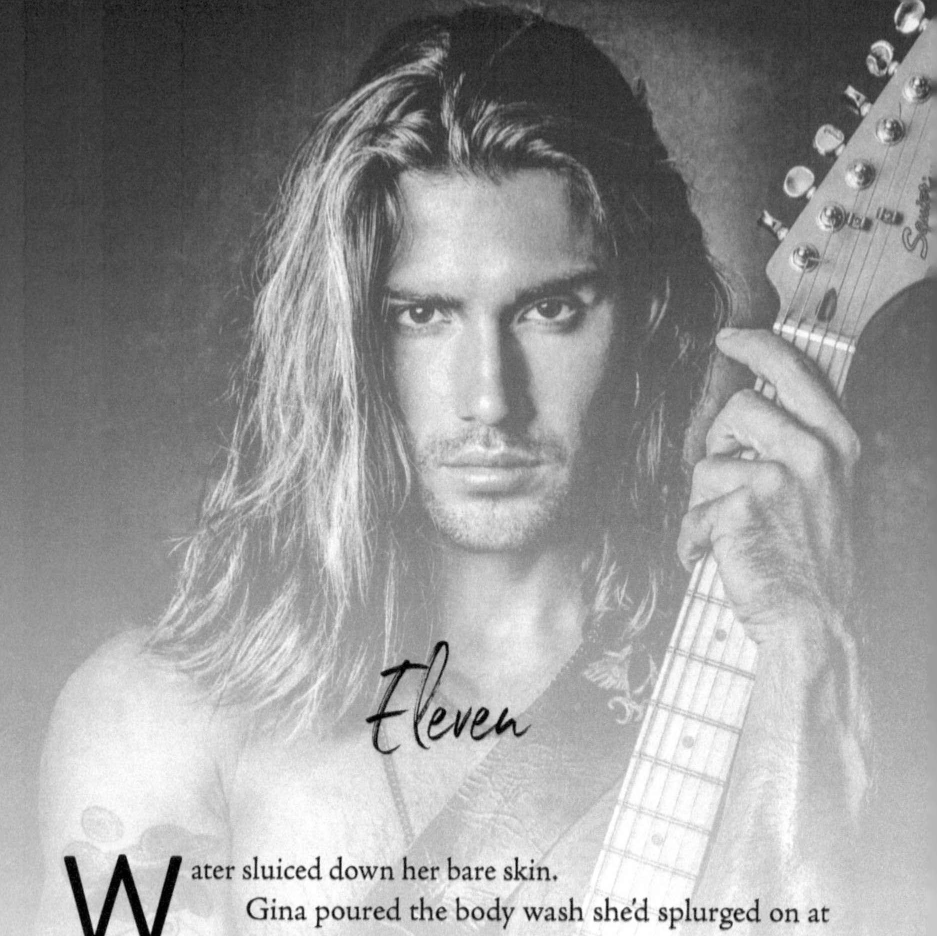

Eleven

Water sluiced down her bare skin.

Gina poured the body wash she'd splurged on at Sephora into a soft, wet body sponge. Neroli. Basil. Shiso leaf. The scent luxurious and sensual, it aroused her, just as he had, so it was worth every penny.

Cleansing her body with meticulous care, Gina reflected on the evening she spent with Matt two weeks ago. At first, she blamed it on the wine, because how else could she explain her behavior? Straddling his lap. Her tits in his face. No doubt, just like every other girl who came before her had.

And there had been a lot of them.

Literally hundreds. Thousands, probably.

She knew that.

Fingertips grazed over her nipples, slippery with soap, and as if awakened by the memory of his touch, her body responded. Beneath the spray, she closed her eyes as heat pooled in her belly.

"God, you're perfect," he'd whispered against her skin, fingers strumming her nipples, his face pressed between her breasts. "But I have to earn the privilege of fucking you by learning your body first."

Learn it quickly, then.

She was crawling out of her skin.

"I want to watch you come." He tugged on her nipple with his teeth. "Just from doing this."

As good as it felt, that would never happen. Gina shook her head. "I can't."

"Yes, you can." He squeezed the twin mounds of flesh. "Look at how sensitive you are."

Licking her lips, she glanced down at her chest. Matt played her like a guitar, plucking at the swollen tips, wet with his saliva. The heaviness building in her belly bade her sink into him. Faded denim pressed against concrete, housed in thin gray sweats.

Sweet, delicious friction.

The rhythmic pulling of her nipples. His voice. Maybe that was what sent her hurtling toward that elusive place no one had ever taken her to before.

Gina held onto his hair.

"That's it, baby. Let go…"

She did.

And for the first time in her life, she had an orgasm she didn't have to give to herself. She *wasn't* broken. Matt did that for her without his fingers ever straying from her breasts.

Why had it been so easy for her to come with him?

Still pondering the question, Gina massaged the matching neroli and basil scented lotion into her skin. The little black dress she'd chosen for the occasion was laid out on her bed. A short, rib-knit tank would work well with a pair of Chucks and her cropped denim jacket in case it got chilly later. Their first actual date. Matt was taking her to Navy Pier for dinner and to see the fireworks.

Her makeup on, hair curled into soft, loose waves, Gina was ready to go with hardly a moment to spare. She breezed past the kitchen, where Teo stood at the stove fixing himself something to eat—a tuna melt, judging by the smell of it.

"Hey." His booming voice halted her. "Where you going?"

"Out."

"No shit. I got eyes in my head, Gina," he said, tapping his index finger against his temple. "I was thinking maybe we could go do something tonight—catch a movie or have a few drinks and listen to some blues at Kingston Mines."

She hadn't known her brother would be here. Everyone else was at Rossi's, but if Tony was there, which apparently he was, then, of course, Teo wouldn't be. For the sake of their sanity, and so they didn't kill one another, their dad tried to keep them apart as much as possible, having them work opposite of each other.

"I can't, babe," Gina said, hugging him. "Sorry, I have a date."

"Serious? When's the last time you had one of those?" Teo looked surprised. Okay, it had been three years, but still. "Well, good for you. It's about damn time. Who's the guy? Is he picking you up? 'Cause I wanna meet him."

"Uh… you already know him."

"Please don't tell me you caved, Gi." He flipped his tuna melt and took it off the stove. "That asshole doesn't deserve another shot after what he did, no matter what Mom says. He's already shown you who he is, and he hasn't changed."

"I'm not going out with Vinny." With a flip of her hair, she glanced at him from beneath her lashes and smiled. "But Matt should be here any minute now."

"Matt?" His head slightly cocked, Teo took a step back as recognition flashed in his hazel-green eyes. "Get outta here. The only Matt I know is… *Madone*, no fucking way."

"Yes fucking way." She giggled.

"You… and Matt McCready?"

Why was that so far out of the realm of possibility? Sure, there was a time Gina believed it was too, but the man had been pursuing her for months now. That had to mean something, didn't it?

"Uh-huh."

"He ain't the guy that lived around the corner no more."

Right, he's a famous rock star on the cover of magazines now, and so? He's still the same Matt, isn't he?

"How'd you ever manage that?" he asked with an incredulous smirk.

She shrugged. "I delivered a pizza."

"Tony's gonna flip the fuck out." Teo grinned, then. "Does he know?"

"No, and I didn't think I needed his permission, either."

"You don't. Fuck him. This is just too good." He grabbed onto her arm and, holding it, plopped a kiss on her cheek. "I'm happy for you, Gi. Truly. I like Matt. He's an all right guy, so don't let Mom or Tony or anyone else make you think otherwise."

"And why would they? It's just a date, Teo."

"C'mon, little sister, I know you're not that stupid." He pushed the hair out of his eyes, head tipping to the side, and his lips curved upward. "Matthew McCready doesn't 'date' anyone. He never has— not that I've ever heard, anyway."

"What are you saying?"

But the doorbell rang, and he failed to answer the question. "I'll get that."

Gina opted to remain in the kitchen. Cowardly? Perhaps. But now that he was here, she was a little nervous and needed a second to catch her breath. And besides, she didn't want to appear overeager.

"Yo, Gina," Teo called out to her from the foyer. "Matt's here."

She took a deep breath in, then blew it out.

Ready or not, here I come.

Slicked into a knot at the back of his head, Matt's caramel-brown balayage blended into darker shades of rich chocolate and polished mahogany. He wore a deep V-neck, the sleeves pushed up to his elbows. Transparent enough to see the outlines of his tattoos, and tight enough to make out the definition of his muscles beneath, its ecru color accentuated his suntanned skin. Faded, olive-green, slim fit fatigues hugged his ass and thighs. Expensive-looking combat boots covered his feet.

Her tummy rumbled and did a flip-flop.

Fuck. Me. I'm in so much trouble.

How in the hell was she supposed to breathe when he looked like that, when he was looking at *her* like that? Wild-eyed, ferocious, and hungry, like she was his dinner.

Matt leaned in and kissed the side of her face. "You take my breath away, bunny."

Teo softly chuckled.

With her cheeks growing hot, Gina slung her fake Louis Vuitton Bumbag over her shoulder. Knowing how much she coveted an authentic one, a co-worker snagged the dupe for her on Canal Street for forty bucks, on a weekend trip to New York City. Maybe it wasn't crafted from genuine Merino shearling, but it damn sure looked like it. If there was a difference, she certainly couldn't tell. Besides, who has four grand to blow on a purse, anyway?

Matt took her sweaty palm and laced his fingers with hers. "You good, babe?"

"Yeah." She smiled at him, her heart hammering so loudly in her chest she swore he could hear it.

Amused by her discomfort, Teo bit his lip to hide a grin. He failed. Miserably. "You kids be safe now."

"*Basta.*" Cut the bullshit. Gina shot her brother a warning look.

"I'll take excellent care of her." Matt's arm came around her shoulders, and pressing his fingers into her skin, he bent to kiss her temple. "I promise."

Matteo tipped his chin and said, "You better."

The Audi R8 parked at the curb was purple, not a vulgar shade like petunias or Barney the dinosaur. This purple was a deep, sexy, sleek metallic, like the color of the sky at night, just before the twilight fades into black.

He opened the door for her and gave Gina a hand down into the low passenger seat. Buttons and controls everywhere, the techy dash looked like the cockpit of an airplane.

"Want me to put the top down?" he asked, buckling her in.

"Will I need a helmet?"

"No." And he looked at her strangely. "Why?"

"Kidding." With a shake of her head, she giggled and fished a hair tie out of her bag. "You put me in a race car, is all."

Matt flashed his shiny white teeth, then, leaning across the console, he took her hand in his. "It's just a car that goes fast."

"Uh-huh."

He kissed her palm and rested it on his thigh, his fingers running back and forth between her knuckles. "You still good, bunny?"

"Yeah," she said, and then pulled her hair up into a messy bun. "Go ahead. Put the top down."

"That's my girl."

Long-awaited, especially after the drudgery of a cold, harsh winter, Chicago summers are incredible. With her hand resting in his, she tipped her head back to let the late afternoon sun wash over her face as they traversed the city streets.

Matt turned a corner that jolted her eyes open. "I thought we were going to Navy Pier."

"We are."

"Then why are we on Cannon Drive?"

He answered with a chuckle, then pulled into Diversey Harbor and backed into a parking spot near the yacht club. "There's more than one way to get there, you know."

"We're going on a boat?"

But the sixty-foot Sea Ray was far too grand to be called a boat. With two bedrooms, seating on the bow, below, and aft, its own galley, and a sky bridge, the luxury yacht could easily accommodate a dozen people.

"Chef has your appetizers ready, and the champagne is on ice, as you requested." Clasping his shoulder, the captain shot Matt a wink. "Our crewman will see to anything else you might need. Enjoy the fireworks."

He sat her on an aft sofa and, with glasses of champagne in hand, snuggled up beside her. She heard an engine then and watched the wake upon the water as they sailed out of the harbor.

"Are we the only passengers?"

"It's just us, Gina. And the crew," he added after a pause, holding her close to his side. "I didn't want to have to share your company with anybody else."

With only a nod and a smile, a uniformed man set a platter of nibbles on the table in front of them. Matt spooned cold shrimp in a creamy dill sauce on a buttery cracker and fed it to her.

"God, that's good," she said after she swallowed. "Are you trying to impress me?"

"Of course."

"You don't have to, you know."

"But I want to." He fed her another cracker and wiped the leftover sauce from her lip. "It's in a man's nature to make sure his woman knows she's precious and cared for."

Not all men. Based on her limited experience with them, anyway.

"Well, you've succeeded and then some." Her tummy fluttering, Gina tilted her head to gaze into his chocolate eyes. "I don't know what to say except thank you."

His lips turned up in a boyish smile and, leaning closer, Matt took the tie out of her hair. "I've been looking forward to today."

"I have, too." *Longest two weeks of my life.* Gina glanced away to look out at the magnificent Chicago skyline. She'd never seen the city from this perspective before, except in photographs. "I didn't want to like you."

"But you do." With a finger on her chin, Matt drew her back to him.

"Yeah, I do."

Smiling, his lips brushed over hers. "Why didn't you want to?"

"My own insecurities, I guess," she admitted. It might be foolish of her to say, but that was the truth, wasn't it? "C'mon, you're famous. I've seen photos of you with lots of beautiful women… I mean, you could have anyone in the world you want, so why me?"

"*You* are beautiful, and it's *you* I want. Nobody else." His fingers slid into her hair, and he dropped his forehead to hers. "Do you know why I've never gotten married or been in a relationship before?"

"No, why?"

"It's only been the past few years since we rebuilt Park Place that we haven't been touring non-stop. Life on the road? Couldn't commit to anyone during all of that, not that there was someone I wanted to commit to." He rubbed her cheeks with his thumbs while skating his lips along her jaw. "And yeah, I've had more than my share of meaningless flings and casual sex, but we learned real quick that girls only wanted to be with us for the story—so they could say they fucked a rock star. I can't say I felt anything for any of them, and I know none of them gave a shit about me."

"That's so sad." Gina held her hand to his face.

"It's not, really." Matt pulled her onto his lap so she straddled it, and his eyes locked with hers. "Sad would have been settling for what was indiscriminately offered and so easily taken."

"What do you mean?"

"See, I don't want a tame love. Shallow kisses and careful touches. Love that lacks passion is a sure way to boredom and the slow path to death." A hint of a smile appeared. He reached for her nape, and bringing her so close to him that their noses touched, his thumb traced along the bounding pulse in her neck. "I need to claim, to own, to feel it in my gut. I need out-of-breath, sloppy, rough kisses. Two sweaty bodies craving each other."

With a swipe of her tongue, she licked her lips. Lost in the heated gaze searing into her soul, her chest heaving, Gina found it difficult to breathe. She craved him.

He knew it.

His smile widened.

And as if to contain it, Matt grazed his lip with his teeth, tenderly stroking her windblown hair.

"I want to hear in no uncertain terms that I'm the only one, grab a fistful of this pretty hair and make you look at me when I tell you how much I fucking love you. I want unleashed passion, filthy desire, and an endless inferno of lust that's downright impossible to douse." His head dipped to the hollow of her throat, and inhaling deeply, he dragged his lips up to her ear. "You can keep that soft and careful shit. I don't want it."

She opened her mouth to speak, but nothing came out. Gina circled her arms around him, and sliding her hands underneath his shirt, she caressed his skin.

"My love is savage and raw, baby. It's so fucking intense, and so damn unreasonable, it seems impossible to keep up with, but for the right woman it makes perfect sense." Matt lifted his head, his gaze seeking hers. "I want that woman to be you, Gina, and if it is, then you will know, without a doubt, that my love is the only love you deserve, and the only love you'll ever need."

Oddio. Oh, God.

He took her mouth then, claiming it with his teeth and his tongue. She allowed it, returning his kiss with the same fervor. When had she ever known such brutal honesty, such vulnerability before? *Never.* He only wanted to be loved, and isn't that what she wanted, too?

The sound of the crewman clearing his throat halted them. "Your dinner, sir. Would you like it served here or down below?"

"Right here is good," Matt answered, unabashedly. "Thanks."

Her cheeks heating, Gina glanced down to see the hem of her dress had ridden up well past her thighs. Mortified, she scrambled off his lap and, pulling it back down, sat like a lady should beside him.

His arm came around her shoulders, and he kissed her crown. "Did I mention how beautiful that dress is on you?"

It was a simple dress, nothing special about it.

"I thought so the moment I saw you." Matt laced their fingers together and brought her hand to his lips. "I was so blown away that I think I forgot to tell you."

"Thank you, but I know what you're doing."

"And what's that?"

The crewman returned, setting covered plates down in front of them. He removed the domed lids to reveal perfectly seared filets, grilled asparagus, and lobster tails with drawn butter, then retreated.

"You were trying to distract me from the fact that my ass was bared for that man to see."

"Did it work?" He grinned, and after opening another bottle of champagne, Matt refilled their glasses. "He didn't look, baby girl. I'd have torn his eyeballs out if he had."

Oh.

He patted his lap. "Now, come back here."

The boat gently rocked with the waves of the lake. They took turns feeding each other their dinner, laughing together between bites. And Gina couldn't recall ever having felt as genuinely content as she did right now.

"We're playing at the festival in two weeks."

"I know."

"I want you to be there." Matt held her chin and softly touched her lips with his. "The boys would like to meet you. Well, I suppose I should say they want to see you again."

"You told them about me?" She hadn't expected that he would— not yet, anyway.

"Of course I did." He cocked his head with a smile, running his fingers through her tangled waves. "Why wouldn't I?"

Gina didn't have an answer.

"Will you come?"

"I'd love to." She laid her head on his shoulder, stroking the stubble along his jaw. "I promised my mom I'd help her that day— Rossi's is crazy busy during the festival—but yes, I'll be there."

"Good," he said, releasing a breath. "Come as early as you can. We'll have dinner together. They put on quite a spread for us."

"Okay, I will."

"Look, it's almost dark." Matt stood and, taking her by the hand, he helped her out of her seat. "Let's go up top for the show."

They reclined together, side by side on a double lounger, gazing at the clear night sky.

And Gina waited.

For the fireworks to start.

To have his hands on her.

His fingers made a lazy trail up and down her arm, catching on her skin. "Damn calluses. Hazard of the trade. I'm sorry, bunny, but you won't feel anything soft with me."

"I like it," she said, turning her head toward him. "I don't want soft from you."

Matt gave her a look.

"Why do you seem so surprised?"

"I'm not sure you know what you're saying yet." He shook his head and turned onto his side, tracing her lips with his finger. "Are you still a virgin?"

Does it matter?

Her gaze returned to the sky above. "No, I've had sex before."

His hand cupped her cheek, forcing her to look at him. "One day soon, I'm gonna fuck you 'til you're crying for me."

"If you can catch me."

He smiled then, and it was a promise. "Oh, my beautiful baby rabbit, I will hunt you down and pin you to the ground until you beg me for mercy."

"Will you now?"

"I said so, didn't I?" His hand ghosted over the curve of her hip. "But right now, I'm going to make you come on my fingers under the fireworks."

"Someone might see." And why did the thought of that excite her?

A husky chuckle fanned her neck. Rough fingertips crept up her inner thigh, heating her blood. "Do you care?"

"Not really, no," Gina said, her breath sawing in and out.

Black silk panties slid down her thighs. "Pull your dress up. Show me that pretty virgin pussy."

"I told you, I'm not a virgin."

"Yeah, you are," Matt said, swiping his fingers through her slit. Then he pushed a finger inside.

"*I haven't fucked you yet.*"

Twelve

Sweat oozed from her pores, trickling down her chest in rivulets to pool inside the cups of her bra. It dripped into her eyes and tickled her scalp, making it itch. She wished she could scratch it, but hunched over a vat of bubbling oil, frying *zeppole*, she'd just have to ignore it.

Drop. Drain. Sprinkle. Bag.

On auto-pilot, after waking at four o'clock this morning to prepare enough dough for a thousand orders of the traditional festival sweet, though monotonous, her task was at least mercifully simple. It was a good thing Gina didn't have to focus on it too much, because her mind kept drifting elsewhere.

Just a few more hours…

Lina was due to relieve her at four. Two hours to wash away sweat caked with powdered sugar and peanut oil was plenty of time, wasn't it? It had to be. The concert started at eight. Her plan was to meet Matt by six. Anticipation thrummed through her veins, and that alone kept her going under the cover of Rossi's tent on First

Avenue as she toiled in this dreadful summer heat. Gina glanced up, and catching sight of Katie serving iced lattes from Beanie's open-air booth across the street, she waved.

Coming toward her, a striking blonde couple wheeled a baby along the avenue. Gina recognized them and came out of the stall to peer inside the stroller.

My Christmas Eve delivery.

She'd never forget it. While all births are beautiful, this one was especially so. The expectant father was so loving and attentive to his wife as she labored with their first child, and with the baby presenting posterior, it was a difficult one. Gina loved it when a new dad was comfortable enough to show his emotions. So many men are afraid to. They hold them back, as if displaying their feelings somehow makes them appear weak. Quite the contrary. It takes a confident man to let his tears flow, and this man shed bucketfuls.

"Oh, wow! She's gotten so big," Gina exclaimed and hugged her former patient. What was her name again? She recalled it as being unique and pretty. *Linnea, I think.* "You look fantastic! How are you?"

"Good." Smiling, the new mom nodded. "I'm good. You remember Dillon?"

"Yeah."

But he wasn't listening. "Hey, Nick. How's it goin', man?"

"You know my brother?"

"Nick's your brother?" His mouth falling open, Dillon did a double-take.

"Yeah." Gina pointed out her mother, who was ringing up customers. "That's our mom right there."

"I went to school with Nick. Tony, too." A tentative smile building, he jerked his head back. "Wait a minute. You're little Gina Rossi?"

Biting her lip, she nodded. "That would be me."

"Well, damn. You couldn't have been more than six or seven when we were in high school," he said, nodding along with her.

"Sounds about right."

"I never got a chance to thank you for taking such good care of my girls." With his arm circling Linnea's waist, Dillon kissed her crown. "So, thank you. I owe you one."

She glanced down at the baby and smiled. *You've got such a wonderful life ahead of you, little one. Your daddy loves you and your mommy so very much.* "She's beautiful. Congrats, again."

Gina turned around to go back to work to find Nick standing right behind her as he watched the couple blend into the crowd on the street. "You know Linnea?"

"Not exactly. I was her labor nurse when her daughter was born."

"So fucking sad," he said with a shake of his head.

"What are you talking about?" She followed him inside the tent, questioning his nonsensical comment. "Any woman would be lucky to have a husband as devoted as hers."

"*Was* lucky, maybe." And halting his steps, Nick shrugged. "Her husband was killed in an accident before the baby was born."

What? That can't be right.

With a hand clapped over her mouth, Gina shook her head in disbelief.

"Kyan Byrne?"

The name rang a bell, but she didn't know him.

"He was Dillon's younger brother, Brendan and Jesse's cousin. Me and Tony went to the funeral."

Oh, my God.

"Dillon's her brother-in-law?"

"Yeah."

"Jesus, I'm an idiot." She smacked herself in the head, then dropped some dough into the fryer. "I mean, they have the same last name, and it was obvious just how much he adores her and that baby, so I just assumed..."

"Linnea was his wife?" Nick's brow lifted so high his forehead wrinkled.

"Yeah." Fresh sweat erupted on her skin. "I gave him the father's baby band and everything. It never even occurred to me to ask."

"Would you have done anything differently if you had known?"

"I don't know." Shrugging, Gina took the fry basket out of the hot oil. "Probably not."

"Don't give it another thought, then." And he squeezed her shoulder. "But if you're seeing Matt, it's likely you'll be seeing a lot of Dillon and Linnea, too."

"How do you figure?"

"The Byrne cousins and the Venery boys have always been… close. *Really* close. Tight, you know?" Nick sprinkled sugar on the batch of warm doughnuts, and with a snigger, he popped one into his mouth. "Heck, they all live together behind that gate on Park Place."

And?

But he left her, rejoining Teo and their dad on the other side of Rossi's doublewide booth.

What she was supposed to make of that, Gina wasn't sure, but what difference did it make, anyway?

Lina didn't show until half past four. *Figures.* She strolled over, putting her hair up in a ponytail, like it was no big deal. "You can take off now, if you want."

"You're late."

She'd been counting on every minute of those two hours before she went to meet Matt, but thanks to her selfish sister-in-law, her calculations were going to shit. Now, Gina would have to rush when she wanted the luxury of taking her time.

"Sorry?" Hands dropping to her sides, Lina's ponytail swished as she slanted away from her. "It's not like you've got somewhere else to go."

"Actually, I do." Wiping sweat from her brow, Gina plastered on a smile.

"Oh, yeah?"

"Yeah, I'm—"

"C'mon, Gi." Before she could say another word, Teo grabbed her by the arm. "We got places to be."

"We?" Gina asked as her brother dragged her away. She glanced back at Lina over her shoulder. Tony stood with her, shaking his head at them.

"Where you're going, who you're seeing, or what you're doing is none of her business." He squeezed her waist, maneuvering her through the crush on First Avenue. "Unless you want that *puttana* running to Mom and Tony."

"Heh. She wouldn't dare."

"You know she would." His brows furrowing, the pain he refused to let go of was there in her brother's eyes. "She'd post it all over Facebook, too—bitch loves to start trouble, and you are so not prepared for that bullshit."

Until then, Gina hadn't given any thought to the fallout of her relationship with Matt going public. Her family? Well, that was a completely different story. Rosemary would never approve, simply because Matt wasn't Vinny Passarelli or a reasonable facsimile of him. And Tony? He'd lock her up in a nunnery and throw away the key if he could. So, seeing his little sister and his old pal together? Livid would be an understatement.

But she'd cross that bridge when and if she came to it. As an adult, Gina had the right to choose her person the same as Tony had. And her mom would just have to learn to accept her choices, whatever they might be. It was her life, after all.

Teo unlocked the back door and ushered her into the kitchen. With everyone else at the festival, the house seemed unusually quiet and still. The clock ticked, the air conditioner hummed, and dappled sunlight danced to its tune on umber-painted walls.

With a parting squeeze to her waist, her brother turned to go downstairs. That was when she heard the unmistakable sound. "Someone's here."

"It's just Luca," Teo assured her, his voice just above a whisper. "Go do what you gotta do. I'm gonna shower."

"But isn't he supposed to be..." And taking hold of her brother's hand, Gina followed the sound.

She almost wished she hadn't.

With a video game paused on the TV, controllers cast aside, Gina found Luca and his buddy, Kevin Copeland, in the family room with their tongues down each other's throats and their hands in each other's pants.

Teo leaned into her ear. "Don't ask."

But she did. "Are you and Kev—"

"Fucking?" Wiping Kevin's slobber from his mouth, her baby brother looked up at her as if to say *duh*. "Would you think less of me if I were?"

"No, Luca, I love you." And she went to him. "I could never."

Truth.

"Don't worry, I'm not gay. I like girls, too." He slung his arm around Kevin and grinned. "We both do."

"Are you bi or just confused?" Gina sat on the arm of the sofa, running her fingers through Luca's glossy curls.

"Definitely bi, *bambina*." He kissed her on the cheek. "And I've known it for a very long time."

How long? Christ, you're barely twenty.

Hold up a minute.

Confused, she looked over at Katie Murray's strapping younger brother. "I thought you had a girlfriend, Kev."

A football player at the university, he and Luca met last year as freshmen. They'd been fast friends ever since. *Well, more than friends, it seems.*

"I do," he confirmed, his lips forming a smirk.

Luca elbowed him in the ribs. "You mean *we* do."

Ohhh.

"I know I can trust you both." Glancing at Teo, he took her hand and clutched it tightly in his. "You won't give my secret away to Mom, right?"

"Of course I won't." Then Gina held Luca close, reassuring him like she did when he was five and had a bad dream. "It's not my story to tell. Besides, it'll kill her."

"Like you fucking Matt McCready won't put her in her grave." He poked her in the chest and chuckled.

"We're not fucking."

"Yet." He winked. "So, you're cool with it?"

"Are you happy?"

And with a huge smile on his pretty boy face, Luca nodded.

"Then I'm cool with it."

"I'm so lucky. I got the best sister ever. I love you, Gina Bobina."

I love you, too.

Then, glancing at his watch, Teo smacked her on the ass. "Unless you plan on meeting Matt looking like something the cat dragged in, you'd best go upstairs and do whatever it is you girls do to make a guy lose his mind."

"Yeah, you're all sweaty and you stink like peanut oil." Sniggering, Luca waved his hand in front of his face as if she actually smelled. "Can't have you throw all my hard work away."

Gina sniffed herself. "What the fuck are you talking about?"

"I got you and the rock star together, didn't I?"

She smiled. "Yeah, I guess you kinda did."

"Go on, now," Teo said. "We'll all wait and walk back to the park with you."

I'm the lucky one. Best brothers ever.

And with that, Gina hurried up the stairs to get ready to meet her man.

Thirteen

He paced the tent with this pent-up, nervous energy, and not because they were going on stage in a few short hours. He just couldn't wait to see her.

Touch her.

Taste her.

Smell her.

Already, the girl had burrowed beneath his skin. She occupied his every thought, invaded all his dreams. From the moment Matt saw Gina standing at his door with that pizza in her hand, he'd been a man obsessed. And he didn't mind it.

Venery's crew arrived early this morning to set up the stage and load in. Matt glanced at the time on his phone and opened a beer while listening to the techs do a soundcheck. Once they finished, the crew would join the band for dinner, where they'd all hang out together until showtime.

Nine months.

That's how long it had been since their last tour ended, and

Christ, he'd missed this. Sadly, it would likely be another year before they were back out on the road again.

Touring was not an option. It was expected. Yeah, five guys living on a bus can get real old, real quick, but they were some of the best times of his life. Nothing compared to the adrenaline rush of being up on that stage. Of all the boys, Matt loved being out on tour the most, but then he didn't have anyone who loved him to come home to.

Do I, now?

Yeah, maybe I do.

Maybe Gina wasn't quite in love with him yet, but she would be, dammit. Matt was a goner, and well, in his mind, they were already there. So, the thought of having to leave her behind for months at a time didn't sit well with him. He'd figure something out. Bo did too, after all.

Kit was the first one to hit up the buffet. His plate piled high, he glanced over at him as he pulled out a chair. "You gonna eat, bro?"

"Not yet." Matt swiped a piece of shrimp off the bass player's plate and popped it into his mouth. As hungry as he was, he wanted to save his appetite.

"Waiting on Gina?" Kit rolled his eyes with a snicker. "You said she was coming."

"Yeah, she'll be here soon."

Kit shook his head, pushing the blond surfer waves from his face. He reached for a fork, then his lips parted, the utensil dangling from his fingers. "How'd Tony take it when you told him you're fucking his baby sister?"

"I'm not *fucking* her."

While Matt should take umbrage at the crass remark, he didn't, considering that's the only thing he'd ever shared with women in the past. He fucked them. Desired them. But he never had feelings for them beyond physical gratification.

With Gina, it was different. So different. Yes, he desired her, and yes, he wanted to fuck her senseless, but instinct told him it was so much more than that. And it wasn't just his dick talking, his heart wanted her, too.

Yeah, man, you are well and truly fucked.

"And… I… uh… I haven't had a chance to talk to Tony yet." Matt could feel his face growing warm at the admission. He'd been meaning to go see him, and he almost went to Rossi's last night to do just that, but he ended up calling Gina instead.

"What the hell, dude? That's fucked up." Kit set his fork down and picked up his beer, taking a healthy swig. "He should hear it from you, and the sooner the better. What if he sees her here with you tonight?"

"I know, man." His gaze shifted to Sloan, who had taken a seat next to Kit, then back again. "I'm going to, all right?"

"It's your funeral, my friend," Sloan quipped, lips curling into a smirk. His shoulder-length, streaked hair was slicked back at his nape—fucker was always changing it. No shirt. Skin oiled. Tight, threadbare jeans torn in all the places guaranteed to make the girls lose their ever-loving minds.

Leaning forward, Kit glanced up at him. "Is she really worth it?"

"C'mon now." His smirk turning into a grin, Sloan rubbed at the oil on his abs. "You know our boy here better than anyone. Look at him. He's salivating at the thought of stuffing that dick of his into sweet, young virgin pussy."

"How about I stuff it down your throat?" His nostrils flaring, Matt bared his teeth.

Kit snorted. "Might shut him up."

"It's not like that," Matt said, softening his voice. Then he straddled a chair across the table from his bandmates. "See, I don't wanna just fuck her."

"Wait, you really care for this girl?" Kit asked.

And with a nod, he smiled. "Yeah, I do."

"Don't look so butthurt about it." Observing Kit's reaction, Sloan chuckled, then he turned his attention back to him and said with a shrug, "I think he might be jealous."

"Get the fuck outta here, Sloan."

"Suck my dick." And with a lift of his chin, he squeezed the denim between his legs. "I ain't goin' nowhere, baby."

"What's CJ doing here?" Maybe he shouldn't have been, but Matt was surprised to see him waltz in as if he still belonged here. He didn't. As agreed, they paid him a nice bonus in lieu of renewing his contract.

"One of two things." Sloan held his beer poised at his lips. "To start some shit or to try and get his job back."

"Fat chance of that." With a toss of his mane, Kit sniggered. "He's got some balls, man."

"Nah." Matt picked up his beer and winked. "He lost those a long time ago."

"Yeah, well, you better hope he's gone before your girl gets here," Sloan whispered a warning, pointing his finger at him. "The fucker would love nothing more than to run to Tony."

"Or sell you out to *TMZ*," Kit added.

It wouldn't be the first time CJ had pulled something like that. He always had a reason—publicity, image, or some such shit. And they let it slide, until Taylor got married, anyway. After that, when they left the label, his intrusive ploys only got worse.

"Hell, he'd do both." His blue eyes narrowing, Sloan stabbed at a piece of prime rib. "Right after trying to get his stubby little fingers into Gina's pretty white panties."

Like no-nuts tried to with Ava? Over my dead fucking body.

"I'll fucking kill him if he so much as breathes near her."

"Think he wouldn't know that?" Sloan steepled his fingers beneath his chin, and tilting his head, he grinned. "Fuck's sake, Matt, he'd be counting on it."

Right. CJ would get a story for the media, no matter what. He couldn't let that happen. Matt would not subject Gina to his bullshit, and needing to know how much time he had left to get him out of here, he sent her a text.

Matt: How much longer until I see your gorgeous face, bunny?

Gina: Lina showed up late, but I'll be leaving my house in about fifteen minutes.

Matt: Hurry, I need your lips on mine. Be safe on your way over.

Gina: Teo, Luca, and his friend are walking me.

Matt: Good. They can hang out here if they want.

Gina: They'd like that. I'll tell them.

"Let's help CJ move along, shall we?" He stood. "Gina will be here in about thirty minutes, and I don't feel like going to jail today."

Kit rose alongside him. "Looks like Taylor and Bo could use some help with that, yeah?"

Neither one appeared to be pleased at the arrival of their former manager, especially Bo.

"Hey there, Curtis," Sloan taunted him, knowing all too well CJ hated to be called that. "What brings you here?"

"Did you think I'd miss a gig just because I'm not your manager anymore?"

Sure, you would. The asshole had missed plenty of them. CJ didn't even come out on the last tour.

"We're still friends, right?" He clapped Sloan's back, flashing a bitter smile.

"I don't know." Matt glanced over at Bo. "Are we?"

"He's no friend of mine," the drummer said with a shake of his head.

"You heard him." Matt held up his hands and shrugged. "Guess not."

"Is that what all this bullshit's been about, drummer boy?" His stance wide, CJ thrust his chest out and sneered. "You still got a hard-on for the babysitter?"

Matt saw the veins in Bo's neck twitch. His fingers curled into fists, the muscles of his forearms flexing. It took every ounce of strength Taylor possessed to hold him back.

"You fucked with us one time too many, Curtis James." Sloan snatched the bottle of whiskey that CJ held in his hand. "And after everything we've done for you."

"You ungrateful fuck, I'm the one who got you where you are."

No, motherfucker, we did that in spite of you.

"What in the hell did you ever do for me?"

Then, oblivious, CJ made an unrecoverable error. He poked Sloan's chest and woke the bear.

"We made you rich as fuck, that's what." His expression murderous, Sloan bellowed the words like the metalcore screams he was famous for. Then, to drive his point home, he pushed him into a table. "Penthouse apartment overlooking Lincoln Park. Two Maseratis. You think your whiny-ass girlfriend would stay with you otherwise? Think again."

"If she only knew," Matt muttered under his breath.

The countless number of women CJ fucked behind her back for starters.

"Is that supposed to be a threat, rhythm man?" He glared at him, then, wiping the spittle from his mouth, his countenance changed. "C'mon, we've been friends since the first grade. I busted my ass for you guys and this is how you repay me?"

"You got paid," Matt reminded him. "And very well, I might add."

A lot more than you deserved.

"We made you millions upon fucking millions, but that wasn't enough for you, was it? So, you betrayed us." And Sloan came at him again. Gripping the collar of his shirt, he seethed through gritted teeth. "Tell me, Curtis, how much did you get for the story that sent Dominy spiraling? For letting the paps in on Tay's wedding?"

Mic drop.

A ruddy flush crept across his cheeks, and CJ's eyes popped open so wide that white sclera was visible all the way around the iris.

Sloan's deep chuckle filled the silence. "Oh, did you think I didn't know about that?"

"Bloody hell." It was Bo holding Taylor back now. "Was he in on it with Salena?"

"Are you high?" CJ waved Sloan off. "I have no idea what you're talking about."

"I know people, Curtis, and people love to talk. Did Vanessa Parisi pay you to get to us, too, or did she just fuck you for the privilege?" Sloan spat on the ground at CJ's feet, and with a shake of his collar, he let him go. "I hope she wasn't too disappointed."

"This is how you do your *friends?*" Flabbergasted, Matt could only shake his head.

"You're going to regret this. All of you." But CJ was looking right at him. "I made you, and I can ruin you, too."

"Bollocks!" Taylor shouted. Matt couldn't recall ever seeing him this angry. "You didn't make us, you slimy bastard."

"C'mon, CJ, you've had a lot to drink," Brendan said, escorting him toward the exit. "I think you should go home before you say something you'll regret."

"You knew what he did and never said anything?" Bo asked, his jaw going slack.

"Just a hunch," Sloan said, pouring CJ's whiskey into a glass. Then, he drank it. "But I'd say the look on his face confirmed it."

"Damn." Bo took the glass from Sloan, refilling it. "CJ knows people, too. You think he's gonna start shit?"

"Let him try." Slinging his arm over Taylor's shoulder, Brendan didn't appear to be concerned. "I'll have Phil send him a strongly worded letter, and if he does, we'll sue."

"I think now's a good time to tell them, mate."

"Tell us what?" Matt asked, his gaze going back and forth between the two men.

"A friend of a friend put me in touch with UMG." Brendan reached for his shoulder with a broad grin, then he shook it. "And they want Venery."

"Universal Music Group?" Bo took a step back, rubbing his forehead. He muttered the very thought in Matt's head, "I thought we were done with record labels."

"The deal's to our advantage. We should at least consider it," Taylor said, oddly enough, being that he was the one who convinced them to part ways with their old label, and it had proven to be a wise decision. "They only want to back us—license our music. We get to stay in control and retain ownership of the masters."

"We're doing just fine on our own." And slumping down into a chair, Sloan picked at the tattered rips in his jeans.

"You are, but they've got a marketing team with tremendous reach and you don't," Brendan offered, but Sloan already had tuned him out.

Matt turned his gaze on Taylor. "They'll want us touring a lot more than we have been."

"Probably."

"And you're good with that?" It would stun Matt if he said so. Taylor was a grumpy motherfucker when he was away from his family. "What about Chloe, Jesse, and the kids?"

"We haven't negotiated a contract yet." And he handed him a beer. "Besides, if anything, Bo has shown us there's a much better way to travel. Universal's a major label—one of the big three—so I'm sure they'll accommodate our needs."

Then, glancing at the path outside, Sloan got up from his chair. "And here comes trouble."

Brendan followed his gaze. "Who's that?"

She wore a little white dress. Hips swaying, long, dark hair swinging in the breeze, her brothers and Kevin Cofield walking alongside her.

Matt smiled. "My girl."

"You remember Tony Rossi's little sister, don't you?" Pressing his lips together, Sloan attempted to contain his snicker. He failed. Miserably.

"Gina?" Brendan arched a brow, sighing. "Oh, boy."

Fourteen

She shimmied into the white cotton dress, slipping its thin straps over her shoulders. Flouncy, flared, and daringly short, she smoothed the hem down her thighs, checking out her reflection in the full-length mirror. With an open back and a corset-like bodice that pushed up her breasts. Normally, she'd throw on a T-shirt and a pair of jeans to go to a concert in Coventry Park, but tonight Gina wasn't just going to see the show now, was she?

Fearing the humidity would melt any makeup off her face, even with setting spray, she kept it to a minimum, playing up her eyes. With her hair curled into loose waves for the same reason, Gina tucked a clip into her Bumbag in case it turned into a frizzy, hot mess. At least then, she'd be able to put it up. With a cute pair of blush open-toed ankle boots, she took one last look in the mirror and made her way downstairs.

Freshly showered, Teo sat waiting for her in the kitchen, scrolling through his phone. High cheekbones, a strong jawline, and hazel eyes like hers—he was so handsome. Her brother had girls panting after him everywhere they went, not that he ever seemed to care. His happiness was stolen from him, which saddened her, because he deserved it and had so much to offer.

"Where's Kev and Luca?"

Glancing up at her from his phone, Teo shrugged. "In his room, I guess."

"Doing what?"

"Do you really have to ask?" With a toss of his inky mane, he snickered, his gaze returning to the screen.

Did not need to know that.

"Jesus, Matteo." Gina flicked him on the head. "You knew already, didn't you?"

"Yeah, I've known for a while," he said and went back to his scrolling.

"Why didn't you tell me?"

"Sorry, was I supposed to?" He cocked his head, hazel-green eyes locking on hers. "I would never betray our brother, not even to you. Luca loves you more than anyone, so give the kid a fucking break. He wanted to confide in you. I know he planned to. He was trying to figure out how, I guess."

"But he didn't have a problem telling you."

It hurt to think he'd felt even a moment of angst, or shame, or fear over sharing his truth with her.

"He didn't have much of a choice." Her brother stood, forcing Gina to look up at him. "I found him downstairs with a dude when he was fifteen, and they weren't just making out."

"Oh, shit. What did you do?" She was almost afraid to hear the answer.

"They were so into it, I just turned around and left." Pursing his lips to the side, Teo shrugged. "Didn't want to embarrass him, you know?"

I know.

"I talked to him later that night, and he explained it to me the same way he did to you." His arm came around her in a brotherly bear hug. "Luca's not gay. He's always known who he is."

"I'd love him the same even if he were," she said against his chest.

"I know." And smoothing the hair down her back, he kissed her crown. "Don't know how long this girl of theirs will stick around, but I'm glad he and Kev got each other."

"Are they serious?" They were too young to be, right?

With a parting pat on her head, Teo exhaled and took a step back. "Looks that way. They wanna get a place together, but neither of 'em can afford it yet."

"Yeah, working after school at Beanie's and delivering pizzas wouldn't cut it, I suppose."

"Nope. I told Luca they can hang out downstairs when I'm not at home," he said, sliding his phone into the back pocket of his jeans. "I remember what it's like to want to be with someone so fucking bad and having nowhere you can go."

"And we love you for it, bro." How long had Luca been listening from the hallway? He rushed in and hugged their brother from behind, smiling at her with his chin on Teo's shoulder. "Damn, Gina, you look—"

"Hot as all get out. And gorgeous, too," Kevin said, his blue-green gaze sweeping over her frame. "Hell, if you weren't my boyfriend's sister…"

"Well, she is, so don't even think about it." Taking her by the hand, Luca grabbed Kevin with the other. "Let's go. Time to deliver Gina to the rock star, and then my mission will be complete."

To avoid the throng on First Avenue, the four of them walked down Third most of the way. But even from two blocks over, the festival's din reached Gina's ears as if she were in the midst of it.

Was that the amplified rat-a-tat-tat of a snare drum in the distance? Check, one. Check, two. The aggressive reverb of Matt's guitar?

Her stomach dropped.

"Fuck!" She glanced at the time on her phone. Ten after six.

Damn you, Paulina. If not for her, she would've been there by now. "C'mon, we've got to hurry!"

"Don't worry, Gina." Luca pulled her back in step with him. "It's just soundcheck."

"But I don't want to miss anything."

He squeezed her hand and chuckled. "You won't."

"So, who's this girl the two of you are, um… *dating,* anyway?" she asked to distract herself as they left Third Avenue at Ash Street. That, and Gina was genuinely curious.

Kevin smirked, a wicked glint entering his eyes. "It's okay to say fucking. That's what it is."

The hell?

"Don't look at us like that." Luca nudged her with his shoulder, trading a glance with his boyfriend. "It's not how you're thinking."

Sure, it's not.

"Lexi's a senior on the cheer squad," Kevin said as if that should explain everything.

It didn't.

"We have a good time together, but she's going back to Ohio after grad next year, and that'll be the end of it." His shrug halfhearted, Luca sighed. "It's cool, though. We all knew it couldn't be a forever thing going in."

And he was okay with that? Luca wasn't a player. Sweet and sensitive, Gina couldn't bear the thought of another brother's tender heart breaking.

"How long have you all been together?"

"I met her a month or so after I got with Kev." Luca's lips quirked up as he dipped his chin, ebony hair falling into his eyes.

"The football team threw this sick Halloween party." With his head bobbing, Kevin dug his teeth into his lip and grinned. "Lexi was there, and we—"

"Yeah, okay, I get it."

She didn't need the graphic details, but with the seed planted in her head, Gina tried to picture what it might look like.

Kevin poked her side and winked. "It's been us and her ever since."

"Good luck finding another girl that can put up with the two of you," Teo murmured with a soft snort.

"I know, bro. I miss her already." His shoulders slumped, Luca glanced her way. "Lexi went home to visit her folks for a few weeks."

"She's coming back right after the Fourth," Kev said, slinging his arm around her brother.

"Sounds like she's missing you, too." Gina figured the girl didn't have to return until classes resumed in August. That had to mean something, right? "Maybe Lexi will change her mind and stay in Chicago."

"Maybe." But Luca didn't sound convinced.

"Not getting my hopes up and neither should you," Kevin said as they walked past the red double doors at the corner of First and Ash.

The smell of funnel cakes, popcorn, and saltwater taffy greeted her nostrils. High in a hazy western sky, the sweltering sun beat down on the pavement. And smashed between her brothers and Kevin, their clammy bodies cramped together like sardines in a tin, they got caught up in the horde, inching their way toward the midway and Coventry Park.

"Don't look now, Gi." Teo clutched her hand tightly, leading her through the never-ending sea of people. "Just keep going straight ahead."

"Look at what?" She wrinkled her nose. The guy in front of her reeked of body odor and cheap cologne, cumin radiating from his pores. "God, I can hardly breathe."

"Asshole over on the left," Luca said, tipping his head in that very direction.

She looked. Vinny pushed a girl off his arm and, breaking away from his group of friends, came toward her.

Dammit.

"Gina." He was the last person on Earth she wanted to see.

With her hand encased in Teo's firm grasp and Luca's arm around her shoulders, she quickened her pace.

"Gina, hold up." Vinny sprinted out in front of her. "Where you going in such a hurry?"

She skirted around him without bothering to answer.

They kept on walking.

And swallowed up by the crowd, he just stood there.

Kevin looked back over his shoulder. "Who was that guy?"

"*Morto di figa.*" Teo held his middle finger high above his head. *Accurate.*

"It means manhoe, more or less," Luca explained. "Vinny Passarelli, Gina's ex-boyfriend."

"Gotcha." Kevin nodded, leaning forward to look at her. "He cheat on you?"

"Don't know. Don't care." There are worse things, but she wouldn't be surprised to find out that he had. "What happened between us was ages ago."

"You think he wants to get back with you?"

It's what her mother wanted. Hell, his mom probably did, too. But not Gina. She'd rather join a convent than be with that man ever again.

"He's wasting his time if he does." She lifted her chin with a smirk. "See, Vinny had his shot, but disrespect me once, and I'm done. I don't do second chances."

"Fucker doesn't deserve one," Teo agreed. "Besides, it never works out like you think it will."

She saw him before he saw her. A beer in his hand, Matt stood in a huddle with the band, and suddenly, her mouth went dry. Nerves rioting in her heart, the saliva caught in her throat. Gina took a deep cleansing breath, her pulse skyrocketing, to calm the whirlwind in her tummy.

There's no reason to be so nervous.

But this was tantamount to meeting Matt's family, because good God, that's what these people were to him. The guys likely thought of her as just Tony's brat of a little sister, but that wasn't who she was anymore.

Stop. Everything's gonna be okay.

And it was.

He glanced up, and the most dazzling smile Gina had ever seen spread across his face. Matt didn't wait for her to get to him. He sprinted from the tent and scooped her up, wrapping her legs around him.

His forehead dropped to hers. "Give me that mouth."

She gazed into warm brown eyes, the pupils dilating, and offered him her lips. Then, with one hand cradling her bottom, the other at her nape, he took her breath and gave her his.

It didn't matter that her brothers and Kevin were on the running trail beside them, that his bandmates and total strangers might be watching. So enthralled by the taste of his tongue, the feeling of his hard body molded against hers, Gina gave no thought to the breeze at her backside.

With his fingers threading through her hair, Matt softly growled in her ear.

Teo cleared his throat.

Matt smiled, and pressing another kiss to her lips, he eased her down and fixed her dress.

Her brother's boyfriend held up his hand, wiggling his fingers with an amused grin. "Hiya, Matt."

"Hey, Kev."

"You two know each other?"

Duh. Of course, they do.

"Why are you so surprised, bunny?" Matt brushed the hair from her face, tucking a strand behind her ear. "Kev's sister is married to one of my dearest friends, and his aunt has a thing going with another. We're just one big, beautiful, happy family here, and now, you're all a part of it, too."

She glanced over at her brothers' eager faces.

"C'mon, let's say hi to the boys and grab some food." His hand dropped to curl around her shoulder, fingers pressing into her skin. "You've got to be starving. I know I am."

Gina wasn't sure what she expected inside the band's tent, but it wasn't anything quite like this. Plush sofas. Fancy catering and blessed air-conditioning.

The man approaching them was so tall that her neck bent back to look up at him. Dark auburn hair. Ice-blue eyes. From the recesses of her childhood memories, only one person fit the bill. "Gina, so good to see you again."

"You remember Brendan, don't you?"

"It's been a long time." With a wink to Matt, Brendan leaned in to hug her. "The last time I saw her, she was just a little girl."

"You drove a 'Vette," Gina said. "Silver, as I recall."

"Still do." He chuckled.

"This is my brother, Matteo." The introductions probably weren't necessary, but Brendan hadn't been around since they were kids, and she reasoned he might need a refresher. "My brother, Luca, and his friend, Kevin."

"Uh, Gina." Kev tapped her shoulder. "Brendan's my brother-in-law. You know, Katie's husband."

"Yeah, I know." *Gosh, I'm such an idiot.* "Not sure why I said that."

"Nerves, huh?"

Shut up, Kevin.

"I know she remembers me." The goofball Gina once enjoyed pestering wrapped her in a warm embrace. "Don't you, pizza girl?"

She giggled. "How could I forget you, Bo?"

"You couldn't." And he tugged on the ends of her waves. "I forgive you for pulling my hair, by the way. Now, where's my kiss?"

She went to place one on his cheek, but the bare-chested drummer turned his face, and it landed on his lips instead.

"Don't mind him. Dude wants a kiss from everybody." He pressed one of his own to her temple, and laughing, Matt moved her along. "It's too bad his daughter is home with a tummy bug, or you could've met her—Ava, too. You will soon, though. I have a feeling the two of you are going to be the best of friends."

Her gaze flicked up to meet his. Eyes of rich, warm chocolate invited her inside their fathomless depths. They alone told her what words never could.

With an infant on his chest, Venery's lead guitar player lounged on one of the comfy-looking sofas. He seemed larger than life to her when he was a teenager, as had all of Tony's friends, and that hadn't changed. His jet-black hair was longer than it used to be, and ink covered his mocha skin, but even if she hadn't seen those photos in *Revolver*, Gina would've known instantly it was him.

"Hello, Taylor," she greeted him, smiling down at the baby. "It's been a while."

"Gina Rossi, it has indeed. You've turned out to be quite the lovely young lady." He sat up, holding onto the baby, and lifted his chin toward the man leaning against the sofa's arm, a toddler balanced on his hip. "Do you know my husband, Jesse Nolan?"

She knew his marriage wasn't of the typical variety, and according to the media, Taylor wasn't married at all—not legally, anyway. He and Jesse shared a wife. They had children together. As unusual as that might be to some people, it must work for them. One evening, when Lina stayed home and their parents had gone up to bed, Tony told her he envied them for the love they had for each other. He may have been a little drunk, but it struck her as oddly telling.

Gina extended her hand. "Nice to meet you."

"Good to meet you, too." Jesse shook it. "I went to school with your brother, Nick."

Jeez, did everybody know the Rossi brothers? Apparently, so.

They might live in a big city, but their neighborhood was relatively small.

"Jesse is also Brendan's cousin," Kevin whispered, dipping into her ear. "Dillon's too, but I don't see him here."

Ah, the Byrne cousins. Got it.

"Tony said he went to your wedding," she said, still shaking hands. "You've got a couple of kids now, too, I see."

"Yeah, our son, Chandan, will be three on Wednesday. Ireland's fifteen months." Then, Jesse called out to a stunning redhead across the room, "C'mere, babe, Matt's girl is here."

"Our wife, Chloe." Her brother didn't exaggerate. The adoration he held for Jesse and his wife was there in Taylor's eyes. "Chloe, this is Gina."

"Oh, I've been dying to meet you." The bubbly girl, who couldn't have been much older than herself, hugged her like a lifelong friend she hadn't seen in ages. "I know you from somewhere, don't I?"

She looked familiar, but if she attended to her baby's delivery, Gina didn't remember it. And with two husbands, she surely would have.

"You, I know." Chloe giggled. "How's it going, Luca?"

"He's Gina's brother," Matt said, slinging his arm around the boy's neck.

"Rossi's, of course." Nodding, Chloe took the baby from her husband's arms. "That must be where I've seen you before."

Could be.

"Well, welcome to the madness."

Thanks?

"Let's get you some dinner." Leading her away from Chloe, Matt took them toward the buffet. "Besides, you seem a bit overwhelmed."

"Maybe a little."

"C'mon, I got you." And with a squeeze around her shoulders, he kissed the top of her head. "It can be a lot all at once."

Rock stars ate well. Prime rib. Shrimp the size of prawns in a lemon-butter sauce. While Matt piled everything there was on his plate, Gina took a small serving of the scampi and some salad. With her belly still doing flip-flops, she didn't dare eat more than that.

"Well, if it isn't little Miss Trouble." Half-naked, the godlike cretin appraised her, strumming his fingers up and down his sculpted chest. "My, my, my, you *have* grown up, haven't you?"

"Cut the shit, Sloan." Glaring at him, Matt pulled out her chair.

"What? She's quite pretty." Sloan waited for Matt to sit down, then leaned into his ear. "I get it now, man."

"Hey, Gina." Kit raised his bottle of beer in a salute. "Ignore him. That's what we do."

"I will not." With a sharp thrust of her chin, she set down her fork, and taking a deep breath, Gina haughtily stared into haunted blue eyes. "Why'd you call me that?"

"Because you're both asking for it." Sloan just smirked, his head dipping to the side. "How's Tony been? Haven't seen him in a while."

"Oh, I see." And ignoring Matt's hand squeezing her thigh, she flashed the voice of Venery her coldest smile. "Tony's not my dad; he's my brother, but even if he were, like you said, I'm all grown up."

"Heh, guess she told you." Kit leaned back in his chair and drained his beer.

She should've expected it. Gina couldn't be mad at Sloan for it. He just had the balls to come out and say what everyone else was probably thinking, and suddenly she lost what little appetite she had.

"Is there a restroom somewhere?"

"Our bus is here." Matt laced his fingers with hers. "C'mon, I'll take you."

Gina took a few calming breaths in the tiny bathroom. *Fuck Tony.* Matt was worth any trouble that might come her way. Then, she blotted the shine on nose and opened the door. "Sloan doesn't like me."

"He likes you."

"Well, he doesn't like us together," she countered, stepping past him.

Matt pulled her to his chest and cradled her face. "No, he's concerned Tony won't like us together."

"My brother doesn't get to have an opinion."

"I've been friends with Tony for most of my life, and you're his baby sister. He loves you." Matt caressed her cheeks. "He's going to have one."

"It won't be good."

"It'll be fine, baby, I promise."

Then his lips were on hers. Slipping his tongue inside her mouth, fingertips skated down her spine and up her bare back to grab a fistful of hair at her nape. Matt pulled on it and pushed her into the lounge at the back of the bus, deepening their kiss as he went.

"You're so beautiful. I can't decide whether to tear this pretty dress off you or fuck you in it." His teeth scored down her neck, a deep rumbling sound coming up from his throat. "God, I'm dying to fuck you."

Like she wasn't? It had been a month since she'd stood at his door with that damn pizza. Every cell in Gina's body was screaming at her to give herself to him. She wouldn't, though, because somehow she knew Matt didn't want an eager offering. He needed to claim her.

"So, is this where all that legendary rock star sex happens?"

"Nope." And catching his breath, he chuckled. "We have a rule. No fucking on the bus."

"Seriously?"

He pulled the thin white straps down her shoulders, and exposing her breasts, Matt lowered his head to suck on her nipple.

"But some rules are made to be broken," he rasped, sliding his hand underneath her dress. "Give me that pussy, bunny."

His fingers felt so fucking good inside her.

"But you've got a show in twenty minutes."

"And I can make you come in five."

Fifteen

They couldn't have been gone more than fifteen minutes, but in that short span of time, the vibe inside Venery's makeshift green room had changed. An electric energy in the air, the boys weren't chilling out on the sofas anymore. Standing by the portable air conditioner, long blond hair billowing about his face, Bo twirled a pair of drumsticks. Kit stretched his wrists while Taylor's fingers danced over the fretboard of a silent guitar.

Only Sloan appeared unfazed. Propped against the bar, he casually sipped a glass of whiskey. "Welcome back."

"Don't even start, man."

"Start what?"

Matt took the glass out of Sloan's hand and swallowed its contents. "Just don't."

"I'm on your side, you know." The singer set his gaze on Gina, then. "Believe it or not."

Maybe he was, but she hadn't quite forgiven him for being such a jerk, so she wasn't altogether convinced.

Reaching into his back pocket, Sloan retrieved a small plastic bottle. He sprayed whatever it contained into his throat and tossed it to Matt.

Gina glanced up at him. "What is that?"

"Vocal Eze."

"It coats the vocal cords. Keeps them lubricated," Sloan explained. "Tastes like shit, but it works."

Her nose wrinkled watching Matt's face contort as he swallowed. "What's in it?"

"Herbs, mostly. Ginger. Aloe vera. Honey. Glycerin."

"But why do you need it?" she asked Matt.

With a shake of his head, the voice of Venery chuckled. "For the screams, Trouble."

Ohhh.

She probably should've watched some YouTube videos of Venery playing live, then maybe she would've known that. Until that moment, she hadn't known Matt contributed vocally at all, but now that Gina thought about it, Sloan couldn't be the only voice on the record now, could he?

"Five minutes," Brendan announced.

"Time to go, bunny."

Glancing over to the tent's open flap, Gina watched Taylor kiss his daughter's cheek as he handed her off to Jesse. His family accompanied him outside, the bassist and drummer following along right behind them.

With eyes of the deepest brown looking into hers, Matt tucked a curl behind her ear and smiled. "Walk me backstage and kiss me for luck?"

"All right," she said with a nod.

Teo and Luca waited just inside the opening with Kevin, his aunt, Kelly, and some guy who looked like a bad-boy version of Jesus. *Holy hell, that's Kodiak?* Brendan joined them, Katie and their son at his side. Gina had never been more relieved to see another familiar face than she was right then.

It was twenty feet to the tall metal stairs that led up to the stage. Her brothers walked in front of her, Matt and Sloan tethered at her sides. Brendan and Katie took up the rear. Security personnel kept determined fans at bay, while men with cameras positioned themselves nearby, aiming for a photo opportunity. Of what exactly, Gina wasn't sure.

"Fucking ridiculous." Sloan tucked her under his arm, blocking the men holding cameras from view. "Remember when it was just the local crowd?"

His fingers squeezed into her hip, and Matt snickered. "How many times have we played this gig now?"

"Tonight makes five."

"See? They expect us now." Those fingertips traveled to her rib cage, rubbing up and down her side. "People travel from all over to inundate our little neighborhood festival. It'll never be just the local folks ever again."

Brendan chuckled from behind them.

"Paps hiding in the fucking bushes amuses you?" Sloan turned around to glare at him. "You're the one on the festival committee. You got us into this gig in the first place."

"Don't look at me." Holding his hands up in mock surrender, Brendan grinned. "Tay's the one who offered."

"I remember. He wanted to get to Chloe." Matt glanced down at her, and with his arm circling Gina's shoulders, he pressed a kiss on her temple. "Long story."

She was so out of the loop. These people shared a history, a lifetime of memories she'd never been a part of. Gina smiled up at him, and, laying her head against Matt's shoulder, she found she wanted to hear all of his stories. More than that, what she longed for was to be in them.

"Everyone's just waiting on you two," Jesse said, hitching his thumb behind him at the bottom of the stairs. "Here, I snagged some drinks for the rest of you. Chloe's out front holding your seats."

"Showtime." Matt held her out in front of him, his hungry gaze taking her in. "Meet me here right after?"

As Gina nodded, he brought her chest to his, and threading his fingers into her hair, his thumbs caressing her face, Matt kissed her. On a hot summer night, goose bumps sheeted her skin. Electricity sparked at the back of her neck and ran along her spine. Tingles popped between her thighs. How could a simple kiss do all that?

Sloan poked her shoulder, shoving Matt to the side. "Hey, what about me?"

Gina pecked the singer's cheek.

Then, hurrying up the stairs, Matt blew her another kiss and disappeared.

"Champagne slushy." Jesse pressed a plastic souvenir cup with a purple straw into her hand and winked. "Festival tradition."

"Thanks." Tentatively, she took a sip, the icy libation going down easy. "Mmm, I like it."

Katie took them to a section in front of the barricade cordoned off for the media and VIPs. The security guard ushering them through, Gina filed in behind her with her brothers, Kevin, his aunt, and her boyfriend, and followed to where Chloe waited for them.

"There you are," Chloe exclaimed and hugged Katie. "Were the kids okay?"

"They're fine. The guys got it handled."

"Aren't they coming?" Gina peered past the guards, looking for Jesse or Brendan.

"Too many decibels for delicate little ears," Chloe said with a giggle. She did that a lot. "The boys will have fun hanging out backstage, and besides, I need an hour off from Mommy duty."

"Won't it be just as loud back there as over here?"

"We got them Loops and baby earmuffs." She waved off her concern and giggled again, the sparkly silver hoops in her lobes dancing to the sound of her laughter.

I guess not, then.

Anticipation lodging in the pit of her stomach, Gina glanced around the rapidly filling VIP area. "Who are all these people?"

"City aldermen, festival committee members, and invited press mostly."

"What in hell is *she* doing here?" Katie pointed toward the crowd gathered right of the center stage.

Chloe followed her gaze. "Who?"

"Look, that's psycho-bitch Kelsey over there at the barricade, isn't it?"

"Heh, yeah." Her lip curled in disgust, Chloe turned away. "Thank fuck Dillon dipped out to take Linnie home."

"Oh, shit." Katie gasped as if she'd just remembered something. "What if Matt sees her?"

And?

Gina glanced over at the Barbie doll wannabe, her eyes drawn to the diamond flashing on her ring finger. Brown hair up in a tight, high ponytail. Makeup that didn't melt off her severe-looking face. Trendy designer clothes. Prada bag—authentic, no doubt. While the woman seemed confident, she appeared out of place.

"It's not like that. At all," Katie explained, mistaking Gina's perusal for concern. "Kelsey used to date Dillon."

"She's a horrible person," Chloe added, nodding.

"We were all at the club's Halloween party—it was the first time we could get Dillon out of the house after Kyan died—and he brought Kelsey."

"Big mistake." Spreading her fingers apart, the redhead mimicked an explosion. "Huge."

"Why?"

"The wolf pack performed last year." Katie smirked, her breath tickling Gina's ear. "They staged a hunt."

"And Kelsey's easily offended."

"Bullshit." With a roll of her aquamarine eyes, Katie cocked her pretty blonde head. "C'mon, Chloe, she was dating Dillon, for fuck's sake. Besides, she was well aware the Red Door's a sex club."

"Sex-positive."

Gina knew that. While nobody spoke of it much, nearly everyone did. Still, she was clueless. "I'm so confused. A hunt?"

"Every year, there's an act that goes with the ball's theme. Brendan even let the vamps out once," Chloe explained.

"Vamps?"

"Vampires. They have a blood fetish." With a shudder, Katie wrinkled up her nose. "That didn't turn out so well."

"I know, and I'm sorry." Chloe hugged the girl and, thankfully, continued with her story. "But the wolf pack, they're primal, and they were something else, let me tell you. A lone girl in the center of the platform and a wolf waiting in each corner. The club was made to look like a haunted forest, you see."

Okayyy.

"It's a competition of sorts." With a slow smile building, Katie's skin flushed, and a wicked glimmer shone in her eyes. Lowering her voice, she inclined her head. "The wolf that catches the girl gets to claim her for everyone to see."

"Claim her?"

"Mate."

Huh? Ohhh.

Chloe looked at her and winked. "Wolves mate for life, you know."

"The wolf is a hunter, the rabbit its prey… I will catch you."

"And what happens then?"

"I get to keep you."

Gina grinned.

"Anyway, Kelsey had been rude all evening, so things were tense between her and Dillon, which made it uncomfortable for the rest of us," Chloe said, and then shrugged. "Matt was just trying to lighten things up a bit. He gave her a growly."

What the fuck is that?

"She lost it, then." Katie glanced at the woman, her nostrils flaring. "Called Matt 'Fido,' like he was some mangy, flea-infested dog."

"He set her straight, though, didn't he?" With a toss of her long beach waves, Chloe giggled.

"I was so fucking proud of him." Turning to Gina, Katie held onto her arm and smiled. "You've got such a good man, Gina. A *real* man, unlike the lame excuse for one Kelsey's got with her now."

Oh, I know.

Dressed in golf shorts and a polo amidst the throng of concert-goers, the man standing with that *puttana* appeared uncomfortable in his surroundings and woefully out of place. He tugged at his collar. Sweat beaded on his brow. Balding, and his features nondescript, Kelsey latched onto the guy like he might take off if she didn't. Gina almost felt sorry for him.

Matthew McCready wasn't just a gorgeous rock star. He was beautiful inside and out. A man of integrity, she'd describe him as kind, confident, and funny. Honest, authentic, and unapologetically himself, he was comfortable in his skin. An alpha through and through, the man who commanded her body with the slightest touch could never be anyone's bitch boy.

Gina dipped her head into Teo's ear. "What does primal mean?"

"Huh?" Dark eyebrows pulling together, his head flinched back. "That's random. Basic urges. You know, instinct."

"Not the general definition, silly." She bit her lip. "Say you were at the Red Door."

"Primal sex?" A pink hue crept across her brother's cheeks, and unable to meet her gaze, Teo furtively glanced around, then cleared his throat. "Chrissakes, Gina, don't be asking me about that shit."

"Jeez, I was just curious."

He expelled a loud breath and lowered his voice. "The definition still applies. Primal is savage and raw—unrestrained, unfiltered, uninhibited."

"Like animals?"

His lips parting, Teo hesitated. He turned toward her, pupils dilated. "In a sense. But then, that's what we truly are, isn't it?"

The kabuki dropped.

And as the fog lifted from the stage, Matt saw her.

Bathed in flashing technicolor light, her pretty white dress glowed in red. With those beguiling eyes fixed on him, Gina looked up at him eagerly, and so adoringly, but not in the crazed fangirl kind of way he was accustomed to. In a sea of unknown faces, their heads banging, hands held high in the air, her intimate gaze screamed unspoken words deep into his chest.

I love you.

Matt knew that look. He'd seen it between Chloe, Jesse, and Taylor. Bo and Ava. But he'd never had it directed at him before. And for the first time in his life, the adrenaline rush of performing on stage was eclipsed by something even more profound and wondrous.

She loved him.

High on the feeling, he skip-danced across the stage to join Kit and Taylor at its center, the three of them tipping the necks of their guitars up in unison as they came in for the break. Holding onto Teo and Katie, he watched Gina jump up and down. Matt couldn't hear what she screamed, the mix in his in-ear monitors playing Bo's kick and snare over a soft click track, Kit's bass, and the boosted sound of his guitar.

"Chorus, two, three, four."

Upon hearing the monotone cue, Matt went up to the mic, eyes locked on hers, his voice a unique harmony to Sloan's insane baritone.

The setlist trimmed down from last summer's headline tour, they played a dozen of their most-loved songs and closed with an instrumental version of the unreleased track that featured Bo's sick blast beats. A sound bite of what was to come, and though the audience didn't realize it, their positive reception was the feedback that kept the band going in the right direction.

Matt flicked a monitor out of his ear, leaving it to dangle at his neck.

"Sweet home, Chicago," Sloan crooned to the crowd. "We love this town. Thank you."

One more song.

One more song.

One more song.

The words echoed, repeating over and over again.

Playing a riff, Matt stepped up to the mic. "You want another one?"

And before the crowd could respond, he heard a woman shout, "Hey, Fido," then, mocking him, she howled, "Ahoooo."

"Left barricade," Brendan said via the monitor that remained in his ear, not that he had to look to know who it was.

Fucking cunt bitch.

Matt glanced at Sloan, and with a wink, the lead singer grinned. "What the fuck was that pitiful wail? You've gotta do better than that if you want one more. Show them the beast, rhythm man."

Expectant silence hung in the air, a single beam of murky light illuminating the fog that swirled at his feet. He took a deep breath, releasing a low, drawn-out snarl into the mic, followed by the loudest, most menacing growl he could muster.

Kit's deep bass and Bo's kick joined in, the crowd roaring with their approval. Then, Taylor strummed the opening chords of the encore.

"Scream, two, three, four."

On impulse, he changed the lyrics. "*Fuuuuck youuuu.*"

And with the last song over, the stage went dark, the fans still chanting for more. Ripping the monitor out of his ear, he handed his guitar off to a tech. Kit handed him a beer. "Did you see the look on that bitch's face?"

Kelsey was irrelevant to him, so he hadn't bothered to.

Sloan high-fived him. "Smooth move. That was fucking great, man."

Slinging his beer back, he took to the stairs. The girl who loved him waited at the bottom, and right then, the only thing Matt cared about was getting to her. He pushed past security and, ignoring the city officials and VIPs waiting to shake his hand, he sprinted right over to Gina.

"You were so—ah—"

But he didn't let her finish. Instead, Matt scooped her up, and spinning with Gina in his arms, he kissed her.

And he didn't stop. He kept right on kissing her until they were back inside the tent. "I love you, pizza girl."

"Yeah? That's a good thing," she panted, smiling from beneath her lashes. "Conisdering I love you, too."

In his soul, Matt already knew that, but hearing her say the words made all the difference. A flood of warmth infused his limbs as Gina nuzzled her cheek against him. She'd given him her heart and taken his. He'd get to be the one to care for her, provide for her, protect her, and support every one of her dreams.

With a tender smile, he combed the sweat-dampened hair from her face. "C'mon, let's go home."

"But Katie invited all of us over for drinks and nibbles." She glanced at his dear friend's wife and shrugged. "It's their anniversary, I guess."

"Tuesday," Katie said, planting a kiss on his cheek. "You know, I ran into Brendan in this very park during Venery's concert three years ago."

"We got married a year to the day later." Brendan moved in and, hooking his fingers inside her jeans, pulled his wife to his chest. "I love you, Katelyn."

"I love you, baby." And she kissed him.

With the foil to his plans taken care of, Matt grinned. He wasn't about to share Gina's company with anyone tonight—not her family, nor his. "Another time. We've got a celebration of our own to get to."

"Yeah?" The corners of her mouth turning up, Gina bit her lip.

"Didn't I tell you I'd catch you, bunny?" He looked into those hazel-green eyes, and skimming his nose along her pulse, Matt inhaled her distinctive scent. "I'll be fair and give you a head start."

He always did have an excessive amount of leftover energy to burn off after a show.

Fuck it.

"Run."

Sixteen

"Run."

Was he serious?

Gina glanced down at her feet, cursing the trendy booties she wore. They were so *not* designed for a frolic through the woods. But not one to back away from a challenge, she lifted her chin and met his wolfish gaze. "Catch me if you can, rock star."

Matt grinned.

"One hundred. Ninety-nine…"

Calmly, she moved past her brothers, securing the bumbag around her waist, and inhaled thick night air steeped in the smells of popcorn, beer, and cotton candy. In front of her, a crew carried equipment off the stage. Behind her, the band's tour bus and a line of town cars idly waited. She could stick to the smooth, paved running trail that meandered through the park. Whether Gina went left or right, either direction would take her to First Avenue, but that's not where she wanted Matt to find her.

"Ninety-three. Ninety-two…"

Gina took off her boots, and with one in each hand, she looked toward the trees and ran.

One second, warm asphalt heated her feet, and the next, cool, tender blades tickled the bottom of her soles. Crazy how this swath of forest grew amid towering concrete and steel. Scrambling through bushes, she rested her frame against the rough bark of a mighty oak. Gina couldn't hear him anymore, but she counted along to the rhythm of his cadence in her head.

Sixty-nine, sixty-eight…

She closed her eyes. The distant din of the festival had faded, replaced by the call of a cricket, the faint, whirring buzz of cicadas. Gina could almost imagine herself in the middle of a haunted wood, mist coiling around her ankles, the big, bad wolf on the hunt for his prey, closing in from behind her.

Would he take her with a ferocious hunger and tear at her pretty clothes?

Or lay her down gently on the forest floor and lift the hem of her dress?

With anticipation mounting, her heart thumped wildly in her chest.

Forty-seven, forty-six…

She'd lost her bearings, and unsure which way she should go now, Gina darted to a tree up ahead. Eventually, she would come upon the tall iron fence that bordered the park on the south, the east, and the west. While Coventry Park didn't come close to Lincoln Park's twelve hundred acres, it was sizable enough. Densely forested at the rear and along its winding trails, how would Matt ever be able to find her?

Twenty-five, twenty-four…

Should she pick a spot and stop running? Because zig-zagging from the trunk of one tree to another in her bare feet had her winded already. Nothing looked familiar. Sweat clung to the fine hairs standing on her skin. Dried leaves crunched beneath her toes.

Three.

Two.

I'm coming for you, bunny.

Gina stood still. She looked around and, seeing no one, hid herself beneath the brambles, nestled in a stand of trees. Something small, dark, and furry scurried out from under her, and drawing her knees up to her chest, she let out a shriek.

Did Matt hear it?

The swaying old oaks groaned in response.

She was alone.

Minutes felt like hours. Where the fuck was he? Shouldn't he have found her by now? Perhaps Matt had meant for her to stay on the lamplit path. Maybe she'd hidden too well. Second-guessing herself, Gina crawled out from beneath the tangle of branches.

A soft, deep chuckle.

She whipped her head around, scanning the trees in every direction, but no one was there. "Matt, is that you?"

Even the crickets were quiet.

A twig snapped.

The hair on the back of her neck prickled. Her heart pounding, Gina took a careful step, and then, with a surge of adrenaline, she ran.

Something or someone was behind her. Was it a coyote? Because just the other day, they spotted one in the subway—it was on the news! Gina couldn't see it or hear it, but she could feel its eyes on her.

And whatever it was, it was getting closer.

Fanculo! Fucking hell.

Her feet stung. A thorn piercing the tender skin, she yelped. Tired and out of breath, she didn't see the gnarled root protruding from the ground and fell onto her knees.

Panting, Gina rested. Just for a moment. Just until she could catch her breath.

Who's afraid of the big, bad wolf? Not me. A coyote, though? Yeah, maybe.

She wet her lips and, digging her fingers in the dirt to gain purchase, Gina sought to get back up again.

An arm shot around her middle, gripping her against solid warmth like a vise. She smelled the familiar, masculine scent of him, and with relief flooding through her, Gina sagged in his hold to rest her head back on his chest.

He didn't say a word.

Warm breath fanned her hair, fingers pulling up her dress. Matt reached inside her panties, a soft growl in her ear. She was soaked.

The hardness inside his jeans pressed into the split of her ass. Clutching his forearm, Gina pushed back against him in a silent invitation to fuck her. Here. Now. Amongst the trees. Let the stars above be witness to her undoing. Right then, she didn't care who might see.

With his fingers pumping in her cunt, he leaned her forward. She braced herself on the wide trunk of a giant oak, the rough bark biting into her palms. Matt kicked her feet apart, and plunging deeper inside her, his teeth raked across her neck.

Fuck me. Please.

As good as it felt, Gina wanted more than his fingers.

She heard the button pop, his zipper open.

Hot, hard flesh prodded at her needy, wet hole.

And with one savage thrust, he drove his cock inside her.

This wasn't exactly how Matt had planned it.

He'd intended to chase his beautiful bunny to the house, corner her in the back garden, tear off that pretty white dress, and fuck her beneath the silver moonlit canopy, on a bed of soft, green grass.

But then, she fell.

And with her pliant body cushioned against his, he realized Gina didn't know the code to the park gate, anyway.

So, this would do. It was better, even. Hidden inside the arms of an ancient oak, nobody could see them here. No one would hear her cries when she came.

She taunted him, rubbing her sweet little ass against his dick. And after four months of pursuing her, Matt was done waiting. His baser nature prevailed and, wrapping her hair around his fist, he slammed himself home.

Fucking Christ.

Gina tightened around him, her silky, wet warmth fitting like a glove that was one size too small. Matt could stay here, inside her like this, not moving, and die a fortunate man. But the animal that dwelled within had other ideas.

He wanted to rut.

To conquer.

To claim.

Moonlight flickering through the leaves made patterns on her skin. He released her hair and watched it fall to the side, then pressed his fingers down her spine, tearing through the thin white straps that crisscrossed her back as he went. In appreciation of the delicate beauty before him, a growl rose from his chest. Matt tried to hold back, to keep himself in check, but he'd been wanting Gina for so long, and now, he'd never get enough of her.

He gripped her hips, driving his cock even deeper inside. Gina met him thrust for thrust, and every time, a sound he'd never heard before bellowed from deep inside her throat. He wasn't sure how to describe it. A whimper? A cry? A moan? None of those were right, but no matter what the sound was, he didn't want it to stop. They spurred him on, urging him to go faster. Harder. To make her come for him.

Sweat dripped from his brow to sting his eyes. Matt tipped his face up toward the sky and closed them, savoring the sublime sensations of her body. Gliding in warm butter, he could feel the tiny grooves of her wondrous walls stroke the head of his dick.

His pleasure and hers.

Submerged inside Gina, nothing else mattered.

Matt could feel it. Every ridge of her insides. Balls tightening, his cock heated and swelled. Close to the point of no return, he pressed into her clit as electrical pulses shot up his shaft, and that indescribable sound she made—a keening cry. It echoed in his ears, drowning out the roar that came with his release.

Matt lifted Gina into his arms, legs shaking, her knees close to buckling. He kissed her. And holding her close to his chest, he carried her home.

"What happens now?" she asked as he set her feet down on the mosaic tiles of his bedroom en suite.

Smiling, he plucked a twig from her hair. "Now, I get to take care of you."

Gina clutched her dress to her breasts, her gaze clouding, as if she didn't quite understand his meaning, and that was okay. He'd show her. The loving doesn't end with an orgasm. It's only the beginning.

Matt took her hands in his, and as he kissed her fingers, the tattered cloth she held within them drifted to the floor. He kissed her neck, along her jaw, and when he reached her tender lips, he whispered, "I love you."

Skin to skin, he held her to his chest. With those enchanting eyes gazing up at him, her fingers twined in his hair, and he kissed her, soft and deep and slow. She was his now, and nothing could ever take her from him.

He reached into the walk-in shower and turned on the water. Then, taking Gina by the hand, Matt led her inside. She stood just out of the spray, watching him as he poured some Japanese hinoki body wash into his palm. "C'mere."

Gina came closer, and starting at her nape, he massaged the fragrant cleanser into her skin. His fingers traveled over her shoulders, along her collar bone, and down between her breasts to her tummy. Gently, he pressed in until her shapely ass rested against his thighs.

With a dreamy sigh, her head fell onto his shoulder. "God, what are you doing to me?"

Fine mist falling onto her beautiful face, Matt poured more soap into his hands. "Has no one ever seen to your needs before?"

"No."

"Then he was a fool." He turned Gina to face him, his thumbs grazing her nipples, and she gasped. "But I'm not."

His knees dropped to the tile floor, and with his soapy hands sliding between her thighs, Matt spread her legs apart. He buried his face in her pussy, inhaling the musky scent of what he'd left inside her, and, with no hesitation at all, his tongue sought her sweetness.

"Matt," she squeaked, trying to wiggle out of his hold. "We just…"

But ravenous, he held her firm. Licking her slit. Slurping on her opening. Juice from her cunt flooded his mouth, and he groaned. Her thighs trembling, Gina held onto his shoulders. Matt pushed two fingers inside her, then with his free hand, retracted the hood of her clit, exposing the extra-sensitive glans. His lips brushed over the sentient nub of flesh before sucking it into his mouth. He held onto it with his teeth, all the while pumping his agile fingers in and out of her.

Gina's knees gave way. Matt caught her, and easing her body down onto his, they lay together on the shower floor, its warm, gentle rainfall washing over them.

"Didn't I tell you I'd catch you, bunny?"

Her face burrowed into his neck.

He pressed his lips to her brow.

"You're mine to care for now."

Forever and always.

Seventeen

t had to have been a dream.

A fantastical concoction of repressed longings that resided somewhere in her head.

Replete, Gina curled into the cool, soft linens, ignoring the light that seeped through her eyelids. She didn't want to wake. Once she did, the dream would have to end.

He carried her from the shower, laid her on his bed, then took his time rubbing a woodsy, aromatic oil into her damp skin. She couldn't move—didn't want to. Her limbs felt far too heavy. Matt cradled her, naked in his arms, ice-cold water at her lips, soothing her scratchy, dry throat, made raw from running and panting and screaming his name.

But she needed to touch him. So, with great effort, Gina lifted her hand to stroke the stubble along his jaw. He turned his head, and soft lips brushing her cheek to meet hers, Matt kissed her.

It was as if he'd woken her from a long winter's slumber.

With renewed vigor, she held Matt's face, plundering his mouth with her tongue. Wedged against her belly, his dick grew hot and hard. He took her lip between his teeth, and slick with a need of her own, she pulled back.

The feeling was visceral.

She wanted to devour him.

Matt licked the blood from her lip, and as she laved a trail down his chest, Gina smiled.

His cock twitched.

She tasted his skin, inhaling the subtle scent of him. Warm and sweet and spicy, an ambrosia of cypress, citrus, and fresh herbs commingled with an alluring masculine musk. Drawn to it, her nose pressed into his navel, and breathing in deep, she stole the pearly drop that leaked from the smooth mushroom head.

"Fuck," he groaned.

And that negative noise, the constant hum she'd heard in the recesses of her mind these past three years, went quiet.

Gina sucked him like she was dying for his dick.

Because she was.

They made love in his nest of a bed all night long, falling asleep in each other's arms as the first signs of morning appeared in the eastern sky. Gina couldn't count how many orgasms Matt had given her. His fucking was intense; wild and savage one moment; gentle and tender the next.

Unleashed passion.

She got it now.

Vivid and raw and so incredibly real, it couldn't have been a dream. Besides, her imagination was never that good, anyway.

With his arm draped across her middle, Gina gave in and opened her eyes. From the paint colors to the artwork, black and white and cream covered the bedroom walls. Animal-print throws and an assortment of accent pillows lay scattered on the floor where he'd tossed them. She stared at a portrait of Queen Elizabeth II mounted beside a stuffed faux zebra's head, and giggled.

The hand on her stomach moved, his fingers reaching for her

nipples. She felt the contact in her clit. One touch from him, and her needy, swollen cunt was ready to be filled again.

"Mmm, fuck me."

With your fat cock, your fingers… anything.

Even the sandalwood candle on the table would do. The way she was feeling right now, she'd gladly take all three.

Matt's answer was to suck her nipple. He latched on, feeding from her as if she had milk to offer him, while he toyed with the other.

"Please, baby," Gina begged, hooking her leg over his.

Infatuated with the morsel in his mouth, he only suckled harder. Matt loved her breasts and how he could get her off just by playing with them.

It was such a turn-on to watch him, holding him there, her fingers running through his hair.

He kept on with his sucking until she came.

"Good morning, bunny." Then, tugging on her nipple with his teeth, Matt pushed two fingers inside.

Best fucking morning of my life.

She spread her legs farther apart.

"That's it," Matt crooned into her neck. "Give me that pretty pussy."

Then, he rewarded her, adding another finger.

Before him, she'd never felt this way. Rabid. Reckless. She never could've imagined it either. *God, what's he doing to me?* As he slid his thumb over her clit, Gina's nails dug into his muscled flesh.

He groaned in what sounded like approval, his teeth nearly piercing her skin. And in that moment, she wanted him to draw blood. To see crimson on his lips. For Matt to leave his mark on her, a tell-tale reminder that body, heart, and soul, she was his.

Grabbing the ends of his hair, Gina pulled his mouth to hers. "I said, fuck me." And she kissed him as if he were the air she needed to breathe.

He rolled her on top of him and drew his knees up, laying her back against his thighs. "I'm going to watch my dick stretch you open, bunny."

Gina closed her eyes, head tipped back, as he notched himself at her entrance. It stung, and she hissed at the contact, the tissue still swollen from hours spent fucking.

"I want you to see it, too," he said, nudging her. "Look, baby."

She gazed into molten puddles of chocolate, the pupils blown, then down to the rigid part of him breaching her little hole. With only the head of his cock inside her, she traced the pulsing veins in his shaft with the tip of her finger, thighs trembling, her entire body tingling in anticipation.

He pushed his hips upward, the lips of her cunt parting for him, until he was all the way inside her. To be filled with him had to be the most incredible feeling in the world.

"You're mine, Gina." With his thumb rubbing her clit, Matt slowly moved in and out of her. "Forever and always, you're a part of me. I hope you know that."

"I do," she moaned, biting her lip, a profound ache building in her core.

And along with his cock, Matt wedged his fingers in her pussy. "I mean it."

Stretched thin, she whimpered.

"Like that, baby?"

Fuck, yes. But she could only nod.

"You're bleeding a little."

Gina glanced down. She must've torn. Blood stained his fingers and cock. "I don't care. Don't stop. It feels too good."

"That's my girl. You can take it." He rubbed her clit, pressing in deeper. "You're not a virgin anymore, are you?"

Like I was before?

But in many ways, she had been.

Only Matt made her bleed, made her come, and she was glad. "No."

"I love you so fucking much." His dick stilled, while fingers unfurled inside her. "I'll never have enough of you."

She liked the sound of that.

I fucking love you, too.

She must've dozed off.

Gina opened her eyes to dim, gray light coming in through the bedroom windows, the zebra on the wall, and his callused fingers lazily stroking the curve of her hip.

"Hey, sleepy girl." The mattress shifting beneath her, Matt leaned over and kissed her neck. "Hungry? I can fix us an omelet or something."

"Uh, yeah." Stretching as she rolled over, Gina nestled into his chest. "We need to eat, I suppose. What time is it anyway?"

"Three."

Fuck.

She sat up in a panic, scrambling to get to her phone on the nightstand. "Shit, I gotta go."

"Whoa, whoa, whoa." With his arm encircling her waist, he pulled her back toward him. "Relax, babe, it's Sunday, and you don't have a shift tonight."

"You don't understand," Gina said. Her voice elevated, the words tumbled out of her mouth choppy and quick. "The festival… I was supposed to be there at noon to take over for Lina. Jesus, my mom's gonna kill me."

"I don't think so." And with his fingers running through her hair, Matt kissed the top of her head. "Look outside."

She turned toward the window. A gentle summer rain fell from the thin gray sky to tacitly cascade down the glass.

No festival to worry about.

"See?"

"Still…"

Gina glanced at her phone. Missed calls. Text messages.

> Teo: Whenever you decide to get your ass home, I told Mom you took off with a friend after the concert, and you were probably spending the night. I didn't say which friend. You're welcome.

She showed Matt the message. "I'm so dead."

"Stop it." He ruffled her hair with a chuckle. "You are not."

"You don't know my mother."

"Yeah, I kinda do." Nodding, his lips pursed to the side. "She never liked me."

"I don't think she likes anybody, least of all me," Gina said and sighed.

"That can't be true."

"Trust me, it can." She lay her head on his shoulder, tracing the ink on his bicep with the tip of her finger. It soothed her. "There's no pleasing her. I can't do anything right in her eyes. She's never approved of my choices."

"You went to college, became a nurse. You've got to know she's proud of you."

"Heh." She scoffed with a toss of her head. "That's the last thing she wanted me to be."

Sad but true. And why?

"My mother wanted me to be just like her." *There it is. And I'm not.* Her chest tightened. "Work in the bakery, marry a nice Italian boy, and pop out his babies. But that's not what *I* wanted. So, I'm just a disappointment."

"You don't wanna make some babies?" He sounded hopeful. Would he be disappointed if she didn't?

"Someday, I guess."

"Listen to me," he said, and lifting her to straddle his lap, Matt lowered his forehead to hers. "I think all that any parent wants is for their kid to be happy and loved."

She shrugged.

He smiled.

"If your mom believes you're truly happy, then she'll be happy for you, too."

I doubt that.

"Maybe."

"C'mon, we need to get some food in your belly." He kissed her lips. "You didn't eat much last night."

"I need to get home."

With bands of steel wrapping around her, Matt held her to his chest. "I don't want you to go."

"It's not that I want to…"

"I understand." His lips brushed her forehead, and he loosened his hold. "It's okay. I get it."

God, I must sound like a child.

Rubbing his pec, Gina bit her lip and looked into his eyes. "I can come back tomorrow if you want me to."

"There's no *if* about it, bunny."

"Yeah?"

He kissed her. "Yeah."

"I'll cook dinner and then we can watch a movie," she offered, her smile so wide her cheeks hurt. "Put that fancy kitchen of yours to good use."

"Sounds good to me." Matt grinned, his fingers pressing into her hips. "Plan on staying the night."

"I will." Gina grabbed his cheeks and smacked a kiss on his lips before clambering off his lap. "But for now, it's time for me to take the walk of shame to my parents' house."

"You will not." He took hold of her wrist. "I'm driving you home."

"They'll see you."

His midnight-purple car wasn't easy to miss. How would she explain it?

"So?" Cocking his head, Matt released her. "They have to find out about us sometime, Gina."

"I know, but not like that," she said over her shoulder as she padded into the en suite.

Their judgments, the arguments, and their inevitable disapproval could come later. Gina wanted to enjoy this carefree time with Matt without them knowing.

She walked into the bedroom, holding the torn remains of her once pretty white dress. "Shit, I can't go home in this."

"Sorry about the dress." Matt sat naked at the edge of the bed, his boyish smile unapologetic. He took it from her, caressing the fabric between his fingers, then placed it beside him.

"I don't care about that, but I can't walk in the door wearing nothing but my underwear."

He pulled her to stand between his legs. "Do you really think I'd let you?"

"No, but I can't show up in a pair of your sweatpants and a T-shirt, either."

He reached for his phone.

She looked at him, confused.

"Problem solved." And glancing up at her, Matt grinned. "Bo and Ava are just next door. You're about the same size she is. So, she's going to drop off some clothes for you to wear home."

"Oh, God." Gina winced, heat sweeping across her cheeks. "That's so embarrassing."

But what other choice did she have?

"There's no reason to be." He kissed her tummy, then, gazing up at her, Matt smiled. "I told you, you're among family here, and we look out for each other."

"Okay." And biting her lip, she nodded.

"Now, c'mere." He spread her thighs apart. "I need to be inside you again."

His fingers strummed through her slit, and her breath hitched.

"I need you, too."

And I always will.

Eighteen

H e woke up alone, and he didn't like it. Not after knowing what it felt like to wake up beside her. Sheer contentment. Utter bliss. Peace.

Her scent lingered. Wrapped in sheets that smelled of warm earth and sex, Matt held the pillow she'd slept on to his chest. This house wasn't a home until Gina walked into it.

It's where she belonged.

And right where he needed her to be.

Patience, man. Six hours.

But that wasn't soon enough.

Eager to get the day started, Matt reached for his phone and, after sending Gina a 'good morning' text, he reluctantly stripped the sheets off his bed. If she weren't coming over later, he would have left them on to keep her scent with him, but thankfully, that wasn't the case. And so, his beautiful bunny would return to an inviting bed made up with freshly laundered linens.

Once he was showered and dressed, with the sound of water

cascading into the washing machine down the hall, there wasn't much left for him to do but kill time. He'd just pulled two rib eyes out of the freezer for dinner when he felt a tap on his shoulder.

Matt jumped, and the frozen meat slipped from his grasp. "Jesus, dude. Anyone ever tell you not to sneak up on people like that?"

"It's not my fault you didn't hear me come in." Kit leaned against the island and snickered. "You gonna grill us some steaks tonight? Good choice, man."

"Gina's coming."

"Oh." And the smirk left his face. "That's cool, I guess."

Matt just stared at him, not sure what to make of the statement. "So, what's up?"

"Not a fucking thing. Just bored," Kit said, and tapped out a beat on the quartz countertop. "Thought we could grab drinks or something later, but it looks like you've got other plans."

He did indeed.

"Sorry, bro." A flutter of guilt swept through his chest. Matt took a step forward and laid a hand on Kit's shoulder. "Another time?"

"Yeah, sure." Kit wet his lips, and rubbing them together, his chin dipped once. "You really like this girl, huh?"

"Told you, I do." He glanced at the ceiling, and releasing a breathless chuckle, his gaze landed on his friend's gentle puppy-dog eyes. "But see, I don't just *like* Gina."

"What are you saying, man?"

"I'm in love with her, Kit." With emotion gathering in his throat, Matt drew in a much-needed breath. "I swear I'm gonna marry that girl someday."

Yeah.

The startled look on Kit's face when he said that was burning in his brain as Matt walked along First Avenue. He hadn't planned to say it out loud; the idea of making Gina his wife only just beginning to take root. She was his person, and he knew it, but their relationship was still too new to speak of such things.

Kit was his person, too, though. He always had been. There'd never been a time either hadn't felt safe confiding in the other. So, while Matt wasn't quite ready to give voice to his thoughts with anyone else just yet, it was natural for him to share them with Kit.

He stopped at the drugstore to ditch his single electric toothbrush for a duo model so Gina could have one at her disposal, too, and stocked up on condoms. They hadn't used them on Saturday. Maybe she was on the pill. The unprecedented, exquisite sensation of taking her raw had stopped him from asking though. Besides, he got off on the thought of breeding her, of his baby growing in her belly. But while he'd welcome it, Gina might not.

They had a lot to talk about.

Dreams. Desires. A future to plan together.

And he knew they would.

Bright summer sunlight assaulted his eyes as he exited the shop. Matt rubbed at them, catching a flash of white on a mannequin in a storefront window. The dress wasn't like the one he'd torn from her body, but he could see her in it, the silky fabric clinging to her curves.

"Excuse me," he said, approaching a middle-aged saleswoman who was busy arranging shirts on a display. "I want to get that dress."

"And which dress would that be?" She looked over at him with a ready smile.

"The one in the window."

"It's lovely. You have excellent taste." Elegant, confident, and poised, the woman approached him. "What size?"

"Uh, I don't know," Matt replied, glancing at the racks of colorful clothing. How was he supposed to know such things?

"I see." The woman's smile widened, her eyes crinkling at the corners. "Let's see if we can figure this out. How tall is she?"

He held his hand level, midway between his pecs and his chin.

She giggled. "And her shape?"

Perfect.

"Slender, but not skinny." Lucious breasts. Plush bottom. Gesturing with his hands, he tried to show her silhouette. "She's got curves, you know?"

"I think I do." The saleslady winked, then went to the rack, and returned holding the dress he'd seen in the window. "If it doesn't fit, you can exchange it for the proper size."

"It looks like it will, but I'm just a dude, so what do I know?"

"It seems to me you know how to make a girl feel special." She smiled at him, her glossy lips shining under the overhead lights. "She's just going to love this dress."

By the time Matt got out of the high-end boutique, the saleswoman, who was damn good at her job, had added shirts, pants, a couple of sundresses, and God only knows what else into the shopping bags. He couldn't stop himself. Didn't want to. Gina deserved the world, and he wanted to be the one to give it to her.

His cheeks aching from a smile he couldn't contain, Matt cut through Coventry Park to make his way home. The sky looked bluer. The sun shone brighter. Old ladies taking their afternoon stroll smiled back at him.

Juggling shopping bags, he punched the code to the park gate, then latched it closed behind him. Except for the music wafting out of Kit's open upstairs windows, Park Place was quiet. He whistled along to the tune until he reached the walkway to his front door and glanced up.

Shit.

Arms folded across his chest, Tony stood waiting.

And he didn't look happy.

"You motherfucker!" Tony thrust his pointed finger at him, taking a slow step down the porch stairs. "And you're supposed to be my friend."

Matt met him on the second step. "C'mon, man. I am your friend—have been since kindergarten."

"She's my baby sister," he fumed, spittle flying from his mouth with every word.

Gina was going to be here in an hour.

"I've been wanting to talk to you." Matt led him toward the door. "Let's do this inside, all right?"

She came bearing bags of groceries, her brother not five minutes gone.

He hoped he appeared unruffled because the talk with her brother did not go as he'd imagined it would. Not at all.

"Let me get that." Matt kissed her cheek, relieving Gina of her burden. "I've got steaks to throw on the grill."

"Perfect," she said, following him into the kitchen. "We can have dinner out on the patio."

He watched her unpack ripe tomatoes, fresh mozzarella, and olive oil in a dark glass bottle. She wore a pair of drawstring khakis similar to his own. A crop top in warm cream bared her summer skin. Matt couldn't stop looking at this girl who'd captured his heart. He pushed every angry word Tony uttered from his head. If he lost him as a friend, so be it. Gina was worth fighting for.

"What all do you have there?" He moved in beside her, his lips dipping to her neck.

"That tickles." She giggled, scrunching up her shoulder. "Just stuff to make Caprese salad and Pasta al Pomodoro."

"I see." Matt chuckled, emptying a bag that held vanilla gelato and a bottle of prosecco.

"What?" She snagged the ice cream and put it in the freezer. "That's for dessert. I'm going to put your espresso machine to good use."

"Oh, yeah?"

"Yeah."

"C'mere." He grabbed her hand and brought it to his chest. Hazel-green eyes looking up at him, Matt held her for a moment. "God, I love you."

Then, with his fingers sliding into thick, silky-soft strands, he lowered his lips to hers. Gina opened for him without hesitation, her sweet tongue slipping inside his mouth, and an overwhelming sense of peace came over him. She was his, and he was hers. That's the only thing that mattered.

They sliced tomatoes together. Chopped garlic. He found joy in the simple domesticity of it. After seasoning the meat and brushing it with olive oil as Gina instructed, Matt took the steaks out to the grill while she boiled pasta and assembled the salad.

He could get used to this. More than that, it's what he wanted. Gina in his house, in his heart, in his bed.

"How're the steaks coming?"

Matt glanced over his shoulder. She looked so happy setting a cozy table for the two of them. He had to tell her about Tony, but he didn't want to see that smile disappear.

"Five minutes."

With her arms wrapped around his middle, Gina kissed his shoulder. "You okay?"

"Yeah, why?"

"You seem… I don't know, preoccupied?" Fingertips strummed up and down his abs. "Like your mind is somewhere else."

He turned around, gripping her by the shoulders. "Believe me when I say this, no matter what I'm doing, or whatever else I might think about, my mind is always on *you.*"

"Yeah?"

"Yeah." And he kissed her. "If you like medium-rare, I think these steaks are done."

After filling their bellies, they sipped on Aperol spritzes in the waning twilight, a candle flickering between them. Matt reached across the table, and taking Gina's hand in his, he raised her fingers to his lips and kissed them. "We need to talk, bunny."

"See? I knew it." She pulled her hand away. "Something's wrong."

"Nothing's wrong, baby, I swear it. Now, c'mere," he said, patting his lap. Gina went to him and sat. "Tony came to see me today. He knows about us."

"You told him?"

With his cheeks puffed out, Matt released a breath. "No, but somebody did."

"Who?"

"He wouldn't tell me."

But I've got a pretty good idea.

Worrying her lip, Gina gazed at him. "He's mad, isn't he?"

Heh. You could say that.

"Don't worry, he'll come around." Matt tightened his arm around her and sighed. "But I need you to be prepared."

"For what? My mother's wrath?" With a shake of her head, she turned her face away.

He touched her chin and brought her back to him. "Yeah, and for what's likely to happen next."

"And what's that?" She wet her lips. "You're scaring me."

Matt tipped his head toward her, smoothing Gina's hair down her back. "There are photos of us together, so expect to see them circulating out there."

"Oh, I don't care about that."

She didn't understand. Not yet. He'd protect her as much as he could, but like Ava and Chloe, Gina would need a thick skin to deal with the media and the parasocial dissection of their relationship.

"You will. The media can be… let's just say they don't always play nice." Matt adjusted her on his lap so she straddled him, then lowered his forehead to hers. "You've got to tell your parents before Tony does, or before they see it in *The National Enquirer.*"

"Okay, now I'm scared for real," she said, rubbing the khaki that covered her thighs.

"You have nothing to fear, baby." He stilled her fidgety hands, covering them with his own. "I'll tell them with you if you want me to."

Gina pulled her head back, giving him a pointed look.

"Or not." With a chuckle, Matt tucked a wave of dark chocolate behind her ear. "Do you know what I love most about you?"

"No, what?"

"You're fearless. Independent," he said, tipping her chin up. "You don't need me. You want me. There's a difference."

"I don't feel all that fearless at the moment."

"I know, but you are." He pressed a tender kiss to her forehead. "You're free to be yourself with me, bunny, and I wouldn't have it any other way. I don't want to stifle you ever. I don't want to change who you are or what you feel, but I want to watch you grow. Because growth can't change who a person is at their core."

"But you have changed me, Matt. In all the best ways." She collared his neck, clasping him against her. "I'm not the same girl who carried a pizza to your door."

"I've changed, too, Gina."

He kissed her.

I'm a better man, and it's all because of you.

Nineteen

Primal sex is honest sex.

Gina understood it now. The hunter inside him didn't want only her body, and he'd said as much.

"I want the shiver in your voice when you realize I see you, fully. I want that ache you feel when your mind's being pulled open before your legs ever are."

He did see her.

Matt saw her like no one else ever had, not even her.

What they shared together was special—a most sacred bond. And now that she had it, Gina wasn't about to let it go. She'd fight tooth and nail to hold on to it forever, so too fucking bad if Tony or anybody else didn't approve.

It's their problem, not yours.

Coating her lashes with mascara, Gina leaned into the mirror. That's what she told herself, anyway. Everyone, including her eldest brother, was downstairs. She could hear him. His voice, louder than the others, drifted down the hallway.

Even though she was exhausted, she dragged her ass out of bed at three in the afternoon. Her mother expected her to join the family for dinner before she had to work her fourth of six twelve-hour shifts in a row. She'd skipped Mass again this morning, so she knew better than to further her ire. Besides, with Teo, Nick, and Luca here to back her, this might be an opportune time to tell them about her and Matt.

If any photos had surfaced, Gina hadn't seen them.

And if Tony had said anything to her parents, she'd certainly know it.

But even she knew, time was not on her side. In the eight days since the concert, her brother had been marinating on what he knew, waiting for the perfect moment to strike. It's how he rolled.

You're fearless, remember?

Gina wasn't going to let him have it.

She grabbed her work bag and strolled down the stairs to pour some coffee and ready herself for what was sure to come. Teo stood at the kitchen counter, muttering to himself as he slammed down the remains of a bottle of Lambrusco.

"That bad, huh?"

"No worse than usual," he said, tossing the empty bottle into the trash with a shrug. "Tony's in there, all full of himself, bragging about how he got us a deal for a place over on Clark Street."

"So, Wrigleyville's a go, then?"

"Looks like it." Teo turned away from her and pulled Mom's salad bowl out of the fridge. "Dad's talking about opening by September."

"But that's a good thing, right?" With her hand on his forearm, Gina glanced up at him. "You won't have to work with him anymore."

He scoffed. "Yeah, well, at least there's that."

"Has Tony said anything about Matt? Made any underhanded comments? Hinted at all?"

"Oddly, no, but you gotta know he will." With a snicker, Teo put the bowl in her hands. "He's probably been waiting for you so he can make a grand spectacle out of it."

Yeah, 'cause he's a dick like that.

"I'm gonna tell them before he does."

Teo's brow lifted, his hazel eyes widening. "Right now?"

"Might as well."

"Oh, shit," he muttered with a chuckle, then, composing himself, Teo hugged her to his side. "It's gonna be all right, Gi. I got you."

The room went silent as she took her seat at the table. She spooned a couple of meatballs onto her plate and helped herself to some salad while wondering how to broach the subject. Gina just wanted to get this over with and go to work.

She didn't have to wonder long.

"Tony was just telling us that a friend of his saw you at the concert last weekend."

"Yeah, so?" she said, glaring at her brother.

He sat back, his hands clasped behind his head, and smirked. "Quite the little metalhead you've become, *bambina*. Since when?"

Gina tilted her head and smiled. "Since I started seeing the rhythm guitarist in the band, but you already knew that."

Eyes bulging, nostrils flaring, Tony leaned across the table. "Well, you won't be *seeing* him anymore."

I'm fearless, I'm fearless, I'm fearless…

She didn't so much as flinch. "And who's gonna stop me? You?"

"If I have to," he bellowed, slamming his fist into the table.

"*Basta!*" Her mother's shrill cut through the room. Then, patting the arm of her firstborn, she softened her voice, placating him like she always did. "What are you saying, Anthony?"

"Your daughter's messing around with my old pal, Matt McCready, that's what," he said, the engorged veins in his neck twitching. "I wanna castrate the sonofabitch."

Her hand falling away from Tony, Rosemary looked at her over the frame of her horn-rimmed glasses. A single eyebrow lifted, and she cocked her head. "Gina?"

"I love him." And as far as she was concerned, that was the only response necessary.

"You don't know him." Tony's fist hit the table once more, and she held onto her glass. "He's a dog."

Fanculo! Gina flipped him off and popped a meatball in her mouth. Maybe that was childish, but her brother was an ass, and she didn't have the mental energy to deal with him right now. Let him throw his hissy fit. She didn't care what he thought, anyway.

"Matt's a pretty cool dude. I like him," Luca said, throwing his arm around her. "He's good to Gina."

"You knew about this?"

"I got them together." With his shoulders back and his chest thrust out, his grin was so wide he showed every one of his pretty white teeth. Then he noticed their mother's frown, and it faded. "Sorta."

"And you…" Wagging her finger inches from his face, Rosemary moved on to Teo. "How could you lie to me—your own mother?"

He settled back in his chair with a sigh, the fork in his hand clattering to the plate. "I didn't."

"Yes. You. Did." Wag. Wag. Wag. As if the words sneering out of her mouth needed any more emphasis. "You told me your sister was spending the night at a friend's."

"And that's what she did." He folded his hands on top of the table and leaned in, tipping his head with an upward tick of his lip. "So, not a lie."

Poor Teo. Being the middle child, if he wasn't ignored, it seemed he always got the brunt of her bullshit.

"I thought you meant one of the girls…"

"Never said that."

Defeated, and with no one else left, she turned to her husband, who'd been silently observing the latest installment of the family soap opera while he twirled spaghetti onto his fork. "Anthony, say something to your daughter, will you?"

"What do you want me to say, Rosemary?" Her dad threw up

his hands, then rubbed the crinkled skin at his temple. "Gina's got a mind of her own—always has. She's gonna do whatever it is she wants to do, so just leave her be. This will run its course in due time."

Let him think that if he wanted to, she wasn't going to correct him. Because the only conceivable outcome in her mind was forever.

"Gina, baby, you *cannot* get involved with this boy." It sounded like a plea, or perhaps a prayer.

"I already am." She reached across the table, and taking her mother's hand in hers, she squeezed it. "And he's not a boy, Mama. Matt's a grown man."

"And far too old for you."

"Really? Try again." Pulling away, Gina rolled her eyes. "Daddy's fourteen years older than you."

"Times were different when I married your father."

Oh, the hypocrisy!

Of course, she'd expected Rosemary to bring up the age difference, which was silly in her opinion.

Love is ageless, and Gina was prepared to defend it.

"Yeah, okay." She scoffed, staring down her brother. "Tony's got eight years on Lina. Why, she was barely legal when—"

He stood, his hand coming down on the table so hard her mother's glass tipped over, burgundy liquid spreading on the pristine white tablecloth.

"You better shut your mouth, little girl."

Fuck you.

"Why should I?" She tossed him a napkin. "It's the truth, and everyone here knows it."

Lina blanched.

Rosemary sent the kids into the kitchen for a cookie while urging her precious son to sit back down. Then, patting Gina on the hand, her voice took on this dulcet tone. "The thing is, sweetheart, Matt McCready isn't the right man for you."

No, Mom, you're wrong. He's the perfect man for me.

"You belong with a nice Italian boy like Vinny."

"*Vinny* is a pretentious asshole," she said with a snicker, stabbing at the meatball on her plate. "I'd rather take vows."

"Good idea," Tony muttered under his breath as he cleaned up the mess he'd made. Then, pausing, he lifted his chin at her. "You'd be safe in a convent, at least."

"Safe from what?"

"Predators."

Oh, for fuck's sake.

"You're being ridiculous." She burst out laughing.

He tossed back his head, shaking it, and huffed out a breath. "You don't know him like I do, Gina."

"C'mon, Tony, I've known Matt as long as you have." Sighing heavily, Nick pushed his plate away. "He's a good guy."

"Oh, yeah?" Tony shifted in his seat, his head half cocked as if their brother had spoken blasphemy by disagreeing with him. "Would a good guy prey on your baby sister? That motherfucker betrayed us."

"Little ears, Tony." Lina drew three-year-old Mallory up onto her lap, holding the child's cookie-smeared face to her chest.

Teo snickered, his scorn obvious, at least to her.

Tony glanced over at him. "You think this is a joke?"

"Nah." Teo wet his lips, swallowed the wine in his glass, and smirked. "It's just real funny hearing it come out of your mouth."

"What?" It sounded like a challenge.

Exchanging glances with Nick and Luca, Gina chewed on her lip.

"Who the fuck are you to talk about betrayal? Tell me, Tony, would a *good* guy knock up his brother's girlfriend?" Teo got up from the table, shaking his fist and pointing at the person he'd once loved and trusted the most, the same person who'd hurt him like no other. "*You're* the motherfucker."

"Matteo!"

"I know, Ma. What's done is done, right?" With his hand

scraping through his umber waves, he looked at her and shrugged. "Just leave Gina alone. Trust her to know what's in her heart."

He stormed off, the kitchen door slamming shut behind him.

So, there it was, the ever-present elephant in the room, out in the open at last. Teo and Lina dated all four years of high school. They used to be that sickening couple who finished each other's sentences and couldn't keep their hands off one another. Until the autumn after their graduation, that is.

Gina was fourteen, a freshman in high school then.

It was nothing big—a little tiff. They'd break up one day and make up the next, as they had a million times before.

But they never did.

Lina was gone for a while. She reappeared at Christmas, a diamond ring on her finger. The wedding was a rushed affair for obvious reasons. A small ceremony in St. Vincent's chapel, with only the parents of the bride and groom in attendance.

In all the years since, it hadn't been spoken of or addressed. Teo had been forced to squash it all down for the sake of "appearances" and a baby that wasn't his, but should have been, while having to look at the face of his betrayer every day.

"Fuck's sake." Tony waved his hand in the air as if his brother wasn't worth a second thought. "He knows it wasn't like that."

The fucking audacity…

Maybe he'd convinced himself otherwise, because how else could he live with what he'd done? But no matter how Tony spun it, an ultimate betrayal is exactly what it was.

With her mouth hanging open, Gina's gaze went from her brother to her parents. "Did any of you ever stop and think about it from Teo's perspective—or even acknowledge his feelings?"

"They were over, Gina," Tony shouted, not allowing anyone to speak.

"Were they?" She glanced over at Lina, who had the decency, at least, to hang her head in shame. "Well, you made sure of that, didn't you? Regardless, Teo's entitled to feel the way he does."

"Yeah, you can't blame him for it," Luca said.

Nick nodded in agreement. "You forgot the bro code, dude."

"See that?" Tony abruptly stood, knocking his chair over, and pointed a finger at their youngest brother. "He's gone and torn this family apart."

"You mean you just noticed?" And Luca rose from his chair.

"No, Tony, it wasn't him. You and your wife did that." Gina glared at him, then, turning to her mom, she lowered her voice. "You and Dad, too."

"That's not fair, Gina," she whispered back.

Pathetic.

"You still don't get it, do you?"

"People can't help who they fall in love with, dear."

She glanced at the clock on the wall. Gina didn't have to leave for another hour, but she didn't want to be here a minute longer.

"Right." And she let a sardonic laugh escape. "I have to get to work."

"I'll take you," Luca offered, putting his arm around her.

Nodding, Gina picked up her work bag and paused when she reached the door.

She turned around.

"And Mom, don't ever tell me who I can and cannot love, because I'll be sure to remind you that you said that."

Twenty

On the days Gina worked, or rather slept, the hours passed by slowly until he knew it was late enough to text her. Afraid of disturbing her rest, Matt rarely sent a message before three. He'd think of her curled up on her bed alone in the attic bedroom, shades drawn to block out the sun. Did she dream of him as he did of her?

You should be here with me, bunny.

If she were, he'd take care of her and make sure she got enough sleep.

She rarely did.

Of that, he was certain.

Just this past Wednesday, the morning dawned stormy, thunder cracking so loudly it woke him. Not wanting Gina to get caught in the rain, he went to the hospital to give her a ride home. Exhausted after her sixth twelve-hour shift in a row, she passed out beside him before he could make the right turn onto Halsted Street from Wellington.

There was something about this girl, and it fueled a desire within him to protect and provide for her. So, instead of taking Gina to the townhouse on Willow Street, Matt brought her home to Park Place. He wrapped her in a blanket, carried her in his arms, ran through the rain, and laid her on his bed.

And through all of it, she slept.

Gina didn't wake until ten hours later, when she sat up in his bed, rubbing her eyes. "Where am I?"

"Home." And he kissed her, sleepy breath and all.

Now that Tony and her parents were aware of their relationship, Gina spent most of her time off with him. She even brought some clothes and personal items to keep there. He couldn't help but smile every time he stepped into the bathroom and saw her shampoo in the shower and her perfume by the sink. They went grocery shopping together, weeded the flower beds, and picked out a tree to plant. Japanese cherry, because according to the salesperson at the garden center, it represents the sweetness of love and new beginnings.

"I can't wait to smell the blossoms in spring," she said, her hands sliding down inside the seat of his jeans as she held him against her.

Matt didn't have the heart to tell her it would be a year or two before she saw them, so he kissed her instead.

"Can we plant peonies in the fall?" Gina held onto his shoulders, bouncing on the balls of her feet. "They're my favorite."

"Whatever you want, bunny."

She smiled. "Some hostas, too, I think."

He'd do anything, buy her the moon if she asked for it, just to see that smile.

A gentle breeze blew onto the balcony where they'd spent the night watching the rain and making love on the outdoor bed. It would heat up later, but for now, in this hour before sunrise, the July air was comfortably cool. Matt watched her as she slept. Wisps of dark hair fluttering about her face. The even rise and fall of her chest.

He hated to wake her, but it was a long drive up to the lake house, and with the holiday traffic, they'd have to leave early if they wanted to get there before noon. His fingertips skimmed the curve of her hip while he leaned over to kiss the tender skin beneath her ear. "Time to wake up, baby."

"Nooo." Gina rolled over with a groan, her hand reaching for his dick. She held it against her belly, cuddling the stiffening organ like a security blanket. "I'm not ready to get up yet."

"Is that why you're getting me up?" He placed his hand over hers. "You wanna fuck, bunny?"

"You never have to ask." And her sweet lips swept across his. "I always want you."

"Oh, but I do." Staring into those hazel eyes that changed color, Matt brushed the hair back from her face. "See, I need to hear you say it."

"I want you."

That's my girl.

Her appetite was as insatiable as his own. Gina could keep up with him and still cry for more. Matt pushed two fingers into her hot, wet hole, the swollen, well-fucked tissue clamping down on them. "Does it hurt?"

"Ah," she moaned, holding his wrist between her legs. "Please don't stop."

He gazed at the marks left behind on her skin. His fingerprints at her throat. On her hips. Had he taken things too far, too fast, last night? She was such a delicate flower, but it made him crazy to be inside her.

"And don't hold back."

"I don't want to hurt you."

I want to tear this pussy apart.

"I love you, and I love what you do to me." Gina cupped his cheek, her thumb stroking the stubble on his jaw. "You promised, remember?"

He did.

But she wasn't ready. At least, not yet.

"I always know what you need, don't I?" Matt pushed another

finger in, and with her thighs already shaking, she spread her legs apart to give him more room. "That's the way, my darling. Relax."

He loved watching her derive pleasure. How her teeth pressed into her bottom lip as she got closer to the edge. The sounds she made. How she screamed, then lost the ability to breathe, her mouth forming a silent O as she came.

Beyond the trees of his back garden, the sky was turning into a pale shade of pink as the sun made its presence known. Light flickered through the leaves to waltz upon her face. Matt held her still-trembling body, his lips pressed against her skin. "You okay?"

"Better than okay." He could feel her smile on his chest, hear it in her voice. "I guess we should get up now."

As loath to leave their love nest on the balcony as he was, Gina didn't make a move. Bailing out of a day at the lake house briefly crossed his mind. Matt dismissed the thought just as quickly. He'd be a shitty friend to do that. *Selfish.* It was something they did together every year, and this was the first Fourth of July without Kyan. Dillon and Linnea might need their support, and this would be the perfect opportunity for Gina to bond with the girls and take her place within his family of friends.

Matt sat up, taking Gina with him, and brushed the hair from her eyes. "I'll make coffee and fix us some breakfast while you shower."

"Or you could shower with me."

God, I love you.

"As tempting as that sounds, if I did, we'd never leave the house." Then he stood, extending his hand. "C'mon, Kit said they'd be by for us around eight."

"Hello, Trouble." Sloan smirked at Gina over his shoulder as Matt guided her inside the rear door of his sporty new M3.

"Hey, Sloan." She returned the greeting with a roll of her eyes, scooching across the black leather seat. "What is it with you guys and purple cars?"

"It's Daytona Violet Metallic, thank you very much." Of course, he had to correct her as if violet and purple weren't the same thing. "Special order. Cost me an extra five grand, I'll have you know."

"For paint?" With a toss of her thick chocolate waves, Gina glanced at him in disbelief as he slid into the seat beside her. "That's insane."

"Call me crazy, then," Sloan said.

Matt shrugged. "Custom paint for the Audi was eight."

Worth every damn penny, too.

"Jesus, you're both nuts." Then, she directed her attention to their bassist, who sat idly staring out the passenger side window. "What color is your car, Kit? And please don't tell me purple."

"Okay, I won't," Kit muttered, still staring. After a moment, he turned away from the window. "It's a yellow AMG GT 63."

Yeah, yellow like a canary or a neon highlighter.

Trading glances, he and Sloan shared a chuckle.

"What?" Those puppy-dog eyes of his flicked back and forth between them. "Yellow's a happy color, and I think if you're spending a hundred grand on a car, you should get whatever the fuck color you want."

If yellow meant happiness to him, and his blinding ray of sunshine on wheels gave him one iota of joy, that's what mattered. Kit earned it, after all. And hell, if he didn't deserve it.

Matt leaned forward and squeezed his shoulder. "Damn right, brother."

Sloan took Diversey to the expressway, driving past the neglected building that was once Mickey's Place, its "For Rent" sign barely visible through the dirt-streaked glass. He glanced at it and the corner of his mouth quirked up, no doubt remembering how they'd shown up in that beat-up old Chevy they'd worked on all summer to convert it into something resembling a touring van. Brand-new cars, big houses, and the luxury of an air-conditioned tour bus were nothing but dreams back then.

Swallowing back a chuckle, Sloan merged onto the Kennedy. "Tony coming around yet?"

"Don't know." Gina flashed him a smile. He could feel her muscles grow taut beneath his fingertips. "And I don't care."

"I, uh, haven't seen him since…" Matt shrugged a shoulder, his hand running up and down Gina's arm to comfort her. "He just needs some more time."

"I saw him," Kit said, looking back at them.

The hell?

"I ran into him grabbing a coffee at Beanie's the other day."

Odd that he hadn't thought to mention it until now. "Why didn't you tell me?"

"I would've, asshole, but I haven't seen you." Kit's eyebrows drew together, and he made a face, his right nostril lifting along with his upper lip. "You've been… uh… occupied."

"What did he say?" Gina wanted to know.

He did too.

"Nothing much," Kit said in a tone that almost sounded evasive. "He didn't mention you or Matt at all."

"He's still mad then." She leaned back, her gaze wandering to her phone, and opened up TikTok. "Not that he has any right to be."

"Doesn't he?" Sloan glanced at her in the rearview mirror. "C'mon now, Trouble, try to look at this from Tony's perspective. I bet you'd throw a hissy fit if he started dating one of your little friends seemingly out of the blue—especially someone he's known since she was in pigtails."

"He's married, Sloan." Taking their bandmate's case in point literally, Kit waved his hand through the air and dismissed it. "So that would never happen."

"No shit."

"You must not know him as well as you think you do." Gina

smirked and put her phone back in her purse. "Tony's done a lot worse."

The last thing Matt wanted was to come between Gina and her brother, but something else was going on here. Something personal and private she hadn't shared with him yet. What the fuck could Tony have done to turn her so adamantly against him when once she worshipped the ground he walked on? Matt pulled her closer and kissed the top of her head. Whatever it was, he hoped it wouldn't fuck up a decades-long friendship. Of course, not realizing this, and in defense of their friend, Sloan went Team Tony on her.

"I remember the guy who hurried home after school for a ridiculous tea party with you and your stupid dolls instead of hanging out with his friends. You know, the same guy who taught you how to ride a bike after you begged him to take off the training wheels and patched up your bloody knee when you fell?" Sloan relaxed his grip on the steering wheel, and with a subtle shake of his head, a broken laugh rose from his throat. "Yeah, I know that guy."

Gina blanched for a moment, but quickly recovered because she was far from done.

"Jesus Christ, I was what? Five?" She leaned in through the space between the two front seats, her finger wagging at Sloan a mile a minute. "My parents were always working, Nick had football after school, and Nonna's hands were already full with Luca, so who else was I supposed to go to?"

"Right." He tipped his chin up at her. "You know, I used to think it was weird. How he practically raised you. Tony always put you and your brothers first, but I'm an only child, so what the fuck do I know? But I know this, his world revolved around his precious baby sister, so yeah, I think he has a right to care."

"Maybe when I was little, but…" With a sad shake of her head, she moved back into her seat. "… when Tony got married, everything changed."

"He has a wife and kids of his own to take care of. That's to be expected, no?" Kit asked.

"Sure, but that's not what I'm talking about." Gina crossed her arms, her gaze meeting Sloan's in the mirror. "Did you know Tony's wife was Teo's girlfriend first?"

Shit.

"I wasn't aware of that, no."

"That's right, you weren't around then, touring the world, and becoming a rock star." It was Gina's turn to shake her head and laugh. "Teo and Lina were together for four years—practically engaged, for chrissakes. Long story short? Tony got Lina pregnant, so he married her instead, while Teo was told to just deal with it. Tell me, how are you supposed to get over something like that?"

No one answered.

Then, Kit softly murmured, "You don't."

Gina squeezed Kit's hand, and he let her.

"I don't think I can ever forgive Tony for what he's done to our family. So, no, Sloan, he doesn't get to play the caring brother anymore when he's already proven that he isn't."

Twenty-One

She stared at the text on her phone.

How odd.

Tony rarely messaged her.

Even stranger, he asked Gina to stop in at Rossi's on her way to the train. Something was up, and it wasn't the *Spaghetti ai Carciofi* he said he'd made especially for her to take to work for dinner. He'd done nothing like that before, either. Was it a peace offering? As if it could make up for his bullshit. But she loved artichokes, dammit, and that creamy, lemon-infused pasta sauce was her weakness.

The fucker knows it, too.

Gina was of a mind to tell him what he could do with his spaghetti, but why waste a perfectly delicious meal? Besides, come two in the morning, she'd be starving. Then, she'd be kicking herself in the ass for having to make do with a wilted salad from the hospital's cafeteria—if she even had the time to take a break, that is.

Most often, physicians scheduled their inductions on Tuesdays or Thursdays, but since it was Friday, the shift shouldn't be too crazy.

Unless the moon was full—crazy shit always seemed to happen then. Or if the charge nurse assigned her to a mom who failed her induction and needed a C-section. That would mean circulating in the OR and hours spent in the recovery room afterward. She'd be lucky to grab a crummy cafeteria salad then, so she might as well take her brother up on his offer.

At the height of the dinner rush when she got there, Rossi's was jam-packed. Her dad and Teo slid pizzas into brick wood-fired ovens while Nick manned the counter. A takeout and delivery establishment, the only seating was some stools along a ledge looking out the window, where patrons could scarf down a quick slice, and a few small tables. Tony sat at one of them, and he wasn't alone.

"Gina." He glanced up at her, pulling out the empty chair beside him. "You remember my old pal, Curtis, don't you?"

She didn't.

"CJ," the man corrected him, extending his hand with a smarmy grin. "Hello again, Buttercup."

Is this dude for real?

"Excuse me?"

"You were prancing around in a Powerpuff Girls getup the last time I saw you."

"Oh." She sat down, heat flooding into her cheeks. "Yeah, well, Buttercup was the one most like me."

"Because of her dark hair?"

"No, she was the tough one."

Who was this guy, and what was he doing here? Amused by her discomfort, he chuckled. "With all those brothers, I guess you'd have to be."

"CJ went to school with me and the Venery boys," Tony explained. "I'm surprised you don't remember him. He hung out with us all the time."

Her gaze traveled back to the man in question. His dark hair was pulled back into a small knot at the base of his skull. Shifty gray eyes. Prominent hawk-like nose. He wasn't unattractive, but

Gina wouldn't say he was especially good-looking either. Maybe he'd changed a lot since she was a kid, because she still couldn't place him.

"I was their manager until a few months ago," he said as if that should somehow impress her. "Made them who they are, and then they fire me? Ungrateful fucks."

What did he expect her to say? Gina glanced at her brother, and he shrugged. "Sorry to hear that, but unless you made the music for them, I'd say they made themselves."

"And what do you know about the industry, huh?"

Not a fucking thing.

"They're talented musicians, I'll give you that, but there's plenty of kick-ass bands out there who never get to see the inside of a recording studio, let alone sell out arena tours. See, I'm the one who made that happen."

Okayyy.

"I'm gonna get your dinner, *bambina.*" With a squeeze to her shoulder, Tony stood. "Be right back."

"It's who and what you know." CJ settled back in his chair, a booted foot casually crossing his thigh. "Negotiation is a skill, and I'm a master at it. They'll be sorry."

"I know nothing about all that." Hoping to end the conversation, Gina looked down at her phone.

"Of course you don't." He leaned in, demanding her attention. His breath tickled her ear. "So, a little birdie told me you've been hooking up with Matt McCready."

"Oh, really?" Feigning interest, she forced a laugh. "Wait, don't tell me. Let me guess. That little birdie is my brother, right?"

"Wrong." His head tipped to the side, and he smirked. "Told you, I know people."

"Well, CJ, you've been misinformed," Gina said, and crossing her arms, she smirked right back. "Matt and I aren't *hooking up;* we love each other."

What have you got to say now, asshole?

"I've known him a helluva long time, Buttercup, and trust me, fucking is all he's good for." He leaned in closer, taking her palm in his. "Chicks. Dudes. He doesn't care. A hole is a hole to him."

As if his touch burned her skin, she pulled her hand away. "You're lying."

"But I'm not." Undeterred, CJ invaded her personal space, his face mere inches from hers. "I've had to endure watching him—hell, all of them, and their depraved sexual escapades for years. And let me tell you this, that selfish motherfucker isn't capable of loving anyone. He doesn't know how."

"Matt is anything but selfish," Gina shot back, her finger poking his chest with every insistent word. "He's loving and generous and kind and…"

… *perfect*.

Well, to her he was, anyway.

"Sweetheart, that's what he wants you to think. He's just playing you." CJ patted her arm, looking upon her with something akin to pity. "You're a beautiful girl, and you're convenient while Matt's bored here at home, but I know him. Once they cut their next album and go back out on tour, he's gonna forget all about you. I heard a big label is looking to sign them, and if that's true, he'll be gone sooner rather than later."

"Sounds like sour grapes on your part to me." Gina schooled her expression to one of indifference. She knew the boys were working on a new album, and that meant eventually they'd leave home again. Matt never mentioned a record deal, but then why would he? The business side of Venery wasn't a topic they typically discussed.

"Nah, see, I've already picked up some new bands. I don't need them; they need *me*." His tongue slowly swiped across his too-thick bottom lip. "If you weren't Tony's sister, I wouldn't even waste my breath. But I don't want to see you get hurt, and if you keep messing around with him, you're going to be."

"I tried to tell her, but all I did was piss her off." Her brother placed a Rossi's bag filled with enough food to feed ten people on the table in front of her and reclaimed his seat. Then, he pulled her hand into his lap and squeezed it. "I'm not the villain here, Gina."

She glanced over at Teo, who looked on from behind the counter, shaking his head. "And Matt is? He's one of your best friends, Tony."

"You don't know him like me and CJ do." His fingertips traced the skin between her knuckles. "Look, he's a good guy, but he's not the guy for you."

"Rock stars are a different breed." Nodding, those shifty gray eyes looked into hers. "Even before they're famous, they've got girls willing to go down on their knees for them and… well, I don't have to tell you the rest. Fuck's sake, just google him."

Gina closed her eyes. Hadn't she had those very thoughts once?

"*I'd love to see you down on your knees. It isn't what I want, though.*"

"*What do you want, then?*"

"*To earn the privilege to worship you at yours.*"

But she'd been wrong, and so were they.

"You know what the Red Door is, don't you?" CJ asked.

She walked past it nearly every day. "A bougie private club."

"It's a sex club, Gina," Tony informed her with a sigh. "And your boyfriend is a charter member."

"Matt's into some nasty shit. He'll turn you into his pretty little whore, ruin your life and everything you've worked so hard for." Then, he dropped his phone in front of her. "I didn't want to show you this, but…"

Photos of her and Matt taken at the festival a few weeks ago.

Gina swiped through them. "How'd you get these?"

"That doesn't matter." CJ took his phone back and passed it to her brother. "I want you to think about what would happen if these photos were plastered all over the internet. I don't think the hospital would be at all happy to see one of their nurses depicted like this on the pages of some supermarket tabloid, do you?"

"*Cazzo!* You'd lose your job, Gina, and with that kind of

publicity, who would hire you?" Tony was getting angry. She could tell. His cheeks turned the color of ripe tomatoes. "Think of what it would do to Mom if these photos were to get out."

"I'm kissing my boyfriend," she hissed through her teeth. "So what?"

"With your *culo* on display for the entire world to see."

The words came out of Tony's mouth with such vehemence, everyone in the place had to have heard him. Heads turned. Even her dad interrupted his task to look over at them.

Mortified, Gina hid behind her hand. "I've got panties on."

"Couldn't tell."

"Simmer down, man. Your sister didn't know. Now, she does." CJ turned from Tony to her. "Listen to me, little girl, this is nothing—just ask Ava and Chloe."

Gina rolled her eyes. Was this guy ever going to shut up?

"You aren't prepared for what's coming, Buttercup, so you better run. Get out while you still can."

With a toss of her ponytail, she snickered. "Is the moon full?"

"I think it was a few days ago, why?"

Crazy shit always seems to happen then, and you, sir, are out of your fucking mind.

"Uh, no reason."

"I better go or I'll be late for work." She stood and, collecting her bags, Gina kissed her eldest brother on the cheek. "Thanks for dinner."

Twenty-Two

Matt watched her from the hallway.

At the kitchen island, with her hair in a loose braid down her back, Gina drenched her hands in olive oil and pressed her fingers into the dough, making dimples in it. Focused as she was on her task, she didn't notice him standing there, not six feet behind her. She worked in quiet contemplation, gnawing at her lip as she went, and he wondered what was going on in that beautiful mind of hers.

Something stirred. She'd been preoccupied—almost pensive—since he'd picked her up at work Wednesday morning. Matt thought of asking her about it, but other than catching Gina musing when she thought he wasn't looking, nothing felt amiss. She gazed at him, love and longing in her eyes, and kissed him with unquestionable desire. Not one to hold back, she'd give voice to her thoughts once she was ready to, and when she did, he'd hold her and listen.

He wound his arms around her middle, his nose nuzzling into

the graceful curve of her neck, as she washed the oil from her hands. "You smell so damn delicious. I want to devour you."

"Again?" And with a giggle, Gina turned around, her wet hands dangling over his shoulders. "It's got to be the *focaccia* you're hungry for."

"No." He lowered his lips to hers, their noses touching, and tasted her sweetness. "It's definitely you."

Gina cinched her arms around his neck and, drawing him even closer, slipped her tongue inside his mouth. Enthusiastic. Engaged. Connected. She kissed him the way every man wants the woman he loves to kiss him.

"I love you." Soft lips swept over his cheek, then she turned back around, sprinkling salt and fresh rosemary on the dough. "Twenty minutes in the oven, and we should be good to go. I whipped up some ricotta with olives and roasted red peppers to take along, too. It's amazing on warm *focaccia*."

"Isn't that what the eggplant stuff we made last night is for?"

Gina had him chopping the baby variety into little cubes, along with onions, garlic, peppers, celery, and olives. She insisted each ingredient had to be sautéed until caramelized separately. Matt didn't understand why that mattered so much, but he rolled with it. Bo was having a cookout so the boys could work on the songs for the new record while the girls hung out together, and he understood she wanted to make a good impression.

"The *caponata*?" She threw him an amused grin, sliding the baking sheet into the oven. "I figured we could bring both."

"Why not?" He picked her up and sat her on the quartz countertop, wrapping her legs around his waist. "Variety's a good thing, right?"

"It's the spice of life, so I hear."

"What's that supposed to mean?" he asked, detecting the snark in her tone.

She only shrugged. "That's what they say, isn't it?"

And just who the fuck is 'they'?

"If there's something on your mind, Gina, then say it." Matt squeezed her shoulders with a heavy sigh. "Because watching you wrestle with it is making me nuts."

"It doesn't matter."

"I can see that it does." With his finger caressing her cheek, he kissed her on the forehead. "Whatever it is, we can talk about it."

Gina rubbed her lips together and exhaled. "Are you bisexual? And before you answer that, I want you to know it's okay if you are. It doesn't change anything."

The words tumbled from her mouth with such earnestness that his eyebrows shot up, then, holding onto her thighs for support, laughter bubbled up from his chest. "No, I'm not."

"I knew he was lying." She lifted her chin, a smile crossing her face. "Told him so, too."

"Who?"

"CJ."

That motherfucker.

"He's such a dick. I can see why the band fired his ass." Her legs around his waist cinched tighter, holding him between her thighs. "I mean, c'mon, did the guy really think I'd believe that you fuck other men?"

"Uh… well…" He had, and he wouldn't deny it. Matt cleared his throat. "I have in the past."

"Wait, you just said—"

With the fragrant aroma of her rosemary bread filling the kitchen, he sealed her lips with his own. Then he kissed her, pressing the erection in his jeans against buttery-soft silk to remind her who he got hard for. "Because I'm not."

"I don't understand."

With a slight headshake, Gina's hazel-green gaze clouded, and Matt was reminded just how innocent she was until he got his filthy hands on her. This is what Sloan warned him about, and why Tony didn't want them to be together.

He brought her fingers to his lips and kissed them. "Yeah, I've fucked a dude, but that doesn't mean I'm bi."

"What does it mean then? Bi-curious?"

"It doesn't *mean* anything." Holding her face in his hands, Matt looked into the eyes he loved. "I'm attracted to women—you, specifically. And the fact that I've had sex with men on occasion doesn't change that."

She opened her mouth, but nothing came out.

He lowered his forehead to hers. "A person's sexuality isn't as definitive as you might think."

"So, you're not attracted to men?" Gina asked, playing with the hairs on his chest. She sounded so hopeful.

"No."

"But you've fucked them."

"Yes."

Her head flicked back slightly. "Why?"

To let the beast out.

He wasn't about to say that, though.

"Because I could."

There was something about playing in Bo's basement. Familiarity. Comfort. A throwback to the days of their youth. Matt couldn't quite put his finger on why, but down here the music flowed effortlessly, as if the songs were already written in their final form, when in reality they were merely rough outlines of what they would eventually become. With every session, the band of brothers came closer to perfecting their sound.

The deal with UMG was still on the table, and Brendan wanted to have demos ready to go when they asked for them.

After the bullshit with their former label, Matt wasn't sure it was a good idea to sign with another. In the three years since they'd gone indie, Venery had managed to put out two albums that went platinum and sell out a tour on a schedule convenient to them, yet he couldn't deny the advantages Universal could offer. He just hoped they wouldn't have to sell their souls or hand over the masters in exchange.

Jesse came down the stairs, Brendan trailing along behind him. The cousins took a seat at Bo's piano in the corner, listening quietly until they finished the song they were playing.

Taylor put his guitar down. "Well, what did you think?"

"I dig it," Jesse said and then kissed him.

"Same. That's your next hit single right there." Brendan leaned back against the piano, and, giving them a thumbs-up, he released a deep, gratifying sigh. "Those execs at UMG are gonna lose their fucking minds."

"Just you wait." Sloan proffered a smug grin, casually anchoring his hand on his hip. "We've got some tracks we're still messing around with that are even better."

"Sweet. I have a *Zoom* call with them on Monday."

His thoughts froze. It occurred to him then. How did CJ know? Deals like this one are usually kept under wraps until the ink is dry, and the label makes an official announcement.

"Who else knows we're in negotiations with Universal?"

Brendan's head flinched back with a frown. "No one that I'm aware of, why?"

"CJ mentioned it to Gina." With a shake of his head, Matt flicked the snaps open on his guitar case. "He told her a big label was looking to sign us."

"Where'd she see him at?" Bo asked.

"Rossi's." Glancing over at their drummer, Matt explained, "Tony had her come by to pick up dinner to take to work, and he was there."

"Sounds like an arranged meeting to me," Bo surmised.

Funny thing was, he'd concluded the same.

"Trying to scare her off, was he?" Sloan chuckled as if the thought amused him.

"You think?" Matt shoved his guitar into its case and slammed the lid closed. "CJ told her I fuck men, and he had pictures of us together from the festival on his phone. He wouldn't tell Gina how he got them, though."

"Don't be daft, mate."

Taylor threw a sharp glance his way, which Matt rolled his eyes at.

"The wanker took the photos himself."

No shit.

"How bad could they be?" Kit took a step toward him, then, with his eyebrows drawing together, he stopped and cocked his head. "CJ didn't threaten her, did he?"

"No, I don't think so."

"Word was bound to get out. Nothing stays a secret for long." Brendan's hand came down on his shoulder, and he squeezed. "I wouldn't worry about it."

But he was worried. CJ had proven himself to be a slimy motherfucker who'd sacrifice anyone to get what he wanted. And what he wanted now was retribution. Matt wasn't about to stand by and let him make Gina his pawn to get it.

Rubbing his fingers on his shirt, Kit bit at his lip. "Do you think CJ's gonna try to fuck things up with UMG?"

"He can't," Brendan said without hesitation. "The guys at Universal have wanted Venery for years. They would've reached out sooner, except they didn't want to deal with CJ. They can't stand him."

"Heh, and the dude thinks he did so much for us." Exhaling a heavy breath, Kit sneered. "The bastard held us back."

Brendan nodded. "I'm told CJ's still tight with your old label. He's managing a couple of new bands for them."

Well, that explains a lot.

Suckers.

Sloan's lip slowly curled. "Makes me want to sign with UMG even more."

"I hate to bust this up." Jesse leaned in. "But the kids are getting antsy."

"And hungry." With a nod, Brendan chuckled. "The girls asked us to come get you."

"Oh, yeah?" Wiping the sweat off his chest, Bo got up from his kit. "Well, you don't have to tell me twice."

Matt found Gina out on the patio with Katie, Chloe, and Ava, keeping a watchful eye on the little ones who scampered after Chester on the lawn. Nibbling on *focaccia* and eggplant, loose strands from the braid down her back blew in wisps around her face. *So fucking beautiful.* He often wondered what he'd ever done to deserve to be loved by her, but regardless, she did, and he'd never take that gift for granted.

A hair caught on her lip. Leaning over from behind, Matt kissed her petal-soft skin and pushed it out of the way. "Sorry I was gone so long. You doing okay?"

"Yeah." Gina smiled up at him. "We were enjoying the music."

"You could hear it?" He sat beside her with a chuckle.

"The sound was muffled a bit, but yeah, for the most part."

Tucking that pesky windblown curl behind her ear, Matt kissed her. "I love you."

"And I love you."

It stopped him in his tracks every time she said it. Not in a dramatic movie-scene kind of way, but in a quiet, ordinary moment that felt like a soft punch to the heart. God help the fucker who did anything to try to take her away from him.

"I just got a text from Dillon," Jesse announced from across the table. "He landed in Dublin."

"I should call Linnea." Bo pulled out his phone. "Get her to come over."

"Don't you think I already tried?" Putting her hand on top of his, Chloe stopped him. "She said she wants to be alone."

"Jesus Christ, then do as she asked, and leave her be." Taking a seat on the other side of Gina, Sloan set his gaze on the wife of their lead guitarist. "If it isn't Dillon or Kodiak, it's *you* breathing down her neck all the damn time. How the fuck do you expect her to work through her grief and get on with her life doing that, huh?"

"Chloe can't help it." Stroking her auburn hair, Taylor kissed the top of her head. "You know she's just trying to help."

"I know, but this is something Linnea has to do for herself," he insisted, and looked at Chloe again. "*By herself.*"

"Not everyone's like you, Sloan."

He cocked his head, a smirk tugging at the corner of his mouth. "And how's that, Chloe?"

"People need people." Resolute, she did not waver. "But you act like you don't need anyone."

She wasn't wrong.

Sloan's teeth dragged over his lip, and slowly, a contemptuous smile appeared.

"Because I don't." Then, disregarding her, he turned his head toward Gina. "So, Trouble, I hear CJ's been stirring up some shit."

"CJ?" Ava asked as if she'd misheard, her startled gaze flicking across the table. "Jesus Christ, what now? I thought we were done with him."

"Seems he's taken up voyeurism." Sloan popped the cap off his beer with a shrug. "And photography."

Gina's muscles grew tense beneath his fingers, the encounter with CJ apparently weighing on her more than she let on. The motherfucker would pay for this. *And friend or not, Tony will too.* Squeezing her waist, Matt brought her closer against his side and pressed a kiss on top of her head.

"He told me the pictures he had on his phone were nothing." Tucked under his wing, Gina turned her gaze toward Ava with a shrug. "And if I didn't believe him, I should ask you and Chloe. What the hell did he mean by that?"

It was Chloe who answered, "Let's just say the media can be… unkind. And being involved with Matt makes you fair game."

"They get off on drama," Ava said, nodding. "Anything for clicks, you know?"

Staring at the evening sky, Sloan appeared to be somewhere else for a moment. He reached for his beer without looking, then, with a shake of his head, brought the bottle to his lips. "And CJ's the one who feeds it to them."

Betrayal discovered too late. And it was Sloan who'd been impacted by it the most.

Despite the hostility between them, Chloe reached for Sloan's hand. He let her take it. "You'll have to grow a thick skin, sweetie, and learn to ignore it. They'll tear the two of you apart if you don't."

"Is that why you fired him?" Gina asked.

Brendan scoffed. "He told you that?"

"Yeah."

"His contract was up." Taylor rolled his eyes with a shimmy of his head, like the topic of CJ bored him, and knowing him, it did. "We paid him a generous bonus and opted not to renew it."

"Well, he seemed quite bitter about it."

"I'm sure he is," Brendan said, pulling Katie onto his lap. "Venery is looking at a three-album deal with a major label, and as the band's manager, that would've put a helluva lot of coin in his piggy bank."

"He mentioned that."

"Fucker made plenty off our backs." Seething, Sloan drained his beer.

"What else did he have to say?" Brendan, apparently, wasn't bored.

"Besides Matt's sexual peccadilloes." Glancing his way, Sloan muttered under his breath, "Heh, we know all about those."

Dick.

"Nothing much." Ignoring the remark, Gina shrugged. "You'll be sorry. Blah, blah, blah."

"You need to revoke CJ's club membership," Sloan snapped. With his jaw clenched, the veins in his neck twitched. "That's our safe space, Bren, and if he can come in? Well, that's the end of that."

"The Red Door?" Gina asked, glancing up at him. "Is it really a sex club?"

"Sex-positive," Chloe interjected, correcting her.

"It's not at all like you're probably imagining," Katie said, offering Gina a reassuring smile. "You'll see."

"I will?"

"You're coming to the party next month, aren't you?" And Katie grinned.

Shit.

"What party?" Poking his side, Gina looked at Matt with sudden focus.

"I don't know." Matt took her hand and held it to his pec. "We, uh, haven't talked about it yet."

He imagined the delights they could explore together there, and a flush of warmth spread outward from his groin. What would he find when he turned his little bunny inside out?

"We opened the Red Door seven years ago. The club is my baby, my passion project," Brendan proudly explained. "We hold an extra-special event to mark its anniversary every year—an open house, if you will."

"Heh, that's one way of putting it." And Sloan swiped his tongue across his lip. "But if CJ's there, I'm out, dude."

"I can restrict his access," Brendan offered. A conciliatory gesture. "He won't be allowed up in VIP."

"Or down in the pen?" Kit asked hopefully.

Brendan shook his head. "Enjoy your playtime in the club's private areas."

"The pen?" Gina repeated, hazel-green eyes widening.

"Is Kit's peccadillo." Sloan snickered, and picking up a loose strand of her hair, he twirled it around his finger. "The playpen is a clusterfuck. Picture a sea of writhing, oiled, naked bodies. Bassy boy here is into group activities. He doesn't care to know who he's fucking."

Kit flipped him off. "And you do?"

"Touché."

"Shut the hell up, Sloan." Gina would never see the inside of the playpen if he had anything to say about it. "You're gonna have my girl thinking we're just a bunch of freaks."

"But we are," Sloan said with a smirk, then he rested his chin on Gina's shoulder. "Wanna know what I think, Trouble? Be bold. Live epic. Life's way too short to settle for ordinary."

"So, when's this party?" Gina asked, a slow smile building.

Glancing at him, Katie winked. "August twenty-sixth."

"Perfect, I'm not scheduled to work that weekend."

"Looks like we're going then."

Fuck me.

And Sloan grinned. "You're welcome."

Twenty-Three

I t was just the four of them, and that's how she wanted it. Maybe because Matt spent so much time with them, and by that, so did she, Gina felt comfortable attending the party with his bandmates. He glanced around the VIP space, fondly remembering when the room was almost too small to accommodate them all. The days when nine princes reigned were all but gone.

Nothing lasts forever.

Dillon had been licking his wounds in Dublin for more than a month now. Understandably, Linnea opted to remain at home. Kodiak said Kelly refused to watch her niece put herself on display, which made Matt wonder what Katie and Brendan had planned. Bo and Ava surprised everyone, taking off to city hall to get married a few weeks ago. They were down in Florida on a "familymoon" with Emery. Monica and Danielle's son came down with a bug, so they bailed. Chloe was watching Declan for Katie, as well as her own two, and Taylor and Jesse wouldn't come without her.

So, that left him and Gina, with Kit and Sloan on either side of them, swallowed up in cushions of deep plum silk on a U-shaped sofa that was far too big for the four of them.

Kyan's spirit was here, though. Matt could feel it.

The ghosts of yesterday didn't exist for Gina. To her, the Red Door was novel and wondrous. Awestruck by the club's decadent splendor, he watched her curious gaze drift up to the polished wood beams, suspended by chains from the ceiling, and travel down the filmy drapery hanging from them, which provided privacy from the neighboring space beside it. Much like a child's first trip to Disneyland, Matt wanted the experience to be special for her, and it delighted him to see the excitement in her eyes as she took it all in.

"Where does that go?" she asked and pointed to the grand imperial staircase on the other side of the club.

"Up and to the right takes you to a bar and dance floor. See it?"

"Yeah." Nodding, she pursed her lips. "How come nobody's dancing?"

"It's early yet." Matt threw his arm around her and squeezed her shoulder. "Come midnight, you won't even be able to get in there."

"People don't go up there to dance, Trouble," Sloan said from beside her. He stretched his arms and laced his fingers behind his head. "They're on the prowl for someone to fuck."

With a shake of her glossy mane, she tsked. "So crude."

"You do know where you are, don't you?" Beneath his trendy bespoke blazer with its floral brocade and satin lapels, Sloan ran his fingers up and down his oiled chest. Tailored slim-fit trousers. Hermès loafers. The dude was obviously looking to get laid tonight.

"Is that how you do it, Sloan—dance?"

That's my girl.

Not put off by his snark, Gina met him quip for quip.

"The only way I dance is horizontal, pizza girl." And he winked at her as if he needed to make sure she understood what he was implying. "Your man there is the hunter—or was, I guess I should say. I've never had to chase down pussy. It comes to me."

"Christ, you're so full of yourself."

"Nah." He laid his head on her shoulder, and looking up at her with an innocent face, Sloan batted his lashes. "But I am a very talented dancer."

"Dick." She burst out laughing and swatted him.

"Yeah, I'm that, too."

Chuckling at their banter, Matt shook his head. "Club staff offices are to the left."

"What's downstairs?"

"Uh, themed playrooms, the dungeon—"

"Dungeon?" Her pretty eyes went wide, pupils dilating, but Matt wasn't sure if it was because of excitement or alarm. He thought he'd prepared her for what she'd find here, but then again, maybe not.

"It's not a medieval torture chamber, dear," Sloan said with an eye roll and patted her thigh.

Holding her close, Matt pressed a gentle kiss to her lips. "The dungeon is an area that's set up and equipped for BDSM play."

"Oh, like Christian Grey's red room."

Sloan snorted.

"Not the best comparison, but yeah, something like that."

"Is your playpen down there, too, Kit?" Gina asked, trying to engage with him. He'd been mopey and quiet, which wasn't particularly unusual, but she didn't know that.

"Yeah."

All she got for her efforts was one syllable spoken with a glum sigh.

"You'll be all right, bassy boy." Sloan leaned over him and Gina to pinch Kit's cheek. "Just take it to the alcoves."

Trying to be inconspicuous, the blonde server who waited on them the last time he was here slipped inside their space—what was her name again? The only thing Matt recalled was Sloan making a big deal about her saying y'all.

She opened a bottle of champagne and set platters of the typical club fare on the low table for them to nosh on. Strawberries covered in rich, dark chocolate. Figs drenched in honey. Caviar. Melon balls and pomegranates.

Kit smiled at her, which Matt found odd considering he hardly ever did. "Thanks, Savannah."

That's right. Savannah from Denver.

"I'll be right back to set up your bottle service." Friendlier than last time, she smiled back. "Will you be having the usual?"

"You know it."

The fuck?

Was that a grin? Matt could see the dimples in Kit's cheeks, and hell, he almost forgot the dude had them.

"Wait." His hand went up, halting the server's departure. "What do you like, Gina?"

"Don't worry about me. I'm good with champagne."

"Glenlivet it is then," Kit said with gusto.

"Of course." The girl locked eyes with Gina. "Your private bar is stocked, but let me know if you change your mind. I can have the mixologist whip up something special."

"Hey, what's with the new fit?" Sloan took hold of Savannah's forearm before she could make her exit.

A transparent deep plum had replaced the black thong getup.

She didn't flinch. "Ask your friend. He had them custom-designed, I hear. I just put on what they tell me to."

"You match the furniture." And he let her go, sitting back against the cushions with a smirk.

"Yeah, so we blend in."

Hardly. With her nipples, not to mention every inch of nubile skin showing through, there was no blending in wearing that.

Matt couldn't help but notice that neither Kit nor Sloan could take their gaze off the girl as she left the room, and it didn't escape him they were on more familiar terms with each other compared to the night they last held court down in the big purple booth. He realized then, and it surprised him, six months had gone by since he'd been here, and of the nine princes, only two were left to claim.

"Yowza." Once Savannah was out of view and out of earshot, Sloan reached for the bottle of iced champagne. "That girl's got a magnificent pair of—"

"Didn't I tell you to stop talking about Savannah like that?" And the bassist's hand came down on the empty cushion beside him.

"Like what?"

"Like an object." With her jaw going slack, Gina gave her head a little shake. "You're sexualizing her. It's disgusting and dehumanizing."

"You *have* forgotten where you are." Sloan poured a glass of champagne and put it in her hand. "The human body is a most incredible work of art, and I can appreciate its beauty. No need to get so butthurt, Trouble. I think your tits are gorgeous, too."

"You really are a dick."

"Yeah, well, we've already established that now, haven't we?" And he clinked his glass with hers. "Cheers."

They squabbled like siblings, and it warmed his heart to see it. His bandmates—his brothers—were his only family in the world, and therefore an extension of himself. Matt wanted his boys not only to accept Gina but to love her in the same way they'd all come to love Linnea, Chloe, Katie, Ava, and Kelly. Fiercely, unquestionably, and without hesitation.

Gina took a sip of champagne, then let out a sigh. "So, now what?"

"Now, we relax and get comfy." Matt pulled her against him a little closer, leaving a trail of kisses on her skin. "Eat a little. Drink a little."

"And we wait for the entertainment to begin," Sloan said, waggling his brows.

She looked up at him, hazel eyes blinking, as if she wasn't sure what that meant. Her naïveté showing, Matt reminded himself that Gina's only actual experience was with him. That selfish buffoon who couldn't even get her off didn't count. Responsive and willing, it was only now that she was discovering her true sexual self. He wasn't selfish. As the man who loved her, he'd be the one to guide her, teach her, and show her every conceivable pleasure her body was capable of.

"Like I said, bunny, we're early." Discreetly, he grazed her nipple. "Pretty soon there'll be demos to watch on the platform down on the main floor."

Sloan leaned into her ear. "Don't worry, you'll get a close-up view on the jumbo screen."

"What's a demo?" she asked.

Sloan snickered. "Think about it."

"The Red Door is more than just a sex club." His thumb remained on her nipple, and she didn't seem to mind. Not so discreetly anymore, Matt traced circles as he explained, because fuck, he needed her to get it. "It's a safe space, a venue where people can be free from shame to explore and connect in enthusiastic, consensual ways, no matter where their interests lie. See, every single one of us is unique. Some folks are into BDSM; others might like pet play or femme domme worship. And those are just a few examples. There's a wide variety of kinks and fetishes."

"Your man here thinks he's a dog," Sloan said, then lifted his gaze toward the ceiling. "Woof-woof."

"A demo is education disguised as entertainment. It's an open house tonight, so there'll be some vetted guests here as well as standing members." At least Kit was attempting to be informative. "You wouldn't want someone tying you up or wielding a paddle on your ass if they didn't know how to do it properly."

"It's a learned skill. Takes practice." Holding onto Gina's hand, Sloan winked. "I'm good with a whip, too."

"Err, um, I think I'll pass."

"Sex-positive doesn't just mean acceptance, baby." Smoothing her hair, Matt pressed a kiss to her lips. "Yes, we're judgment-free, but safe and consensual is a huge component, so education is of the utmost importance."

"Brendan even holds classes here," Kit said, nodding.

"On how to tie people up?"

"Among other things." He chuckled. "And it's called *Shibari*—Japanese bondage."

"Oh."

Savannah returned with their Glenlivet and, without a word, stationed herself close by. The tables on the main floor, now filled with familiar faces, some dressed to the nines, and some wearing fetish attire, had their gazes on the platform, waiting for the show to begin. Montages of demos past played on the jumbo screen, whetting their appetites.

Brendan had quite the crowd here tonight. With the smell of sex already in the air, Matt watched the guests stroke and fondle each other while he toyed with Gina's nipple. Christ, he needed to be inside her. He got pumped up thinking of all the things they could explore here together.

She had a curious mind. Matt paid attention to her breathing, the dilation of her pupils, and made a note of what appeared to excite her. Rough fingering and fisting didn't surprise him. They'd been working up to it and were almost there. And as much as Gina protested to Sloan, she bit her lip when she saw the paddle.

A little impact play, perhaps? I like it.

But while watching a scene of a girl with a harem of men pleasuring her, Gina audibly gasped. Chuckling, Matt pinched her nipple. He could make that happen for her, too.

She wore the little white dress he'd found that day in the boutique window. He could see her dusky nipples, hard and swollen, through the fabric. His boys could see them, too. He'd seen them looking.

Brendan and Katie walked onto the raised platform.

Matt lowered the strap of Gina's dress, exposing her bare breast, and she let him.

"Here we go, bunny."

"What are they gonna do?"

He bent over and kissed the creamy swell of her breast. "No one touches his wife. Ever. Only him. He'll let you watch, though."

"You get to see your friend get her guts rearranged by Brendan's monster cock." Sloan squeezed the flesh just above her knee. "Katie gets off when people watch."

"Have you?" she asked, staring up at him, her hazel eyes big and round.

"Have I what?"

"Watched them."

"Fuck yeah." He moved her hand to the bulge in his pants. "I like to watch."

She squeezed. "Wow, that's so kinky."

"We're all kinky, bunny. Some of us just hide it better."

"Bren used to do demos all the time—he's a master. He only does them with Katie now," Kit said, his gaze fixed on the jumbo screen. "Katie's a subbie. She gets off by pleasing him, too."

"I see."

No, she really didn't.

Not yet.

But she would.

Gina was watching, too. "God, they're hot together."

And they were.

Naked but for strands of pearls that circled her neck and hung over her breasts, Katie kneeled upon a bed draped in sumptuous, deep plum satin, assuming the *Nabu* position. With her back straight, she placed her upturned palms on her thighs spread wide to signify her willingness and desire to please her master.

"It's because they love each other so much—you can see it. He adores her. She worships him."

Then, the spreader bar came out.

"I don't think I can watch."

"You don't have to, my darling." And he slipped the other strap off her shoulder. "We can distract you."

"How?" she asked. Panting, she watched Brendan attach the cuffs to his wife's ankles.

Oh, I think my baby likes that. Matt decided then and there he was going to get one to bring home.

"Let us worship you."

"You want to worship me?"

I do. Forever and always.

"Yeah." He pushed her white lace thong to the side, the intoxicating scent of her arousal making his mouth water. "Just like the video that soaked these pretty panties."

"Be bold, Trouble, remember?" Laying his head on her shoulder, Sloan ran his fingers through the lips of her wet pussy. Hearing her whimper only made Matt's dick even harder. "You should try everything at least once."

"But what if I like it?"

She already did. He could tell.

"God, I adore you." Matt took her mouth with his, kissing her with everything in him. She deserved to experience every pleasure. "I want you to like it, baby."

She nodded.

"You've got to say it, bunny."

And she did.

"Worship me."

Twenty-Four

"Worship me."

Was she out of her fucking mind?

Maybe the champagne had gone to her head, but at this moment, in this hedonistic place, Gina didn't care. She wanted to take what her man so happily offered her. Freedom. Autonomy. Power. Besides, wasn't it every woman's wild fantasy to have three men in her bed? *Madonna, mia! Especially, these three men.* And she was going to be lucky enough to live it out.

"Lie back on top of Sloan now," Matt said, guiding her onto the singer's chest.

Clad only in tight black pants, he'd taken off his jacket and positioned himself in the corner of the gargantuan piece of furniture she'd hardly call a couch, because surely, it hadn't been designed only to be sat upon.

Sloan gathered up her hair and, after running his fingers through the mass of thick, wavy strands, placed it over her shoulder, while her gaze flitted about the room. Thankfully, the girl who'd been taking care of them was nowhere to be seen.

"It's okay, baby. There's no one here but us. I love you." And kissing her, Matt tore the lace panties from her body. "Open those lovely thighs and let my boys see this pretty pussy."

"That's a good girl," Sloan murmured, kissing the skin beneath her ear. "Nice and wide. They're gonna need lots of wiggle room."

"*The Byrne cousins and the Venery boys have always been… uh… close. Really close. Tight, you know?*"

"*Heck, they all live together behind that gate on Park Place.*"

Is this what Nick meant by "close"?

Grabbing onto the ends of Sloan's hair, Gina pulled his face down to hers. "You've all done this before, haven't you?"

"Do you want me to lie?"

"No."

"More times than I can count," he said, his lips brushing over hers. "But this is the first time with someone we love."

"You love me?"

"Matt loves you." Sloan lowered the straps of her dress even further, kissing along her collar bone. "And that means we love you, too."

"I don't understand." Fingers entered her. She couldn't say whose or how many. "Oh, God."

"You will." He weighed her breasts in his hands, the thumbs circling her nipples. "Shhh… relax now."

Well, that was easier said than done.

Gina looked down to see her lover and his best friend draped across her thighs, sharing the space between her legs. Matt spread her pussy lips open, revealing the hidden pearl. Kit flicked it with his finger, then he moved in, caressing her clit with his skilled tongue. And all the while, Sloan held her, sucking on her skin, the hard bulge in his pants trapped against her flesh.

"Keep your eyes on them, Gina." Sloan slid his hands from

her breasts down to her pussy, and took over holding her open for Matt. "Watch how much they get off making you come."

A sensation she never could have imagined before swept through her. With a hungry-sounding groan, Matt's tongue joined with Kit's on her clit. Slowly, he licked up one side, while his friend stroked down the other.

Fucking hell.

Gina tried to squirm, but Sloan's muscled arms imprisoned her. His husky chuckle fanned her skin. She twisted her neck to glance up at him. Crisp blue eyes stared deep into her soul. The corner of his mouth twitched, and then his lips came crashing down on hers.

Sloan Michaels didn't just kiss; he consumed. Wicked and indulgent, he demanded her submission with every sweep of his practiced tongue. And whimpering into his mouth, Gina couldn't help but give in to him.

To all three of them.

"Christ," he panted, nibbling on the lobe of her ear.

She glanced down to see Matt and Kit's tongues meet as they licked her clit. The most erotic thing she'd ever seen, it almost looked like they were kissing. Then, almost as if he realized what was happening, the bassist moved his mouth to Matt's chin, and he pushed two fingers inside her.

"I want a taste of that," Sloan crooned—dark and smoky— the sound of it almost sinful.

Exchanging a familiar glance, Kit extended his hand, and while Sloan licked her from his fingers, Matt stroked himself, his face hidden in her pussy.

Sloan grabbed onto her breasts and, squeezing them together, licked up the side of her neck. She could smell herself on his breath, feel his big, hard cock poking at her ass.

"You taste amazing," he rasped, pressing himself up against her. "I can't wait to fuck you."

Smiling at each other, Matt and Kit took turns sucking on

her clit, then together, they pushed their fingers inside. With her body on fire, their hands on her everywhere, Gina couldn't hold it in for even one more second.

She screamed.

Then, her eyes opened to see Matt and Kit standing there together, naked at her feet.

He leaned over and, stroking her cheek, Matt pressed a tender kiss to her lips. "Let's get you out of that dress, bunny."

The thing was tangled around her waist in a puddle. Sloan helped her up, and while Matt slipped the dress down her thighs, he took the rest of his clothes off, too.

She glanced from Kit to Matt, and then Sloan. "Are you all going to fuck me?"

"Do you want us to?" Sloan smirked. "You're the one who's calling the shots here."

Wondering if that might take the fantasy too far, Gina raked her lip. "I only want Matt inside my…" Why couldn't she say it? "… you know."

This time.

Oh God, am I really thinking there could be a next time?

"You're fucking perfect." Matt pulled her to his chest, and with his fingers kneading her bottom, he kissed her long and hard. "Hear that, Sloan? This pussy is all mine."

He turned to her with a shrug. "Are you okay with anal?"

"Huh?"

And Sloan chuckled. "Is your ass off-limits, too, sweet cheeks?"

"No, that's fine." Gina looked at Matt for reassurance, and he nodded. "I think."

"Any other hard limits?" he asked.

What was this? Some kind of negotiation? She was getting uncomfortable just standing here looking at three naked men with their cocks at full mast. Gina just wanted to keep going before the vibe was gone, and she changed her mind.

"Not that I can think of."

Sloan took a step forward. "She got a safe word, Matt?"

He shook his head.

"Then give her one."

"Cannoli."

"I like it," Sloan said with a snicker, and taking another step toward her, a wicked glint came into his eyes. "Get her ready for me, will you?"

"Just say the word if you want us to stop, okay?"

Cannoli. Got it.

Gina nodded, but she didn't think she'd need to use it. Because Matt stood behind her with his lips on her nape, sending tingles down her spine. And those sharp blue eyes bore into hers, the pupils burning black when he saw her nervous tremble.

"C'mere now, Trouble." Threading his fingers into her hair, Sloan guided her toward his dick. Gina dropped to her knees. "That's a good girl. Suck me."

Between Kit fucking her pussy with his finger, and Matt lubing up her behind, Gina couldn't say how many orgasms she had, while choking on Sloan's dick the whole time.

"Fuckkk." She wiped the slobber from her mouth.

Matt scooped her up into his arms, peppering kisses all over her damp face, and laid her on a nest of silk-covered cushions. Catching her breath, Gina nestled against him, while he stroked her hair and told her how much he loved her.

"Are you all right?"

She nodded.

"Do you need to rest for a bit?"

She shook her head. "No, I'm good."

"C'mon then, my precious little rabbit. Hop on." Matt held onto her hips as she straddled his waist, and he kissed her. "I want you."

She wanted him too.

Her swollen pussy still throbbing, Gina carefully lowered

herself onto his cock, and holding her face in his hands, Matt swiped at the mascara that stung her eyes, gentle fingers caressing her skin. Then, he pressed his lips to her forehead and whispered, "You've got this, baby."

And once again, Sloan gathered her hair. Fingertips brushing past her nape, he squeezed her shoulders. His hands fell in an unhurried path down her spine, only to travel up again, as Matt moved excruciatingly slowly inside her. Maybe he was trying to relax her, but it felt like he'd branded her skin. Gina closed her eyes, the ache in her pussy flaring, and inhaled their commingled scent. Citrus, spice, forbidden lust, and masculine musk. The effect of which could only be described as heady.

She sensed movement going on behind her, heard the telltale sounds. A foil packet tearing open. Lube squirting into a palm. Kit stretched out on his side beside her, and reaching between her body and Matt's, his fingers sought her clit.

"Take a breath." Then, Sloan pressed his cock into the split of her ass.

Odio. My God.

"Shit." And fisting Matt's hair in her hand, Gina latched onto Kit's dick with the other. "It burns."

"Just give it a minute." Fingertips smoothed over her back, his touch and his voice a soothing caress. "Be a good girl for me now. I know you can take it."

"You're doing so good, baby," Matt praised, her face cradled in his hands.

Sloan pushed past the ring of muscle, and her limbs immediately began to shake.

"So, so good." He sighed, fully seated now. "Fuck dancing, we're gonna make you fly."

So overcome with this feeling of incredible fullness, Gina feared she might die. In tune with each other, they moved in magical synergy, taking her to some faraway place. Spots danced in front of her eyes, visions floating in her mind like lucid dreams.

She saw Kit's tongue on her clit, then lapping at the wetness on Matt's cock as he pistoned in and out of her. With his fingers entwined in the bassist's hair, he held his head to her cunt, a throaty, guttural groan rumbling from his chest.

Matt quickened his pace, and, making sounds like that of a rabid animal, he fucked her fast and furious.

With his arm around her middle, Sloan anchored her to his chest. Sweat dripped from his face, making its way down her neck. He yanked her back by her hair, and sealing her lips with his, the voice of Venery swallowed Gina's screams.

In the oddly quiet hour just before dawn, the car brought them back to Park Place. With a kiss to her cheek, Kit and Sloan returned to their respective houses. Gina and Matt showered the night off their skin, then cuddled beneath the covers.

She glanced at the box containing the spreader bar with a sigh. "I can't believe you got that."

"You wanted me to," he said, pulling her bottom snugly against him.

That she did.

He kissed her crown. "Do you want to talk about it?"

"About what?"

"Tonight." He rolled Gina over so she faced him. "You don't have any regrets, do you?"

"No, not at all."

"Something's on your mind. I can tell."

Not that it was a big deal. She wasn't even sure what she saw was real in her lust-fueled, euphoric state.

"Kit," she admitted, glancing up at him. "I think he was licking you as much as he was me."

"Yeah?"

"Yeah."

"Well, why wouldn't he?" Matt chuckled, planting a kiss on her nose. "My dick was covered in you, and you taste fucking delicious."

Maybe so, but she couldn't get the noises he made out of her head.

"You liked that he did."

And he shrugged.

"I didn't mind it."

Twenty-Five

Matt didn't care much for Sundays.

Before Gina, he rarely gave the day a passing thought, but now, on the Sundays she was here, she'd wake with the sun to go to early Mass at St. Vincent's with her family—her obligation, as she called it. More often than not, she was back before noon, but on this particular Sunday, at well past two, she still wasn't here.

He checked his phone and, finding no text, Matt sent one to her. *Everything okay, bunny? Where are you?*

The bubbles danced, disappeared, and then nothing. His spidey sense kicked into gear. He waited a moment, and just as he was about to send her another, the bubbles danced once again.

I'm still here. I'll explain when I get back.

"When will that be, bunny?" Matt asked himself. And what the hell was going on? Something was. He could feel it. But rather than tell her that, he simply replied, *Okay, I love you.*

Then, he stripped the sheets off the bed.

Matt carried them into the laundry room. Stained with her

blood, a mortified Gina had advised him to throw them away when she got up and saw the mess.

"Shit, that's never going to come out." She gasped at the sight. "Towel or no towel, I knew this would happen. It's my heaviest day."

"They're just sheets, babe." And he kissed her. "Besides, it was worth it."

Didn't she realize he loved every part of her? A little blood didn't repulse him, and quite honestly, with Gina, her period had the opposite effect on him. Was that weird? Maybe. And there was a time he would've thought so. But there was something about seeing them both covered in the mess they made together that made him feel some kind of way.

Undeterred, Matt loaded the sullied white cotton into the washer. Sheets had to be white. *And soft.* It was one of the few odd quirks he had. The fabric could be silk, bamboo, cotton, or linen—that part didn't matter so much as long as it felt good on his skin, but they had to be white as the pure driven snow.

"Do your thing, OxiClean." He lowered the lid with a chuckle.

His grandmother swore by the stuff. Addicted to infomercials, Matt fondly remembered finding her glued to the TV at two in the morning, watching Billy Mays hawk the latest, greatest miracle cleanser. She bought damn near everything she saw, too. Ginsu steak knives. The George Foreman grill. Hell, they had an entire drawer of forgotten gadgets to prove it.

He missed her.

Maybe they didn't have a lot, but his grandmother did her best by him. Matt always had clean clothes, a home-cooked meal waiting on the table, and a hug whenever he needed one. She was often sad, though, especially around his birthday, but then her daughter died the day he was born, and surely, the date only served as a reminder. Twelve years later, her son was killed fighting a fire on St. Patrick's Day. So young, too. He was only twenty-four. God, he'd idolized his uncle. His tragic death completely gutted him.

So, Matt understood why she never made a fuss over his birthday.

No party. No cake with candles. And it was okay, because she'd lost a lot, and he knew she was hurting. More importantly, he knew she loved him. His grandmother was the one who always encouraged him to work hard, fight for what he wanted, and chase after all of his dreams.

She gave him his first guitar, after all.

Ten years gone now, Ellen McCready didn't get to see the band's success. She passed away from Hodgkin's lymphoma just months before they made it big. Matt never got to buy her a big house or the fancy car like he promised her he would, not that she wanted any of those things. In the end, she only wanted to go home and be with her family again.

He just wanted her to stay a little while longer.

Love you, Grandma. Tell my mom, Grandpa, and Uncle Mark hello for me, will you?

Matt heard a knock at his front door, and that was odd, considering people came and went as they pleased around here. It was annoying sometimes, but usually he didn't mind it very much. When he opened it, he found Katie's brother standing on his porch.

"Well, hey, Kev. What brings you here?"

"Hey, Matt." With a lopsided grin, he picked at the hairs that clung to his forehead. A cool day in late September, and here, the poor kid was sweating. "I'm helping my aunt and Kodiak move in next door, and I was wondering if you could give us a hand. I swear, it'll only take a minute."

"Sure thing, buddy. Got all the time you need." Swinging an arm around Kevin's shoulders, they went down his porch steps. "What can I help you with?"

"Stuffing my new uncle's big-ass couch through the front door," he said, pointing to the leather culprit sitting in limbo on the walkway. "I keep trying to tell them it ain't going in that way, but who's gonna listen to me?"

"Hey, Kelly." He greeted the newlyweds, his new neighbors, with warm hugs and a kiss to the ice queen's cheek. "Kodiak. Welcome, my friend, and congratulations on your nuptials."

Dillon rolled his eyes.

Having come to his senses, the dude returned from his so-journ in Ireland a few weeks ago. Like a bookmark holding a place in a story that's moving too fast, Dillon had always loved Linnea. Kyan's death had been a mind-fuck for everyone, but for him most of all. Losing a brother? Playing house with his widow? Caring for his infant daughter? That had to have messed with his head. Matt was just glad they both sorted through their shit and were happy. It's what Kyan would've wanted for them.

"I don't understand why you can't get it in." Linnea studied the couch, Charlotte bouncing in her arms. "Chloe and I moved that sofa into Oak Street all by ourselves."

"As I recall, you had a lot of help, gorgeous," Dillon said, taking the baby. "It took me, my brother, Brendan, and Bo to lift that thing."

"Well, what seems to be the problem, then?"

Oh, here we go.

"Gee, I dunno, Kelly." Dillon returned her mocking stare. "Let me think… the width of the door, maybe?"

"Or maybe you're not as strong as you used to be." She pursed her lips with a shrug. "Been skipping the gym?"

This was going nowhere fast. Before Dillon could open his mouth and no doubt say something he'd regret, Matt stepped in between them. "Why don't we try taking it in through the back?"

"Now, there's a novel idea," Kevin dryly intoned, his hands going up in the air. "I've only been telling them that."

"C'mon, Kev's right," Kodiak said, taking a corner. "It's not that it's heavy so much, but the size makes it unwieldy, so it's gonna take all four of us."

Two pretty fit dudes on each end—piece of cake, right?

Wrong.

Matt lifted, his muscles straining, and he hadn't been skipping the gym. Kodiak lied. The fucking thing was heavy.

"My sister damn near fainted when I told her I was going to be living next door to you, so be prepared." Carrying a box in her arms, Kelly walked along beside him. "Kara still tells anybody who'll listen that you called her pretty."

"And she is, but I've got a girlfriend, so…" *Don't be getting any ideas.*

"Kara's going to be crushed when she finds out."

"I don't think so." Couldn't she see he was focused on keeping his grip on her stupid sofa? "And she already knows because I told her."

He had to tell her to get her to stop fangirling all over him. But that was his own fault for being nice.

"Can't you dudes move any faster?"

Says the nineteen-year-old.

"I promised Matt we wouldn't keep him long, and there's half a U-Haul to unload yet."

"It's okay." *Not like I've got anything better to do.*

"Luca was gonna come help, but he had to bail."

Oh?

And his spidey senses reactivated. "How come?"

"His mom made him stay home because they're having company… and some bullshit about World War III." They put the sofa down in the empty family room, and Kevin shrugged. "But that's every family dinner at the Rossi house. You ever been?"

"Can't say I've had the pleasure."

"Yeah, well, they're loud," he said, his head bobbing up and down. "Luca said his sister might need him for backup—and Teo, too."

"Why?"

Spill it, Kevin.

"Um, uh… shit."

Gina didn't want to hang around here any longer than necessary, and wasn't that sad? She should want to spend time with her brothers and enjoy having dinner with her family, but her mom made that impossible for her. Always shoving Vinny down her throat as if Matt didn't exist. And so, she spent most of her days off at Park Place. Hell, much to her mother's chagrin, she practically lived there.

Rosemary insisted they attend Mass together as a family, though. That was non-negotiable, even for Nick and Tony, who had families of their own. She thought it would look bad if they didn't. Gina couldn't fathom why, but her mom was always concerned about appearances. She and her friends would chit-chat about silly things like how many cars were in old Mrs. Cavarelli's funeral procession. Any number less than fifty made it look as if a person hadn't been that well thought of. Or how could Lydia Santucci allow her daughter to get married in a gown that wasn't white? People will know she wasn't a virgin.

As if.

Chrissakes, the gown was this gorgeous blush.

So, to appease her mother, Gina went to church with them every Sunday and either went to sleep if she was working, or back to Park Place if she wasn't, shortly thereafter. She'd love to stay, help with the cooking, and have dinner if Matt could be here too, but Rosemary made it abundantly clear he wasn't welcome at their table.

"And just where do you think you're going?"

Gina had been gathering some things to take to Matt's when her mother barged into her room.

"I've got plans this afternoon." She didn't, but her mom didn't need to know that. "Matt's waiting for me."

"Well, he's going to be waiting a while." Rosemary meant business. Tapping her foot on the wood floor, she crossed her arms in front of her. "We've got company downstairs, so you'll be staying for dinner."

Dammit!

"It wouldn't look right if you just up and left now, would it?"

"Let me invite Matt to dinner, then," Gina said, tossing an extra box of tampons into her bag.

"Absolutely not."

"Why not?" She had to make her mom see reason. "He's my boyfriend, I love him, and he's not going anywhere."

"Do you think I want people to know you're involved with that man?" Moving in closer, she emphatically shook her head. "No, no, no. Whatever feelings you think you have are going to fizzle out. Mark my words."

"Why do you hate him so much?"

"Hate is such a strong word, Gina. I don't hate him, but I don't want to see you with him, either." Her mom sat on the bed beside her and smoothed her hair. "People will talk, honey. Everyone knows where he came from."

"Yeah, from around the corner. What the hell are you talking about?"

"Never you mind." And back to business, she stood. "Now, put on a pretty dress and get downstairs."

Figuring the sooner she complied, the sooner she could get back to Matt, Gina changed into a casual mid-length burgundy dress. With long sleeves and a scoop neck, it hugged her curves without showing too much cleavage. *Heaven forbid!* She giggled and added a taupe leather belt and a pair of matching boots.

Teo met her at the bottom of the stairs. "I'm sorry, Gina."

"Sorry for what?"

But the moment she glanced into the living room, she knew. "What the fuck is *he* doing here?"

"Guess." She didn't have to. "I was just coming up to warn you. Luca and I can distract them while you slip out the back door."

"Fuck that." She'd had it with her mother's meddling. "I'm putting an end to this bullshit once and for all."

And holding her head high, with a smile plastered on her face, Gina strode into the room.

"Why, hello, Mrs. Passarelli. Isn't this a pleasant surprise?"

Not. Politely, she hugged the woman, then glanced over at her son. "Vinny."

"Wine?" Tony smirked, and putting a glass in her hand, he leaned into her ear. "Don't you dare make a scene and embarrass Mom, *capisce?*"

Wouldn't think of it.

She would, but she'd save it for later.

"Vinny, can we talk in private for a minute?"

"Sure, babe." Vinny grinned like he'd already won. She wanted to smack it right off his face. "We'll be right back, folks."

"It's going to work out." Gina heard his mother say.

"I think so, too."

He followed her into the den, closing the door behind him. Then, she laid into him. "What do you think you're doing, Vinny?"

"Getting my girl back," he said with a shrug, stalking toward her.

"I'm not your girl, and I haven't been for three fucking years."

"Gina, baby, it's what our parents want. It's what I want." Vinny picked up a strand of her hair, and twirling it around his finger, he grinned again. "And when did you get such a foul mouth?"

"Well, it's not what I want."

"You did once."

Gina smacked his hand, watching her hair unravel. "Yeah, and then you showed me who you really are."

"*Madone, do you see the tits on the blonde over there?*"

"*Stop looking, Vin. You've got a girlfriend with amazing tits.*"

"*So?*"

"*Didn't you tell me you're gonna marry her?*"

"*Gotta marry somebody, right? She gives decent head. I could do worse.*"

Disrespected. Humiliated. She threw a drink in his face and walked away.

"C'mon, Gina, you know I didn't mean it."

"You meant it." And with her gaze locked on his, she nodded.

"The look on your face when you saw me standing there told me everything I needed to know."

"I'm sorry, and I swear I'm gonna make things right."

No, you're not.

"You can't. And anyway, it's too late." Her gaze and her voice never wavered. "I love someone else."

"Unlove him, then."

"Impossible."

"Gina?" Luca poked his head in. "Matt's here."

"Take care, Vinny."

And she smiled.

Twenty-Six

He asked her to move in after that.

For real—as in change her address with the post office, real.

As in permanently.

As in forever and always.

And while his blood was boiling, Matt kept his cool and remained civil. It didn't matter what he was feeling at that moment. Rosemary would always be Gina's mother, and Tony was still his friend.

There was one thing Matt couldn't let slide, though, and he made it very clear. Rosemary didn't have to like him or accept him, but Gina was his priority, and he wouldn't tolerate any disrespect toward her. *Ever.* And that meant respecting her choices, from her career in nursing to loving him.

Chugging down a bottle of water, Sloan snickered. "Told you so."

"Told me what?" And with a sigh, Matt cocked his head. The dude could be so annoying sometimes.

"She'd end up being your problem."

"Nah, her attitude is *her* problem." And with a half-hearted shrug, Matt began stretching his fingers. "It might take a helluva long time, but I'll earn Rosemary's trust the same way I earned Gina's love."

Sloan glanced up at the ceiling and rolled his eyes.

"Yeah, man, she'll come around." Sitting behind his kit, Bo stretched his fingers much the same way he had been, but then they'd been playing for hours now. "Eventually."

"Are we finished with the idle chatter yet?" Taylor asked with a lift of his brow. "I promised Chloe I'd be home in time for dinner for once."

Me thinks break time is over.

"Chillax, my dude." Bo stood, raising his arms above his head.

They'd just signed that three-record deal, and being under a label again had everyone on edge. Striving for perfection—Taylor's idea of it, anyway—they'd been spending twelve hours a day in the studio. Matt had Gina to get to. He wanted to go home, too.

"We're recording," Taylor announced. "Tomorrow."

"Tomorrow?" Bo looked as genuinely surprised as he was.

"UMG wants the demos."

"Well, all right." Bo sat back down.

"And they want them now."

"It's all good, Tay. We're ready." And they were. Matt clasped his bandmate's shoulder. "One more play through, and we call it a day. Okay?"

Picking up his guitar, Taylor nodded.

While the timeline wasn't set in stone yet, UMG was looking to release the album in the spring, in time for them to headline at the European festivals, then following up with a North American tour. A year had gone by since Venery's last one, and Matt was itching to get back on stage. But not without Gina. The thought of leaving her behind was unthinkable. She had to go with him.

I'll make her my wife before then.

After they finished, Matt watched Kit mope on a stool in the corner, just plucking at the strings of his bass. He was always quiet, but for the last several weeks, he'd been especially so, and he wondered what could be troubling him. *Must be nothing.* If it were truly something, then he would know, right?

"I'm off." And Taylor bolted for the stairs. "See you in the morning."

"Can't wait." Rolling his eyes with a snicker, Sloan turned to follow him. "Later, dudes."

"Sheesh, is Tay wound up tight or what?" With a slow shake of his head, Bo watched his ascent. "I sure hope Jesse and Chloe work some magic on him, so he comes back chill in the morning."

"Cut the guy some slack," Matt said. "You know how he can get when he's anxious."

"Yeah."

"He'll be all right once we've got the demos down."

"You guys doing anything? Want to come over?" Using his T-shirt as a towel on his sweaty chest, Bo got up from behind the kit. "Ava has to stay late at school—parent-teacher conferences. We can order pizza. Have a few beers."

"Thanks, man." Matt grinned. His pizza girl was waiting for him at home. "I've got plans. I'll take a rain check, though."

Bo looked at Kit. "Another time, maybe. I've got plans too."

That's a damn lie.

Unless he considered taking a nap or blasting his music as *plans.*

"You're not doing shit."

"So?"

Nothing was definitely something. What concerned Matt even more was that he didn't know what that something could be. When had Kit not come to him with his problems?

"What the fuck is wrong with you lately?"

Ignoring his question, Kit set his bass on its stand.

When he straightened, Matt was waiting right in front of him.

Turning away, Kit shrugged. "I'm just… it feels like I don't have my brother anymore."

What? The? Fuck?

"You're wrong." Grabbing him, Matt pressed into solid muscle. "I love you, man."

"Yeah? Well, it doesn't feel like it." Kit cocked his head and snickered. "You even fucked Bo but never me."

"Do you want me to?"

The words just tumbled from his mouth.

"I think I do."

Shit.

He couldn't have meant it.

Kit had to be talking out of his ass or something, because where in the fuck did that come from? Except for, perhaps, an accidental groping during group activities, Matt had never known his friend to touch another guy. And fuck one? *Never.* Hell, the dude plowed through more pussy than all of them put together.

He blamed Courtney for that. Ever since the eighth grade, Kit only knew how to love *her*, and then the bitch ripped the rug out from under him in the worst way imaginable. Matt and the boys helped him pick up the pieces as best they could. Being in a band gave him access to willing women. A *lot* of women. And he'd been numbing the pain inside them ever since.

The last one to leave, he locked the studio behind him and took in a breath of brisk October air. It helped clear his head. Then, feeling lighter, Matt walked home.

He opened the door of his once-empty house and followed the savory aroma of butter and herbs. Bent over the oven in a pair of sweats and a long-sleeved, crop-waisted tee, Gina looked so damn delicious. There was no better feeling in the world—even the stage took a distant second—than coming home to her.

"Hey, bunny." Gina put the hot pan down, and he wrapped his arms around her middle. "It smells good in here."

"I didn't even hear you come in." And she kissed him. "How'd it go today?"

"We're recording tomorrow."

"The demos, right?"

Tucking a wisp of silk behind her ear, Matt nodded. "Yeah."

"What do they need those for again?"

Gina was always asking questions. Because she was interested, and he loved that she was. It meant she cared.

"So many reasons." It would take hours to explain it all. "They help them decide who would be the best producer to make the record with us, for one."

"You don't get to pick?"

"We have a say," Matt assured her, squeezing her waist. "And once they get a feel for the album's vibe, UMG's marketing team will get busy, too. A lot has to happen between now and when it comes out, so the sooner they can get started, the better."

"I see."

She didn't. Not yet. But she would.

Little did Gina realize that once the hype machine was put into motion, she'd be riding on the crazy train with him.

"There's going to be a lot of eyes on us between now and then."

"I know," she said, biting her lip.

"Remember that thick skin Chloe said you'd need?" He tipped her chin up with his finger. "Well, get ready for the parasocial pariahs because here they come."

How Matt wished he could shield her from all that hurtful bullshit. It was impossible, though. Like Chloe and Ava, she'd either have to learn to ignore them or just get used to it.

"I'm going to be okay, you know." Those chameleon eyes locked on his, and Gina smiled at him. "They can't hurt me."

He raised an eyebrow.

"Because I know who I am, and I know who you are."

This girl. How'd he get so lucky?

Then, changing the subject, Gina popped a morsel of deliciousness into his mouth. "Now, eat some of this mushroom bruschetta be-fore it gets cold."

"Fuck, that's good."

"I know." And with a tilt of her head, she tipped her chin. "Just make sure to save room for the chicken, okay?"

"Don't worry, bunny. You know I've got plenty of room in here for dinner." Patting his belly, Matt winked. "And dessert."

"Jesus."

"That was pretty bad, wasn't it?"

Nodding, she giggled.

The sound of it warmed his insides. Gina had to love him a helluva lot to laugh at his offhand jokes.

"God, I'm such a dick." Here he was stuffing his face with mush-rooms with the smell of rosemary chicken roasting in the oven. "Why didn't I think of it?"

"Think of what?"

"Bo's on his own tonight, so he asked me and Kit to hang out and have pizza with him." *I fucked up.* "I should've had them come here for dinner instead."

"You should have. I made more than enough food." She fed him another piece of bruschetta, then plated the rest. "You can still call them over, you know."

He could. And before Matt could swallow the food in his mouth, he pulled out his phone and sent them a text.

"Bo said thanks, but he's already got Rossi's coming."

"Course, he does," she said, and pulled the chicken out of the oven. "What about Kit?"

"No response." Matt shrugged. "Something's, um, I dunno… something's going on with him."

"What do you mean?" Her gaze held genuine concern. "Is he okay?"

"Kit told Bo he had plans, and that was a lie."

He knew it must sound nonsensical, but that was out of char-acter for him. The dude was truthful to a fault.

"Maybe he just didn't feel like having pizza."

"Nah, he's been… withdrawn lately." With a shake of his head, Matt got himself a beer from the fridge. "I even called him out on it."

"What did he say?"

Telling her almost felt like he was betraying Kit's trust, but Gina cared about him too. "That he feels like he doesn't have me anymore."

"Ohhh." Nodding, she bit her lip, and took a seat beside him. "I get it. Kit thinks you're abandoning him."

"But I'm not."

And he never would. They'd been inseparable since they both could walk, so how could he ever think that?

"No, but you're not available as much as you used to be, either."

Stroking her hair, Matt pressed a kiss to Gina's forehead. "Well, I have you to think about."

"Exactly."

"Are you saying Kit's jealous?" *Ridiculous.* "Of us?"

"I wouldn't say that, but see, your dynamic has shifted because of me." Gina had a valid point. "He's going to need some time to adjust."

"Yeah, that explains it."

It makes sense, doesn't it? Course, it does.

"Explains what?"

"My boy thinks he wants me to fuck him." It sounded more absurd saying the words out loud. "He really doesn't, though. Kit's just feeling some kind of way, like you said."

"You sure about that?" Rubbing the back of her neck, Gina wet her lips. "I saw—"

"I think he was licking you as much as he was me."

"Positive."

Only he wasn't.

Twenty-Seven

Bundled up in thick, furry blankets, they cuddled together on the outdoor bed, watching the snow fall. In the shelter of his arms, Gina reclined against his chest, while Matt let his fingers slip through her hair, and fondly remembered all the Thanksgivings that came before this one.

The childhood years at his grandmother's table, when he'd run up to Kit's after turkey for a slice of his mom's pumpkin pie. She'd hand them the can of whipped cream, because they insisted they could do it themselves. They covered the pie, the plate, their hair, and their faces in it, but she never got mad. She'd just laugh, clean them up, and send them outside to play street hockey or dodgeball with Bo and Brendan, Jesse and Dillon, and Sloan. Kyan would watch from his porch, pouting, because, four years younger than they were, he was still too little to join them.

Those years on the road, cramped inside that old, beat-up Chevy van. Back then, Thanksgiving was a turkey sandwich at a gas station, and sometimes Denny's, if they were fortunate enough to be near one. *Good times.* Sure, they missed the comforts of home; even so, they had each other.

Matt kissed the top of Gina's head, and, rubbing his nose in her fragrant hair, he smiled.

She glanced up and kissed his chin. "You all take turns hosting Thanksgiving. How'd that come about?"

"I'm not sure. Brendan and Katie did the first one. Wait." *That's not right.* He closed his eyes, pulling the memory from his head. "No, I take that back. It was Linnea's old place on Oak Street. She and Kyan weren't married yet. That was the day Dillon got us the deal on Park Place. Brendan had Thanksgiving the following year, and Chloe the one after that."

"Then Kit?" Gina giggled.

"You got it," Matt said, twirling her hair around his finger. "Around the block in a circle."

He watched her count on her fingers. "What are you doing?"

"That means in three years it's our turn."

That's right, bunny.

Matt had the ring in his pocket. After stuffing tubes of pasta with ricotta to take to her mother's and Sloan's—yes, they'd be eating twice this year—he was waiting for just the right moment to give it to her.

Okay, and thinking of the right words, too.

I should've had Sloan help me write them.

He was the wordsmith, not him.

"I love you, Gina Rossi."

"And I love you, Matthew McCready." She turned in his arms, straddled his lap, and kissed him.

He held her cheeks, and with his fingers threading into her hair, he brought her lips back to his. "I knew you were my forever when you brought that pizza to my door."

"The first time or the second?"

"The first time, pizza girl." He could still see her ponytail swishing, the way she looked at him from over her shoulder. "All I want is to spend every day of my life with you… so, will you marry me?"

Her breath caught, then, filling with tears, her hazel-green eyes locked with his. "I want to say yes."

Then, say it.

He had a feeling there was a "but" coming next. It never occurred to him there'd be one.

"But I have to say, not yet." Gina held onto his face so he couldn't look away. "You and Kit… well, ever since you cut the demos, I've seen you both… I'm not sure how to put it… struggling?"

"Nonsense."

"I think the two of you need to work out your feelings, even if it means you have sex with him."

Have you lost your fucking mind?

"Maybe you need to." She shrugged. "Look, I know Kit loves you and you love him… you love me, too. But I can't be the Yoko Ono who drives a wedge between you. You'd only end up resenting me for it. So, I need you to be sure that I'm what you want."

"I am sure." Her hair danced in the wind. Taming it with his fingers, Matt kissed her. "You and Kit are the two people I love most in this world."

"I know, baby." *Why is she crying?* "Truly, I do."

No, she didn't. Because he'd been too ashamed to tell her.

"I was the only kid at school who didn't have a mom. She, uh, died a few hours after I was born. And I never knew who the fuck my father was. Still don't." He took a breath and wet his lips. "Well, anyway, kids can be cruel about shit like that, but Kit was always the first one to defend me. He was there for me when my uncle got killed, when my grandma got sick… and when Kit needed me, when he fell the fuck apart, I was there for him."

"Courtney?"

"Yeah," he said, nodding.

"What happened?"

"That's his story to tell, not mine." Matt let go of a heavy sigh and gazed at the falling snow. "I gotta ask you, Gina. If you don't want to get married, what do you want? To break up?"

"Nooo." She clung to his neck, her hot tears branding his skin. "God, no, I love you no matter what."

"I want to marry you, Gina." He tasted the salt on her lips. "And I want to put my babies in your belly."

"I want that, too." She hiccupped. "So much."

One word, bunny. Say it.

"It's going to happen, Matt. Just not yet."

He couldn't even be mad about it. Disappointed, yes. But not angry. If Gina needed more time, he'd give it to her. She loved him, she wanted to stay with him, and for now, that was enough. Matt didn't want to admit it, but her observations were correct. He and Kit *were* struggling, but not for the reasons she thought. It was just awkward being around each other now.

"Do you want me to?"

Ask a stupid question, get a stupid answer. So, why the fuck did he even ask? The mess he was in was his own damn fault.

Matt stared out the cold glass and sighed. The Japanese cherry he and Gina planted, a symbol of sweet love and new beginnings, looked so fragile in the snow. He hoped she got to see it blossom in the spring.

The scent of her struck him from behind, and her arms came around him. "You good?"

"Yeah." Turning away from the window, he kissed her forehead.

"I know they can be a lot."

"They were fine." *Mostly.* "Dinner with your folks went surprisingly well, I thought."

Kevin did not exaggerate. They *were* loud. And boisterous.

"Yeah, I thought so, too," she said over her shoulder, heading into the kitchen where a large tray of *manicotti* was heating in the oven. "Mom said you didn't eat enough."

"Seriously?"

Mangia, mangia, mangia.

Any time Matt cleaned off his plate, there was Rosemary, piling more onto it. The tryptophan coma was already calling his name, but it wasn't over yet.

On to Thanksgiving, part two.

Everything about the house across the street was dramatic, dark, and moody—just like Sloan. Black walls. Avant-garde paintings and kitschy artwork. A tiger-striped sofa. Expressive, explicit, eclectic, and a bit morbid, Sloan's living room looked like a cross between a punk bar and an urban subculture museum. Nothing matched, but somehow it all went together.

Gina looked up at his odd assortment of *objets d'art*. A signed Motörhead album cover in a frame. A vintage embellished leather jacket that once belonged to someone notable—no idea who. "Sloan's style is, uh… interesting."

"Yeah, it's different, for sure."

"I think it's called maximalism," she said, taking it all in.

Matt couldn't help it. He snorted. "Is that what they call cramming shit everywhere?"

"Fuck off, guitar boy." Sloan elbowed him, the *manicotti* he precariously held nearly tumbling to the floor. "I embrace abundance, bold colors, textures, and an excess of accessories. It makes a statement, you know."

"And what's that?" Gina asked.

"More is more," he said, unapologetically pretentious. "C'mere now, Trouble. I need a hug."

"Why?"

"Because I don't like people all that much, but I can tolerate you, so…" Sloan opened his arms and Gina went into them. "I lied. I really wanted to feel your tits smooshed against my chest."

"Dick." She giggled, smacking him.

"You know it." Then, he dipped down to Matt's ear. "Where's the ring? I thought you were gonna ask her—"

And with a subtle shake of his head, he carried the tray into the kitchen while Gina went to say hello to the girls.

"You two all right?" Sloan asked once they were alone.

"Yeah, we're good. I just have some shit I need to sort out first."

And his eyebrow lifted. "If you say so."

Matt took a seat at the impeccably set table, and holding Gina's hand on his lap, he surveyed the room. Everyone he loved was gathered here. His band of brothers. His chosen family—and hadn't they grown? Hell, they might have to pitch a tent in the yard next year to hold them all.

As noisy as the Rossi household, if not more so, food was passed, and glasses were filled amid a bounty of smiles, laughter, and animated chatter. Then, signaling the room to be quiet, Brendan stood. They weren't the kind to make speeches or say grace, so his curiosity was piqued.

With his fingers running through Katie's blonde hair and a hand resting on his son's ginger head, Brendan gazed tenderly at his wife. "Declan wanted me to let you all know he's getting a baby sister in May."

"You're pregnant?" Kelly asked, her mouth hanging open.

Rubbing her still-flat tummy, Katie beamed. "I am."

The news wasn't altogether unexpected. It was common knowledge among them that they were ready for baby number two.

"Well, Declan, guess what?" Kelly exchanged a glance with Kodiak, and he nodded, while the two-year-old finger-painted with his sweet potatoes. "You'll be getting a new baby cousin, too! I can't tell you if it's a boy or a girl, though. It's going to be a surprise."

Two more seats at the table. For sure, they were going to need that tent.

"Ohmigod, when are you due?"

"May fifteenth."

"No way! So am I!" Katie embraced her aunt, giggling. "I'm convinced we made her at the Red Door party in August."

And Kelly shot Brendan a side-eye. "Of course, you did."

"Since we're making announcements…" Clearing his throat, Dillon wrapped his arms around his little family. "Linn and I are taking Charlotte on a trip to Cabo San Lucas. We're getting married on New Year's Day."

Out of sorrow, joy can grow, my friend. They both deserved all the happiness in the world.

Gina squeezed his hand.

Matt pressed a kiss to her cheek.

Yesterday, he thought they'd be sharing joyful news of their own. *Soon, right?* He glanced across the table at Kit. Knowing what he'd been through, the pain he still endured, Matt wanted him to feel worthy and loved. Because he was. And by him more than anyone.

"I drove past Mickey's yesterday. Linn sent me to pick up the ham," Sloan casually mentioned as he poured whiskey into a glass. "The building's for sale."

"If a developer gets their hands on it, they'll just tear it down to build more overpriced condos." Dillon would know. That's what the Byrne cousins did. They bought stuff, made it beautiful again, and then sold it.

Glancing at all of them, Bo shook his head. "That would be a fucking shame."

It would. Art déco in style, the old, rundown building held more than just sentimental value.

"They can't do that to Mickey's." Kit stared blankly, and tipping back his bottle of beer, it looked as if a light bulb suddenly went off in his head. A smirk appeared. "We should buy it."

"And do what with it, pray tell?" Glancing up at the ceiling, Taylor rolled his eyes. "Turn it into a shrine?"

"Yeah, why not?" Matt said with a half-shrug. "It's not a bad idea."

"Have you gone mad?"

"Nope." *Quite the contrary, in fact.* "And before you get your knickers in a twist, hear me out. We gut the inside and get rid of the apartments upstairs. Nobody lives there anymore, anyway. The entire building becomes a club… a bar… whatever you want to call it. Picture an intimate venue where folks can have food, some drinks, and listen to live music from up-and-coming bands."

"I can see it," Sloan said, glancing at the Gothic stained-glass window, and grinned.

Gina leaned into his ear and giggled. "I think he's already decorating in his head."

Uh-oh.

"Mickey's on steroids." Bo high-fived Kit. "Yeah, man, I dig it."

"Hold up. Before you get too excited, let me check the listing." And Dillon held out his phone. "It's still available. The asking price is reasonable, but I bet we can get it for less. If you're serious, that is."

"Are you sure you want to take on something like this right now?" Brendan's bright blue eyes flicked between Taylor and Matt. Always looking out for them, he was wise to question his sanity. Perhaps he was mad. "You've got a record releasing in six months, and you'll be touring all summer, at least."

True, but by the time they completed the sale, gutted the building, and renovated it, the tour would be over and done with. And then what? The way Matt figured, it would be a year to eighteen months before they'd be ready to open. This could be the perfect side-venture to keep themselves occupied with between album cycles.

It sure beats putting model cars together.

"So?" Leaning back in his chair, Matt shrugged and laced his fingers behind his head. "It's not like we have to do it all ourselves."

"You don't. C'mon, Brendan, look at all the people right here in this room. I mean, you have done this before, yeah?" Chloe sounded giddy. "I think it's brilliant."

"It *is* quite a project," Brendan agreed. "And with Venery's name behind it, success is all but guaranteed. Bands will flock to you for a chance to play there. UMG will love that."

"Why would they care?" Sloan asked.

Matt wondered, too.

Swallowing his whiskey, Brendan winked. "Positive publicity for you, and a chance to discover new talent for them."

Win-win.

"Shall I make the call, then?" Dillon asked, picking up his phone.

Everyone looked at Taylor.

He looked at Chloe while Ireland clambered from Jesse's lap into his, and he nodded.

"Do it."

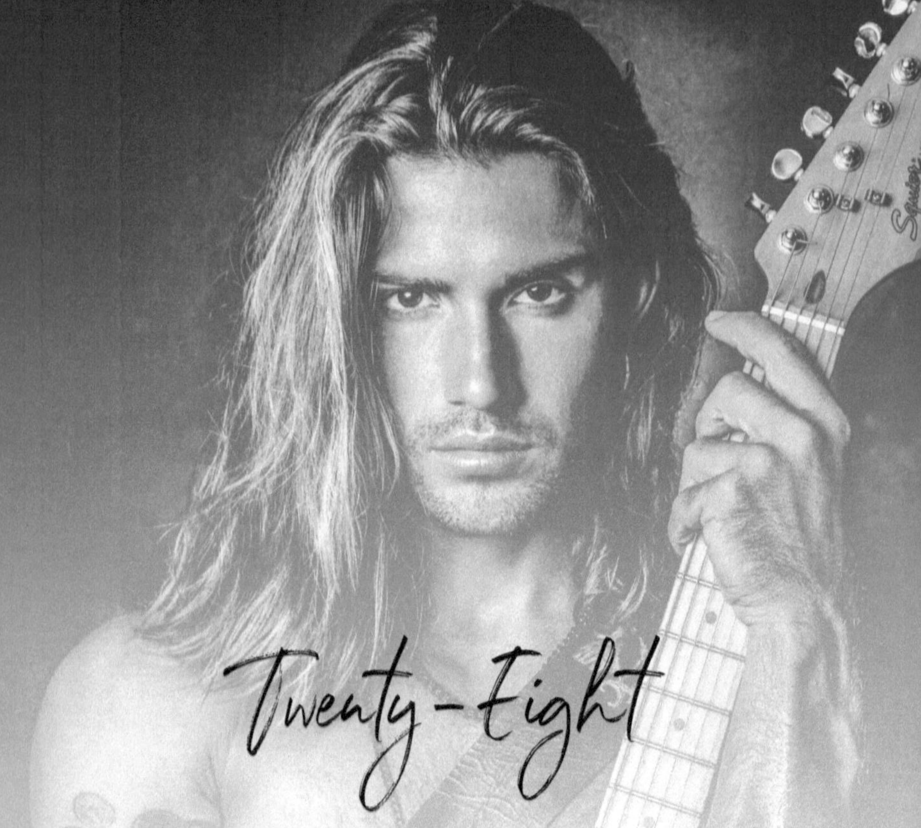

Twenty-Eight

Gina woke up on the couch to a dark house and the TV asking her if she was still watching. *Obviously not.* She couldn't even remember turning it on, and clicked it off. Her six-day stretch at the hospital had been a doozy, and there was no full moon to blame it on.

God, I hate night shift.

This was the day off that didn't count—the one she spent in a coma. Matt picked her up from work, and they had breakfast together before he tucked her into bed. Gina loved how he took care of her. The little things he did, like having a cup of coffee from Stan's waiting for her in the car or warming a towel for her when she was in the shower.

Out of habit, she got up the first time just as the sun was setting. That had to have been around four. Matt had her coffee ready and made sure she was fed before he had to meet with Brendan. The boys put in an offer for Mickey's Place, and it was accepted.

Understandably, there were many details to iron out; hence, the meeting.

Gina tried to stay awake until he got back home. Truly, she did. She washed her hair and straightened it. Threw in a load of laundry. Cleaned out the old leftovers from the fridge. Anything to keep herself occupied. But somehow she ended up on the damn cloud sofa, and once that happened?

Lights out.

She stretched out her limbs and trudged upstairs to brush her teeth and splash cold water on her face. Dark circles. Winter's dry skin. Tired eyes. *Ugh.* Matt should come home to someone who at least resembled a human instead of a sleep-deprived zombie, so she dabbed on some tinted moisturizer and glossed her lips too.

She made yet another cup of coffee. Most likely, she'd be up all night now, which wasn't always a bad thing, especially with Matt beside her. But he kept regular hours, while it took her a day or two to switch back into her normal circadian rhythm.

Hunched over the island, she traced the blue and copper veining in the stone while sipping on the aromatic brew. Sensing a presence behind her, she turned around to see Sloan leaning against the wall.

"Hey there, Trouble."

"Matt's not here."

"I know," he said, strolling toward her. "I'm here to see you."

"Me, why?"

"Make me a cup of coffee. Actually, never mind." He got a bottle of whiskey out of the liquor cabinet. "This calls for something stronger. We need to have a little chat."

The hell?

"About what?"

"You." Taking the bottle and a glass in one hand, Sloan took a seat on the middle cushion of the too-comfortable cloud couch. "C'mon, sit down."

Gina just stood and shook her head. "I'll fall asleep again if I do."

"Not with me, you won't," he said with a wink and pulled her down to sit beside him. "I hardly ever sleep."

"How come?"

"I'm a gaming addict." Laughing it off, Sloan shrugged. "Better than heroin, right?"

What an odd thing to say.

"How come there isn't a ring on this finger yet, hmm?" He took her left hand, studying it, and softly kissed her palm. "When I know Matt popped the question."

"He told you?"

"I knew he was planning on it, silly girl, and when you showed up on Thanksgiving with your finger bare, I got it out of him." The blue eyes staring into her soul were almost as bloodshot as hers. "What the fuck is spinning inside that pretty little head of yours?"

"I didn't say no."

"But you didn't say yes, either."

"I wanted to, but…" At a loss for words, Gina gnawed on her lip.

"You are trouble." With his fingers going through her hair, Sloan combed the freshly washed strands. "I can assure you, Matt is not bisexual—not in the usual sense, anyway. I mean, it's no secret he's fucked a dude on occasion, so technically, he fits the definition, but he's not, you know?"

"That doesn't matter to me."

"What is it then?"

"Kit." And she placed her hand on top of his, halting the perusal of his fingers.

"Oh, him." He waved away her concern. "He's… fucked up. I don't know where his head's at lately."

"But they love each other, Sloan." The looks. The intimate touches. "I saw it with my eyes, and I know you did too."

"We all love each other, Trouble." The tip of his finger traced a slow path down the hollow of her throat to her breast. "And we have for a very long time. You think everyone would put up with me if they didn't?"

"I see through you, Sloan Michaels." Crossing her arms over her chest, Gina sat back. "I don't know why you pretend to be such an asshole because you're really not."

"Figured me out, huh?" Chuckling, he poured himself a hefty shot of whiskey, slammed it back, and then his hands were holding her face. "Matt loves *you*."

I know.

"I told Matt he should fuck Kit." She wet her lips. "I encouraged him to, actually."

"Why?" His eyebrow arched, and that smirk turned into a devious grin. "You wanna watch?"

"No, because I need him to be sure."

His head tilting to the side, he let her go. "Suppose they did, and they wanted to be together, could you love them both?"

"I-I don't know."

"Are you looking for someone to wash your sins away, or do you want permission to embrace them?" He rose from couch and stood in front of her. "Because you sure loved playing with him."

"And you."

"Well, I'm right here, Trouble." Holding her chin, he swept his thumb over her lips. "Should you and Matt ever want to play again."

Matt agreed to this evening's meeting only because he knew Gina needed her rest. She would have forced herself to stay awake otherwise, and she was beyond exhausted when he picked her up at the hospital this morning. When he left, she was eating the Thai he ordered, and knowing Gina as well as he did, she was fast asleep on the couch by now.

He sat on a black leather sofa in Brendan's office at the club, going over contracts that might as well have been written in Greek because he sure as shit didn't understand what they said, and Matt wasn't stupid by any means. It kept the suits busy in their swank high-rise offices downtown, he supposed.

Whatever, man.

The only reason he needed to be here was to hand over the check. If Brendan and Phil said everything looked good, then it was. He trusted them implicitly.

"I drew up a new LLC for the property." Okay, he knew what that was. Venery formed a corporate entity for the studio and their indie label, Euphonia Records. "This way, the band and the club are separate entities—for tax and liability purposes."

"Gotcha." He tossed the stack of paper onto the table in front of him. "Is that what all this gibberish says?"

"Pretty much," Phil said with a polished grin. Why do all lawyers look the same? Starched shirts and silk ties so tight around the collar that they had to be cutting off oxygen. "And now that the contract's been accepted, I'll need a check for the remainder of the escrow deposit."

Matt patted his breast pocket. "I've got fifty k right here."

Insane. Considering there was a time when he couldn't have come up with fifty cents.

"And here's ours," Brendan said, scribbling out a check. The Byrne cousins were partnering with them.

"They want to close in thirty days. Is that going to be a problem?"

"Financing is taken care of."

"Excellent. Then, you're all set." And after returning the documents to his briefcase, the attorney stood. "Well, gentlemen, I've got to get home to the wife, but I'll let the seller's side know you made escrow."

"Thanks, Phil."

"Anytime," he said, shaking their hands. "I'll be seeing you."

While Brendan saw him out, Matt made himself a drink. They just handed over a hundred grand like it was peanuts, and in the grand scheme of things, it was because they'd have millions into this thing before the doors ever opened. He swallowed the whiskey, reminding himself that their plan was a good one, and the investment was sound.

Nothing ventured, nothing gained, right?

Right.

"All right, my brother." And Brendan poured a drink of his own. "It's time for us to get to work. We'll start with the interior demo in February."

We? Matt glanced down at hands that hadn't seen manual labor in years.

"We've got people who do that, you goof. Jesse has a crew lined up already." With a shake of his head, he swallowed the shot. "But we'll have plenty of other things to do that would require everyone's input, like building plans, branding, a name. Anybody come up with one yet?"

"Nope." They'd been tossing names around, but nothing they'd come up with so far had hit quite right.

"We've got time," Brendan said, adding another shot of whiskey to each glass. "UMG sent your dates over a little while ago."

"Yeah?" Though at this point, Matt had a pretty good estimation of the timeline.

"The album is going to come out on Friday, May third, but they want to drop a few songs starting in March."

It's always on a Friday.

"Told ya, didn't I?"

"You were right." They clinked glasses and drank. "Your new producer will be here in January to record."

"I was good with the one we had, but hey, it's their dime."

And UMG had no qualms about spending it. They installed new recording equipment in their studio just last week. World-class. All the latest technology. But the best part was they'd be recording at home, where they were most comfortable, the familiarity of the Park Place studio reminiscent of those days in Bo's basement.

"You're slotted for Germany and Download in June." He knew that. The festivals were announced months ago. "Then, you get July to rest up. Tour starts August first, here in Chicago. They'll announce it in January, and tickets will go on sale in March after the first track drops."

That didn't leave him much time. Matt wanted a wedding ring on Gina's finger long before the tour started.

"I'm gonna need my own bus, dude, because Gina's going with me."

"Figured as much." He winked. "Already taken care of."

Thank fuck.

"How long?"

Brendan just stared at him, his eyebrows squishing together.

"The tour."

"Three months," he said, his deep voice unusually soft. "Fifty-six dates over fourteen weeks, and no more than two shows in a row, as per your contract."

"Yeah, well, okay."

"Katelyn and I will be there with you." He squeezed his shoulder. "C'mon, let's go home."

The club was already vibing when they descended the grand stairs—early for a Wednesday night. Funny how the place held little appeal for him these days. Everything he'd ever wanted was waiting for him at home.

Poor dude.

Teo sat alone at the bar. After learning how Tony did his brother dirty, Brendan comped him a membership, so he wasn't alarmed to see him, but beyond the bar, on a lounge chair in the corner, sat Luca swapping spit with…

Holy shit! Is that Kevin Cofield?

Yup, sure is.

"What the fuck are they doing in here?"

Looking up from his drink, Teo glanced over to the corner and shrugged. "Isn't that kind of obvious?"

"What I mean is, how did they get in?" Matt asked, trying to remain calm.

Brendan would blow a gasket if Teo somehow got them in. Axel kept security pretty tight here. There was no way they'd make it past the red double doors.

"I dunno." And he shrugged again. "They were going to Charley's."

"Wanna bet Kevin snuck them in through the kitchen?" A tick appeared in Brendan's jaw. "Smart-ass kid thinks he knows all the tricks. I'll handle this."

That had to be it. The cousins owned both establishments, and Charley's provided the food served at the club. There was a red-painted service hallway that connected the two.

"Sorry, bro. I had no clue they were gonna do that." Teo shook his head as they watched Brendan exchange words with his wife's younger brother. "It's not like they needed someplace to go."

That's right. Kevin had the loft above Beanie's all to himself now, didn't he?

"It's not your fault, T, but they're not old enough to be in here." He looked glummer than Kit, and that was saying something. "You doing okay?"

"Yeah." And then, he perked up. "Hey, Gina tells me you guys are gonna open up a club. That's pretty cool."

"You know where Mickey's Place used to be?" Matt smiled with him when he nodded. "We bought the building. It's going to be a venue for live music once we're done renovating it."

"Food?"

"Of course—on all three levels and a rooftop bar, too."

"You think maybe I can help run the place when you open, so I don't have to work with Tony anymore?"

The way Teo said it nearly broke his heart. Matt wasn't privy to all the details of what went down between him and his brother, but he knew enough. There's a bro code for a reason, and thinking with his dick, Tony broke it.

"Is it that bad?"

He didn't answer, but his face said it all.

"We'll talk some more when the time comes, okay?" Matt placed a brotherly arm around him. Teo was his family now, too. "But if that's what you need to do, you've got a place with us."

"Thanks, man." Then, his eyes went wide. "*Cazzo!* Here they come."

Not appearing contrite at all, Kevin protested, gesturing wildly with his hands. Obviously, they were in the middle of quite a conversation. "But I need to learn everything I can about the lifestyle, so I can manage the club for you someday."

"Everything?" The telltale tick in his jaw still ticked. Brendan was livid.

"Yeah, I fucking love girls, but I love Luca, too." In an exaggerated huff, Kevin blew out a breath. "Why are you so surprised I'm bi?"

Color me surprised, kid, but I don't think that's what the big guy here is pissed off about.

"I am too," Luca said proudly. "And poly."

"You're barely twenty, for fuck's sake," Matt shouted. *Still a kid.* "You don't even know what that is."

"Yes, I do. I love Kevin." Then, as if to prove it, Luca kissed him. "For real and forever."

"And one day we hope we can find a girl who'll love us like Chloe loves Jesse and Tay," Kevin added.

"Or maybe we'll meet two bi chicks and all four of us can be together," Luca said in all seriousness.

Kevin responded with a high-five. "Yeah, I could get down with that."

Oh, boy.

Matt could just see the shitshow that was surely coming. "Does your sister know all this?"

"Does she need to?" Luca cocked his head, evidently offended. "Yeah, she knows."

"Katie knows, too. I tell her everything." Arm in arm, Kevin took up his boyfriend's side.

Brendan sighed. "C'mon, Kev, you're nineteen."

"Yeah, and my sister was eighteen when she fell in love with you."

Valid point, but this situation had disaster written all over it.

"So, will you teach me?"

"And me."

Matt called the bartender over and asked for a shot.

"I can't let you work here until you're twenty-one," Brendan said, softening, the tick in his jaw now gone. "In the meantime, if you're both serious, there are books you can read and workshops you can attend."

Teo glanced at him. "Mama's gonna shit."

Matt downed his whiskey.

"I know."

Twenty-Nine

Matt didn't want to hurt him, and he couldn't lose him, either. Besides Gina, he loved Kit more than anyone. He'd lay down his life for the guy if it came down to it. Their kinship went beyond friendship or brotherhood or blood in a way he could never explain. But after seeing Luca with Kevin, one thing became quite clear: he didn't love him like that—the same way that Jesse loved Taylor. That kind of love was sacred and reserved for Gina alone.

Whatever the fuck was going on in Kit's head, he'd put it off long enough. Awkward or not, it was well past time to confront it.

Matt didn't bother knocking, but then no one around here ever did, so why start now? He walked right in to find him kicked back on the sofa with his headphones on. "Hey, my dude."

His eyelids slowly opened, and those sad puppy-dog eyes appeared. "Hey."

"We need to talk, don't you think?"

"About what?" And he closed his eyes again.

"C'mon, Kit, we've been avoiding each other for weeks," Matt said, shaking him by the shoulder. "I love you, man."

Kit shrugged.

"Talk to me."

"What do you want me to say?" Ripping off the headphones, he pushed himself up to sit. "Because I ain't feeling it, brother."

It was written all over his face. Even though Matt hadn't meant to, he'd hurt Kit deeply. Why had he let this go on for so long?

"You even fucked Bo, but never me."

"Do you want me to?"

"I'm sorry." Placing his hands on Kit's shoulders, Matt framed him with his body. "I know you didn't mean what you said about us. I shouldn't have responded the way I did."

"What makes you think I didn't?" With a toss of his surfer waves, he glared up at him.

"Because I know you, man, and dudes are *not* your thing."

"They aren't yours, either, but you've fucked a few," Kit said. "More than a few."

"Yeah, and you know why." *So I could let the beast out.* "For my own selfish reasons, nothing more."

Pushing him backward, Kit stood. "So, Bo is nothing to you?"

"Fuck, man." His chest tightened, pain spearing the back of his throat. "You were there. He asked me for a favor, and we had a good time."

"Is that why you fucked him twice?"

Shit.

"How do you know about that?"

A faint smirk curved at his mouth. "I overheard you talking to Bo and Ava at Emmy's party."

"Kiss me."

Grabbing Kit by the belt loops of his jeans, he brought him to his chest. Their lips hovering a hairsbreadth apart, he didn't make a move. Matt inhaled his breath once, twice, thrice. Kit would have to take what he wanted, but he couldn't.

Knew it.

"If you wanted to fuck, that wouldn't be so hard." He took a step back, putting some distance between them. "This really isn't about Bo, is it?"

Kit shrugged as if thinking of the right words to say. Being that he was a man of few, Matt knew how difficult it was for him.

"It's always been you and me, ya know?" He sat down, his fingers raking through his hair. "And everything's different now."

"Because of Gina?"

He hesitated a moment, then shook his head.

"I love her, Kit, and I'm going to marry her." Matt took a seat beside him, an arm going around his shoulders. "But that doesn't mean I love you any less."

"I remember what that feels like," he said with a deep sigh, his voice flat.

Christ, it always goes back to her, doesn't it?

"You can feel it again, and with someone who truly deserves you." Forcing Kit to look at him, Matt held onto his chin. "Courtney never did."

A tremor passed through his body, and he closed his eyes, lashes pressed tightly against his skin. He stayed like that for a moment, then opened them again. The pain Matt saw in their liquid depths was as fresh and raw and visceral as the day Kit stood on his porch all those years ago.

"Let her go."

Kit snickered.

"I won't pretend to know what betrayal like that feels like, but I know what it did to you—what it's still doing to you." Matt pulled Kit against his shoulder, and with sincerity, he said, "See a therapist if that's what it takes. You've already wasted sixteen years dwelling on someone who didn't deserve sixteen seconds in your head. She never deserved your heart. But I guarantee you there's somebody out there who does."

Kit shrugged.

And his tone softened. "Let her go."

"I love you, Matt, and I'm happy for you and Gina. Truly, I am. But I'm gonna miss the way things were before." He threw his head back on the sofa, and shaking it, he croaked out a laugh. "God, now I'm stuck sharing a bus with Sloan."

"It's a top-class ride, though."

Kit elbowed him in the ribs. "Yeah, and at least he doesn't snore."

"I don't either."

"Yeah, bro, you do." He picked up his headphones. "Now, go home to your girl."

And clasping his shoulders, Matt stood. "I'll always be here for you. You know that, right?"

I love you, Kit.

Putting his headphones back on, he nodded. "I know."

He was done decking the halls, feasting on seven fishes at the Rossi's house, singing fa la la la la and "Happy Birthday" at Linnea's, and overdosing on *panettone*, marshmallow frosting, and hot cocoa.

Fun is fun, but two events on Christmas Eve were more than enough.

At least Gina got them out of going to Midnight Mass.

Matt wanted to get to the good part.

A Christmas tree stood in the corner by the fireplace. After his grandmother died, he never bothered with one, didn't see the point, but Gina insisted, and he couldn't say no to her. So, on Black Friday, they went to the tree lot on First Avenue, then spent the rest of the day picking out shiny baubles and lights before going back home to decorate it.

Matt had one more sparkly thing to add. He tied it to a ribbon and hung it from the lowest bough where Gina would be sure to see it.

Then, he opened a bottle of Spumante and waited.

She came down the stairs wearing red Lululemon and an oversized cardigan sweater with one of those sexy little bra tops underneath. No makeup. Dark chocolate waves in a pile on her head. And she looked fucking gorgeous.

He handed her a glass of the sparkling Italian wine, and she cuddled with him in front of the fire. "This is perfect. *Salute.*"

"To us." Matt clinked his glass with hers. "Merry Christmas, bunny."

"I hope we didn't look rude leaving Linn's."

"Nah, it's all good. We sang to Charlotte and watched her make a mess of her snowman cake before we left." Once Dillon showed his sweet pea what to do with it, the baby had marshmallow fluff everywhere—Dillon included. "Besides, everyone's got to get home to play Santa tonight."

Matt tipped his chin toward the tree in the corner, the carefully wrapped packages beneath it, and the lone silver ribbon he was waiting for Gina to discover, but those eyes that changed colors failed to follow his gaze.

"Yeah, I guess you're right." And sipping her wine, she cuddled closer. "It was special for me to be there for her first birthday, you know, especially since I took care of Charlotte when she was born."

"I'm sure you'll be there for her second birthday, too." *And every birthday after that.* "I have a feeling we'll be spending Christmas Eve at the Byrne house after the fish fest at your mom's for many years to come."

"*Festa dei Sette Pesci*—the Feast of the Seven Fishes." Gina giggled, correcting him. "It's an Italian tradition. No meat is served on Christmas Eve. The seven fishes are symbolic of the seven sacraments."

"I thought that was for Lent, but what do I know?" An altar boy he was definitely not. "You're in love with a heathen, baby. The roof might cave in if I ever set foot inside a church."

"Just don't tell my mother." She winked.

With a chuckle, he topped off her glass. "I'm pretty sure she knows."

Gina settled back against his chest, and sipping her wine, she gazed at their first Christmas tree in all its magical splendor. Twinkling white lights. The blue and copper ornaments she chose because they matched the veining in the stone.

Then, she leaned forward, pointing to the ribbon. "What's that?"

Took you long enough.

"Maybe you should go see."

The five-carat Dutch marquis diamond, twinkling like a star on the end, was damn near impossible to miss. She held the ring in her palm, her hazel-green eyes shimmering.

"You're my forever, Gina, so I'm going to ask you again." And with a hopeful smile, he kissed away her tears. "Will you marry me?"

"I will." She didn't hesitate this time. "Yes."

Thank fuck.

He untied the ribbon, and after sliding the ring on her finger, Matt kissed the woman he'd love for the rest of his life. "I love you."

"I love you, too." And she whispered, "I want everything, Matt."

"Tell me what you want, bunny."

"You can't break me." The diamond sparkling on her finger made a pathway down his chest. "So, let the beast out."

And he grinned.

"Run."

Thirty

The roof did not cave in on him.

On the last Saturday in May, three weeks after Venery's album with UMG came out, Matt and Gina were married on the altar of St. Vincent's Church. Despite Rosemary's protests that planning a wedding in five months would be impossible, it was a grand affair.

The bridesmaids wore blush, and Gina's gown was ivory, much to her mother's chagrin. Silly woman, he'd never seen any bride look more beautiful than his. The moment she appeared on her father's arm and came down the aisle toward him, his heart skipped a beat, and the air was sucked from his lungs. Matt was almost certain he wept, because Kit was there at his side, discreetly lending him a handkerchief from his pocket.

Then, Anthony Rossi placed his daughter's hand in his.

Everything passed by in a blur after that.

They had a surprise planned for Rosemary, though. It thrilled Matt that Danielle could capture the look on her face when the long-haired hooligans she'd thought little of in their youth, joined the choir to play "Ave Maria" as Gina laid flowers at the feet of the Blessed Virgin. Sloan sang his cold little heart out. Not a dry eye in the house. Even the priest was crying.

Afterward, in the church's vestibule, where they formed the receiving line, the woman was still shocked speechless. Matt just winked at her. "You okay, pretty?"

Holding her newborn, Katie couldn't hide her giggle.

They left for Germany the next day, and after the festivals there, they traveled to England for Download. Taylor and his family were going to stay on a while to visit with his mom in London, and Jesse's mom in Dublin, before flying back to Chicago to get ready for the tour.

Bo, Kit, and Sloan were going home.

His wife didn't know it yet, but Matt had a surprise planned for her, too. Tomorrow, after Venery finished their set, there'd be a car waiting to whisk them away to Heathrow, and there, they'd board a flight to Italy for a late honeymoon.

Just the two of them in a villa by the sea.

Matt couldn't wait.

Maybe they'd make a baby there. He'd convinced her to toss her birth control pills before they left Chicago. God knows, he'd been fucking his little rabbit every chance he could. And heaven help him, she welcomed it.

"I love how this hot, wet pussy feels on my dick," he rasped in her ear after he came.

Gina's pretty eyes grew wide watching him grow hard again as he pushed his cum inside her. "You like that, don't you?"

"Fuck, yeah. I get off breeding you, knowing my seed is inside you where it belongs. I want to fill you up with it. Fuck you over and over again."

She giggled. "You're fucked up."

"Am I? Tell me you don't get off on the thought of my baby

growing in your belly," Matt said, and rubbing his fingers over her flat stomach, he kissed it.

"You got a pregnancy kink too?"

"Never been with a pregnant chick before, but yeah, maybe." And he pressed his lips to her mouth. "*You're* my kink, Gina McCready. I love you."

"I guess we're both fucked up then." She smiled.

"Oh, yeah?"

"Yeah. Because you're *my* kink, Matthew McCready. Fuck me. Breed me. Fill me up with your cum. Cover me with it. Do whatever you want to me. I love you. And yes, I want your baby."

"*Babies,*" he informed her, and gazing into the eyes he loved, his fingertips memorized her skin. "I want to have a bunch."

"Yeah?"

Why does that surprise you, bunny?

"Like that idea?"

"Yeah."

"Good."

Matt should've known it the day she showed up at his door.

Nice girls do end up with rock stars.

Even a mangy old mutt like him.

Epilogue

Two years later

Matt hadn't set foot in a church since the day he and Gina got married. Out of obligation, she still joined Rosemary every Sunday, but well, he wasn't going to push his luck. St. Vincent's needed their roof.

But today, he didn't have a choice.

He had to go.

His son was being christened today.

Only a month old, Dominic McCready had blue eyes that hadn't changed color yet and a head of dark hair like his mother's. Bo and Ava were expecting a little boy in a few months, and Chloe was due soon after that. Matt smiled. A new generation of hooligans. He already knew the three boys were going to be the closest of friends. Brothers. Family.

Just like their fathers are.

"Here, let me do that for you." Gina tied his tie. He hated the damn things. "Everybody's waiting for you downstairs. If Teo and

Sara don't get the baby dressed before he gets fussy, we'll be late for church."

The godparents have that honor. Along with the blue sugar almonds, it was another tradition he'd never heard of.

"Does he have to wear a dress?"

"It's a christening gown." And patting his chest, she giggled. "My brothers wore it, too. Our *Nonna* crocheted the lace herself."

Rosemary was in *his* kitchen, where she'd prepared a large home-cooked meal for the party afterward. At least he had plenty of good food to look forward to. Matt had to admit that he ate well.

"I know you don't know these things, Matthew, but remember when you carry my grandson into the church, you do it without looking back," his mother-in-law schooled him, wagging her finger. "Then, he'll grow fearless and strong."

Behind his hand, Kit snickered.

Matt didn't believe her superstitious nonsense either, but he'd listen to her just the same.

Gina's family was his family, and his family was hers, after all.

He carried his son across the threshold, a blue ribbon hanging on the door, and then into the church with his wife. *His* family.

His luck held.

The roof remained intact.

And he never looked back.

The End… until *The Bass Line*

Acknowledgments

Can I get a howl, please? All together now, and make it loud—ah-hooo!!!

It's never, ever taken me this long to type 'The End.' Every word made it slowly onto the page. Maybe because the space bar on my Mac keeps sticking, or maybe because there's only two stories left to tell now. Closing the door on this series is going to be the hardest goodbye. But let's not think about that yet…

The Pinterest board and the playlist for *Rhythm Man* on Spotify and YouTube are open. Kit's story, *The Bass Line*, <u>Book 8</u> (Holy shit, how'd that happen?), is next in the *Red Door* series. I've included a short sneak peek following these acknowledgments. But before we get to Kit, Jake Gantry wanted me to let you know he's got one helluva story for y'all. And so, we'll be going back to Brookside, Wyoming for *The Distant Thunder*—soonish. But…I have a bunch of stories with characters you're going to want to meet screaming at me, so I'm not sure which book I'm going to write next. I guess we'll see who screams the loudest, yeah?

As always, there are so many people to thank. I couldn't do this without my Dream Team, you know. And yes, I say it every time, I'm going to keep it short and sweet. After doing this eleven times (and that blows my mind), you'd think I'd have it figured out by now. I probably don't.

My loves—**Michael** and **Raj**, **Charlie**, **Christian**, **Josie Lynn** and **Josh**, **Zach** and **Sam**, **Jaide**, **Julian**, **Olivia**, **Jocelyn**, and baby **Jalina**. I love you forever and always.

Zee, my amazeball bish at *The Blue Couch Edits*. Don't spank me too hard—I might like it! I'm going to get my shit together one of these days, I promise! But you love me, right? xoxo

My ride-or-die, **Linda Russell**, and her fantastic team at *Foreword PR*. I think I gave her gray hairs with this one! Luckily, she loves me, because I don't know what I'd do without her. xoxo

My Cover Queen of Hearts, and my beautiful Aussie friend, **Michelle Lancaster**, *Lanefotograf*. These gorgeous images of **David Bodas** are absolute perfection. My thanks to you both. I love you so, so much! xoxo

Lori Jackson, *Lori Jackson Design*. Dream Team Designer. Magic Maker. We only kept this beauty of a cover under wraps for 2 1/2 years! I adore you, beautiful, and I can't wait for everyone to see what's coming! xoxo

Ashlee O'Brien, *Ashes & Vellichor*. My girly. Book Daughter. Dream Team Graphic Designer. Trailer Maker. Alternate Cover Goddess. Alpha Reader. She's been my everything from the very beginning. I love you the mostest, Ashlee! xoxo

Stacey Blake, *Champagne Book Design*. Formatter extraordinaire!!! She's makes the pages as pretty as the cover, and she's the best at what she does. Thanks so much for putting up with me—I love you! xoxo

My special thanks to **Hydrus**, who graciously allowed me to use his poem, "Rustled", for the epigraph of this book. Filled with vivid imagery, his poetry is evocative, and I encourage to read more of his words. xoxo

My Beta Team—**Charbee Balderson, Jennifer Bishop, Heather Hahn, Kim Lannan, Marjorie Lord, Lee Ann Mathis, Anastasia Meimeteas, Melinda Parker, Sabrena Simpson, Trisha Sparks, Rebecca Vazquez Kinkead**, and **Staci Way**, together with my **ARC Team**—who barely got this book before you did. Thank you for hanging in there, but mostly for being you. I love you big time! xoxo

Bloggers, **Bookstagrammers**, and **Booktokkers**—Mad props for everything you do, every day, and not just for me, but for every indie out there. Your dedication to the book world is invaluable—none of us could fly without you. So, to say thank you isn't nearly enough, but thank you!

My **Redlings**, who hang out with me *Behind the Red Door*. Y'all know how to keep me going and I love you for it! If you'd like to hang with us too, you can find us on Facebook. They're truly some of the most wonderful humans on the planet. We'd love for you to join us!

And, as always, my lovely **readers**. Thank you for being here and loving the *Red Door* world. Your messages and emails make my day—I appreciate all of them so much. Thank you for wanting more Kyan, Dillon and Linnea, Chloe, Jesse, and Taylor, Brendan and Katie, Bo and Ava, Kodiak and Kelly, Matt and Gina, Kit, and Sloan. It's not over yet.

Until *The Bass Line...*

Much love,

Dyan
xoxo

Kit, eighteen years old.

If he had to spend one more afternoon bagging groceries at the Jewel, he was going to lose his shit. It wasn't worth the measly six-fifty an hour they paid him. But a weekend gig with the band here and there wasn't enough to pay the bills, so what other choice did he have?

Life would be a heck of a lot easier if Courtney weren't on his back all the time, and if his parents didn't charge him rent to live in the basement. That was his father's doing. Consequences for his "thoughtless and reckless" behavior.

The fuck?

It's not like he stole a car.

He got married, for chrissakes.

And it had been the best nine months of his life so far. Well, sort of. It would be better without all the bickering. Courtney wanted things—things they couldn't afford yet. Like an apartment of their own. It didn't help that she spent most of her paycheck on clothes at Abercrombie & Fitch. As if her employee discount made it okay. It didn't. She didn't like him playing in the band either, and she didn't care for his boys. Especially Matt, but then he didn't like her either, and she knew it.

Truth be told, if Kit had known it was going to be this hard, he would've waited. But until when? Until he earned a living from his music? Courtney said Venery wouldn't get him anywhere. That he'd amount to nothing if he stayed with them. His dad agreed with her, of course. He always did.

It wouldn't surprise him if that was the real reason his dad made him pay to live in his crappy old basement—so he'd quit the band and get an actual job. Because that's what Courtney kept nagging him to do. Why didn't they understand that the band and his boys were everything to him? They'd been playing together since they were eight years old, and they were fucking good. Couldn't they see that? Kit was certain their big break was just around the corner.

So, for now, he was stuck at the grocery store. They were flexible with his schedule, which gave him the ability to play when Venery picked up a gig. Could be worse, he supposed.

"Hey, Kit." His manager cupped his shoulder. "It's slow. Why don't you go before the storm comes? Looks like it's gonna be a doozy."

He looked through the storefront glass at the dark and menacing sky. Spring thunderstorms. There'd be tornado warnings for sure.

"Sure, thanks."

It didn't matter that Courtney would bitch at him for coming home a couple of hours early. Kit could already hear her screech, "That's thirteen dollars we won't see on your paycheck."

As if.

It's not like he ever saw a penny of it.

Maybe if he loved on her when he got home, she wouldn't be so mad.

Maybe she'd let him. Because Courtney hadn't wanted to in weeks. She always had an excuse. Her period. His parents. A headache.

Thunder rumbled, the first drops of rain stinging his skin as he unlocked the basement door. It was dark, and except for the washer and dryer, the place was quiet. Almost too quiet.

"Courtney?"

Kit heard it as he got closer to their bedroom. The little squeaks she made when she was about to come. His dick twitched at the sound, and that pissed him off.

Nice, you'll play with yourself, but you won't let me touch you?

He turned the knob, and when he opened the door, Kit was so fucking stunned he couldn't move or breathe or react or think.

This was so fucked up.

It couldn't be real.

How the fuck could you do this to meeeeeeee???

But the screaming was not his own.

"Goddammit, you weren't supposed to be home until four."

Kit didn't say a word. He couldn't. He just turned around and closed the door.

He walked to Matt's in the rain, and the only thought in his head was that she didn't even say she was sorry.

About The Author

Dyan Layne is a nurse boss by day and the writer of twisty sensual tales by night—and on weekends. She's never without her Kindle and can usually be found tapping away at her keyboard with a hot latte and a cold Dasani Lime—and sometimes champagne. She can't sing a note, but often answers in song because isn't there a song for just about everything? Born and raised a Chicago girl, she currently lives in Tampa, Florida, and is the mother of four handsome sons and a beautiful daughter, who are all grown up now, but can still make her crazy—and she loves it that way! Because normal is just so boring.

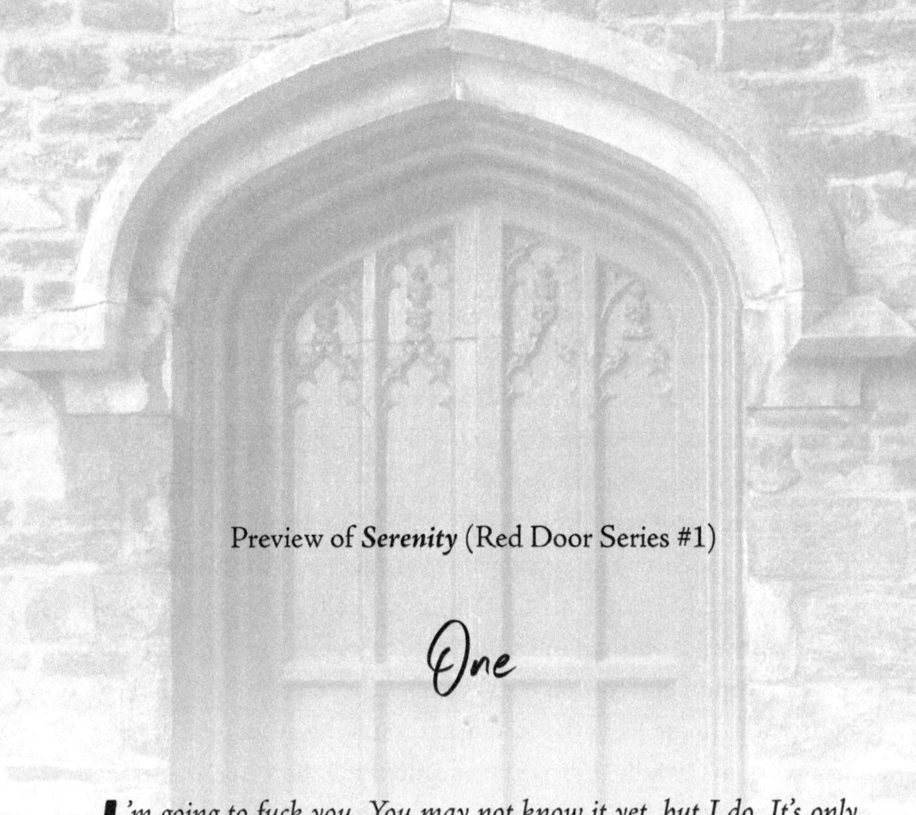

One

I'm going to fuck you. You may not know it yet, but I do. It's only a matter of time. I've been watching you. I swear that you've been watching me too, but maybe it's all in my head. No matter. Because I've seen you, I've talked to you and I've come to a conclusion: You are fucking beautiful. And I will make you lust me.

The words danced on crisp white paper. Her fingers trembled and her feet became unsteady, so she leaned against the wall of exposed brick to right herself, clutching the typewritten note in her hand. She read it again. A powerful longing surged through her body and her thighs clenched.

Who could have written it? She couldn't fathom a single soul who might be inspired to write such things to her. Maybe those words weren't meant for her? Maybe whoever had written the note slid it beneath the wrong doormat in his haste to deliver it undetected?

Linnea Martin, beautiful? Someone had to be pulling a prank. *Yeah. That's more likely.*

She sighed as she turned and closed the solid wood front door. She glanced up at the mirror that hung in the entry hall and eyes the color of moss blinked back at her. Long straight hair, the color of which she had never been able to put into a category—a dirty-blonde maybe—hung past her shoulders, resting close to where her nipples protruded against the fitted cotton shirt she wore. Her skin was fair, but not overly pale. She supposed some people might describe her as pretty, in an average sort of way, but not beautiful.

Not anything but ordinary.

Linnea slowly crumpled up the note in her hand. She clenched it tight and held it to her breast before tossing it into the wastebasket.

Deflated, she threw her tote bag on the coffee table and plopped down on the pale-turquoise-colored sofa that she'd purchased at that quaint secondhand store on First Avenue. She often stopped in there on her way home from the restaurant, carefully eyeing the eclectic array of items artfully displayed throughout the shop. Sometimes, on a good day when tips had been plentiful, she bought herself something nice. Something pretty. Like the pale-turquoise sofa.

Linnea grabbed the current novel she was engrossed in from the coffee table and adjusted herself into a comfortable position, attempting to read. But after she read the same page three times she knew she couldn't concentrate, one sentence blurred into the next, so she set it back down. She clicked on the television and scrolled through the channels, but there was nothing on that could hold her interest. The words replayed in her head.

I'm going to fuck you.

Damn him! Damn that fucker to hell for being so cruel to leave that note at her door, for making her feel…things. The words had thrilled her for a fleeting moment, but then the excitement quickly faded, replaced by a loneliness deep in her chest. Love may never be in the cards for her, or lust for that matter, as much as she might want it to be.

Once upon a time she had believed in fairy tales and dreamt of knights on white stallions and handsome princes, of castle turrets shrouded in mist, of strong yet gentle hands weaving wildflowers in her long honeyed locks—just like the alpha heroes in the tattered paperbacks she had kept hidden under her bed as a teenager. She thought if she was patient long enough, her happily-ever-after would come. She thought that one day, when she was all grown up, that a brave knight, a handsome prince, would rescue her from her grandmother's prison and make all her dreams come true.

Stupid girl.

Her dreams turned into nightmares, and 'one day' never came. She doubted it ever would now. It was her own fault anyway. She closed her eyelids tight, trying to stop the tears that threatened to escape, to keep the memories from flooding back. Linnea had spent years pushing them into an unused corner, a vacant place where they could be hidden away and never be thought of again.

It was dark. She must have been sitting there for quite a while, transfixed in her thoughts. The small living room was void of illumination, except for the blue luminescence that radiated from the unwatched television. Linnea dragged herself over to it and clicked it off. She stood there for a moment waiting for her eyes to adjust to the absence of light and went upstairs.

Steaming water flowed in a torrent from the brushed-nickel faucet, filling the old clawfoot tub. She poured a splash of almond oil into the swirling liquid. As the fragrance released, she bent over the tub to breathe in the sweet vapor that rose from the water and wafted through the room. Slipping the sleeves from her shoulders, the silky robe gave way and fell to a puddle on the floor.

Timorously, she tested the water with her toes, and finding it comfortably hot, she eased her body all the way in. For a time serenity could be found in the soothing water that enveloped her.

You may not know it yet, but I do. It's only a matter of time.

At once her pulse quickened, and without conscious thought her slick fingertips skimmed across her rosy nipples. They hardened at her touch. And a yearning flourished between the folds of flesh down below. Linnea clenched her thighs together, trying to make it go away, but with her attempt to squelch the pulsing there, she only exacerbated her budding desire. And she ached.

Ever so slowly, her hands eased across her flat belly to rest at the junction between her quivering thighs. She wanted so badly to touch herself there and alleviate the agony she found herself in. But as badly as she wanted to, needed to, Linnea would not allow herself the pleasure of her own touch. She sat up instead, the now-tepid water sloshing forward with the sudden movement, and reaching out in front of her she turned the water back on.

She knew it was wicked. Lying there with her legs spread wide and her feet propped on the edge of the tub, she allowed the violent stream of water to pound upon her swollen bud. It throbbed under the assault and her muscles quaked. She'd be tempted to pull on her nipples if she wasn't forced to brace her hands against the porcelain walls of the clawfoot tub for leverage.

Any second now. She was so close.

I'm going to fuck you.

And he did. With just his words, he did.

Her head tipped back as the sensations jolted through her body. The sounds of her own keening cries were muffled by the downpour from the faucet. Spent, she let the water drain from the tub and rested her cheek upon the cold porcelain.

Prologue

"Aidan, baby."

His mother took him by the hand and pulled him along behind her as she hurried out of the kitchen. He'd only eaten half of his grilled cheese sandwich and some grapes when the banging started. It startled him and he knocked over his juice. By the time she went to the front door to see who it was, the banging noise was coming from the other side of the house.

"You can't keep me out, bitch."

It was a man. He was yelling. He sounded angry. Aidan didn't recognize his voice.

His mother seemed to, though. Her eyes got real big and she covered her mouth with her hand. It was shaking.

There was a hutch in the living room that the television sat on. It had doors on the bottom. He hid in there sometimes. His mother opened one of the doors, and tossing the toys that were inside it to the floor, she kissed him on his head and urged him to crawl inside.

"We're going to play a game of hide and seek from the loud man outside, okay, baby?" his mother whispered.

Aidan nodded.

The banging got louder.

"You have to be very, very quiet so he doesn't know you're here." It sounded like she was choking and tears leaked out of her eyes, but she smiled at him.

"Like at story time?"

Aidan's mother took him to story time at the library every Saturday, and afterwards if he'd been a good boy, she would let him get an ice cream.

"Yes, baby. Just like that." She nodded with tears running down her face. "Now stay very still and don't speak a word until I tell you to—no matter what, okay?"

He nodded again. "Okay, Mommy."

"I love you, Aidan."

"I love you, Mommy."

Everyone said the place was haunted. The kids at school. The people in town. It didn't look scary, but nobody ever went anywhere near the two-story white clapboard house that was set off by itself on the cove.

It was to be her home now.

Molly stood at the wrought-iron gate with her mother, holding onto her hand. She clutched her *Bear in the Big Blue House* backpack, that she'd had since she was four, with the other. A boy with sandy-blond hair sat on the porch steps. Aidan Fischer. He didn't pay them, or his father unloading their belongings from the U-Haul, any mind. He had a notebook in his lap and a pencil between his fingers. It looked like he was drawing.

The boy chewed on his lip as he moved the pencil over the paper. Even though he was in the fifth grade, and three years older than her, Molly knew who he was. Everybody did. He was the boy who didn't talk. And six days from today, when her mother married his father, that boy was going to be her brother.

Sneak Peek of

THE Third Son

oming out of the bathroom, Arien stubbed her toe, close to taking a tumble over a stack of forgotten boxes in the hallway. "Ouch. Motherfu…"

She held onto her foot, hopping the rest of the way to her bedroom in the small townhouse apartment she shared with her mom. It was all packed up, cartons neatly labeled, identifying the contents inside. Bed stripped. Closet and drawers emptied.

It wasn't like she had a choice.

A moving van was parked outside.

Holding her towel closed, her back against the wall, Arien sat cross-legged on the bare mattress. She had exactly thirty minutes to put on some makeup and get dressed. It would only take her ten.

This is so not fucking fair.

She blew out a breath. A week ago, her room was pretty and her life wasn't packed away in cardboard boxes. That all changed when her mother and her boyfriend—if that's what you call a man in his forties—took her out with them to dinner.

And that alone should have told her something was up.

Jennifer Brogan had been dating Matthew Brooks for about six months now, but Arien didn't know him all that well. A real cowboy, her mother said. He had two sons and lived on some ranch up in Wyoming, an eight-hour drive from Denver. He'd come into town for business, and to see her mom, a few times a month.

He was the one to break the news to her. "Arien," he said with a smile, taking her mother's hand in his. "First off, I need you to know I love your mama very much. So much, I've asked her to marry me."

She about choked on her green-chili cheeseburger.

Her mom held up her left hand, waving the huge diamond glittering on her finger. "I said yes."

Okay.

Arien was seventeen, soon-to-be eighteen. She'd be going away to college at the end of summer anyway. Her mom deserved some happiness, right?

Swallowing down the cheeseburger, she put on a smile. "At least you won't have to change your monogram. When's the wedding?"

"Next week," her mother announced, biting her lip. "I'm pregnant."

"Three months already," Matthew said proudly, patting his new fiancée on the shoulder. "I'm coming back with the boys. We'll get married and have you all moved in before Thanksgiving."

What? To Wyoming? Nope. Not happening.

"Wait. You want me to move, to change schools during my senior year?"

"I'm sorry, sweetie."

"You're going to love Brookside." Her soon-to-be stepfather patted her on the hand. "We have a superior private school there. The ranch. The mountains. You can take lots of pictures."

"There's mountains right here."

Isn't thirty-six too old to have a baby anyway? Apparently not. And what happened to all those lectures her mother gave her about having sex, taking precautions, and all that stuff? She should've listened to her own advice. If she had, Arien wouldn't be going to a courthouse wedding to leave Denver, and the only life she'd ever known, behind.

Only for a little while.

True. She had her acceptance letter to UC. She'd be back.

"Sweetie, are you ready yet?" her mother asked from downstairs. "Matt and the boys are here."

Dammit.

"Almost," she answered, plucking through her makeup bag.

Clearly a lie. She hadn't even begun.

Holding a compact mirror in one hand, Arien applied mascara with the other, the towel slipping away from her.

She couldn't say for sure what made her look up. A feeling she was being watched, maybe.

Two boys—no, these weren't boys, they were hot-as-fuck men—stood smirking in her doorway.

"Who the hell are you?"

"I'm Tanner." The man smiled, and taking a step inside her room, he hitched a thumb behind him. "That's Kellan."

"And I'm naked." She snatched up the towel, covering herself.

Kellan snickered.

Tanner came closer. "Well now, that's a mighty fine hello, little sister."

Whiteout

Chapter One

Five hours.

That's how long she'd been driving already, and Breanna hadn't even reached the California state line. Maybe she should've stayed on I-5, instead of cutting over to Route 39, but that's the way her GPS sent her, so she took it. Passing Klamath Falls, she cranked up the tunes and grinned. "Seventeen more miles."

Spotify playlist blasting, she excitedly waved goodbye to Oregon, as the 'Welcome to California' sign appeared. The state of her birth, though she wasn't going to be anywhere close to her family in LA. She hadn't even told her mom she was making the trip. She'd only worry. Besides, just hearing the name, Dalton, made Sarah Benjamin sad. Breanna was surprised she got to keep her dad's name.

Bad blood between her mother and her late father's family. Namely, her grandmother, Valerie Dalton, whom Breanna had never even met. She'd never met Shane Dalton either—not that she could remember anyway. He died when she was just a baby.

So when she received an official-looking letter from St. John, Maynard & St. John, Attorneys at Law, requesting her presence at Dalton House, on her grandmother's behalf, Breanna's curiosity was piqued. What did Valerie Dalton want? She doubted it was a desire to meet her son's only child after twenty-one years. But it could be, right? The woman had to be in her seventies now. Maybe she'd had a sudden change of heart in her old age.

Yeah, and maybe shit doesn't stink.

The correspondence, signed by one Derek St. John, didn't say much. No clue as to why she was being summoned. He only stated he was following the wishes of his client and advised Breanna to make arrangements to get there prior to the Thanksgiving holiday—and before the arrival of winter weather in the Sierra Nevada. Mountain roads can be treacherous when the snow comes.

Did he think she was an idiot?

Just because she was a California girl didn't mean she'd never driven in snow before.

After marinating on it for a week, she left word with the lawyer's secretary, letting him know when to expect her. The week of Thanksgiving break would have to do, and too bad if Derek St. John or her grandmother didn't like it. Breanna had friends to see, parties and classes to go to. Okay, she was on the flexible undergrad track for her BA in English. She could log in on her laptop, comfy in her pajamas, from the sofa in her apartment for most of her classes—or from anywhere for that matter, but the old lady didn't need to know that.

Her gaze flicked over to the snowcapped range of peaks to the east. Overcast, the midday sky looked dreary, but the clouds weren't ominous. *Yet.* She'd be fine. But Breanna still had five hundred miles, some seven hours of driving left before she reached her destination, and her ass was already numb.

A hundred and forty miles later, her bottom screaming at her to get up and stretch, gas gauge down to a quarter tank, she got off the highway. Refuel. Restroom. Coffee. There was no time to waste if she wanted to reach Dalton House before dark. Estimating she'd only need to make one more stop after this one, Breanna stood in line, Styrofoam cup in hand, rubbing circulation into her aching backside with the other. As long as the weather held, and barring any unforeseen hazards on the road, she should be good.

Her ass protesting once more, she sat back down behind the wheel, burning her tongue on the steaming hot battery acid that passed for gas station coffee. *Yuck.* Breanna grimaced into the cup, her phone vibrating on the center console.

"Hey, Kay," she answered.

"Just checking on you. You there yet?"

Kayleigh, her closest friend at college, and her roommate, was a worrywart. An old mother hen in a twenty-year-old body. She was the girl who forbade the consumption of jungle juice at parties—especially those held on Greek Row—cockblocked the fuckboys, and forced her to eat something besides cheap ramen noodles for dinner. And Breanna loved her for it. God only knows just how many bad decisions she'd saved her from.

"Hell, no." She expelled some air, tipping her head back against the seat. "Just made it to 395."

"You're not being safe." Breanna could just picture Kayleigh shaking her head. "You should stop. Get a room and rest for the night."

"No, I'll be fine," she assured her. "It's only a few more hours."

"Stubborn." Kayleigh could be heard sighing through the phone. "Have you even bothered checking the weather, Bree? They're predicting—"

"Snow. I know." Swallowing a sip of the putrid battery acid, she glanced up at the sky. "I'll be there long before it gets here, so don't worry, okay?"

"Yeah, I bet that's what the Donner Party said too, and look what happened to them."

"So dramatic," Breanna said, chuckling. "I think it's pretty safe to assume no one's going to be eating me—dead or alive."

Kayleigh giggled. "Well, should that lawyer guy or Grandmama serve fava beans and a nice chianti at dinner. Run. Fast."

"Will do." And she started her car. "I'll text you when I get there."

The cloud cover grew more dense the farther she drove. No longer merely overcast, the sky appeared heavy, saturated in a deepening gray. Breanna wasn't too concerned, though. According to the GPS, Dalton House was less than an hour away.

Like a good, obedient girl, she exited off the highway when the robotic British male voice instructed her to. She preferred him to the Siri-sounding woman. A checkpoint was set up on the road in front of a mom-and-pop store. Coming to a stop, Breanna lowered the window.

"Evening, miss."

She tipped her chin. "Hello."

"You're gonna need to get chains on those tires before I can let you through. We're expecting a doozy of a storm. Can't have you getting stuck out there on the pass."

"But—" *It's not even snowing yet.*

"Sorry, miss." He pointed toward the little store. "Hank's got 'em if you're needing some. Seventy-five bucks and he'll put 'em on for you too. Have you back on the road in a jiffy."

"Okay, thanks," Breanna assented, raising the window. "This is some bullshit. Hank must be raking it in."

Figuring she might as well top off her tank before heading inside the store, Breanna pulled up to the gas pump. A cold gust slapped her face as she exited the car, causing her to clench the unzipped jacket tightly around her middle. Trees danced on either side of the road, their naked branches bending to the will of the wind in the thickening darkness. Gazing heavenward, the slate-gray altostratus ominously churned.

Triggered by a familiar tickle in her nose, she sniffed the air. The scent of an approaching storm mingled with sweet benzene. Breanna zipped her worn, black leather bomber, and winding a scarf around her neck, made her way across the small parking lot. Bells attached to the door clanked into the glass as she wrestled with it, a sudden squall pushing her inside.

It was as if time had forgotten this place. To her left was a small diner with a checkered floor, red vinyl seats, and an old-fashioned soda fountain. To her right, a counter with rows of penny candy—cost twenty times that now—and a cash register. In front of her were several aisles of grocery essentials and sundries.

A balding head popped up from behind the counter. "Need something, miss?"

"Yes. Yes, I do. Chains." Behind her, the door burst open again. Breanna shivered, tingles creeping down her spine. "The officer at the checkpoint told me to see Hank."

"That's me." Pointing a thumb backward at his chest, he cracked a crooked grin, revealing a crooked front tooth. "I'm Hank."

"Can you put them on for me?"

"Be happy to." His head bobbed. "Where's your car?"

"Right outside," she said, handing him her keys. "The white Miata."

Breanna heard a snicker at her back. A voice, rich and deep, muttered low, "Figures. Damn girly car."

She whirled around to find six feet of rugged man standing behind her. Bearded. Suede coat lined with sheepskin. A black Stetson on his head. Dark hair brushed his shoulders. Eyes the color of whiskey. "Yeah, well, I *am* a girl."

"I can see that." Smirking, he dropped his head to the side and winked.

Probably drives one of those big-ass pickup trucks to compensate for having a puny dick.

Flustered by the stranger's boldness, Breanna turned back to Hank. "How long will it take?"

"Not too long," he assured her. The crooked grin fixed to his face, he bobbed his head to the left. "Why don't you get yourself a cup of coffee while you wait? Have a piece of banana cream pie. My wife makes it. Best damn pie in the world, trust me."

"Can't pass that up, now can I?" She smiled at Hank, side-eyeing the tall, dark, imposing stranger. Brushing past him, Breanna took a seat on a vinyl-covered stool at the end of the counter.

Sweet on her tongue, she licked thick, whipped cream from her lips. Hank did not exaggerate. The pie was chef's kiss, the coffee sublime, especially after the gas station sludge she'd been existing off of.

Rubbing his hands together, cheeks reddened, Hank came behind the counter as she washed down the last of her pie with a sip of coffee. "You're all set, miss."

"Great, thanks." Breanna handed him her credit card.

He just held it in his hand, staring at it. "Dalton, huh. You any relation to Valerie?"

"Yeah, she's my grandmother, why? You know her?"

Tucking his tongue into the corner of his lip, Hank nodded. "Well, I'll be goddamned. I had no idea. You have to be Shane's girl then."

"That's right."

Brows cinching together, his eyes flicked to the windows behind her. "It's startin'. Best get you on your way."

The bold one sat in a booth. Hat on the table, a mug of coffee poised at his mouth, he shook his head. "Suicide. Chains or no chains, she's gonna slide right off the mountain in that thing."

Standing from the stool, Breanna sniggered. "It's just a few snowflakes."

Slowly, he swiped his tongue across his lip and grinned.

"And every storm starts with just one."

Cast of Characters

In alphabetical order by first name

Ada Blythe—Jeremy's mother

Aggie—owner of gift shop on Maple Street

Alicia "Allie" Robertson—older sister to Bo

Angelica—vamp (blood fetish) girl at masquerade ball (also appears in Don't Speak)

Anna—Kodiak's client

Anthony Rossi Sr.—husband to Rosemary, father to Tony, Nick, Matteo, Gina, and Luca. Owner of Rossi's Pizzeria & Italian Bakery

Anthony Rossi III—eldest child of Tony Jr. and Lina

Ashton Michael Thomas Kerrigan Nolan—youngest child and son of Chloe, Jesse, and Taylor

Austin—boy at camp

Ava Liane Harris Robertson—wife to Bo, elementary school teacher

Axel—head of security for the Red Door

Barbara "Babs"—Kodiak's therapist in California

Bea—hospice social worker

Becky Brinderman—Taylor's date to senior prom

Bernie—Kodiak's Bernedoodle

Bethany—former high school sweetheart to Jesse

Elizabeth "Betsy" Bennett—mother to Michael, grandmother to Chloe

Billings—Kyan's friend from high school, now with the state attorney's office

Robert "Bo" Robertson Jr.—drummer of Venery, husband to Ava (also appears in Don't Speak)

Brandy Sullivan—Kodiak's mother

Brendan James Murray—eldest of the Byrne cousins, runs the Red Door/CPA, husband to Katie

Brigitta Thurner—wife/submissive to Hans, hostess at Red Door

Brittany McCall—high school classmate of Chloe, former fiancée to Danny

Cameron Mayhew—Katie's college classmate/former boyfriend

Casey—boy at camp

Catherine Lucille Martin (deceased)—grandmother to Linnea

Chandan William Arthur Kerrigan Nolan—eldest child and son of Chloe, Jesse, and Taylor

Charles Alexander "Xander" Byrne—son of Dillon and Linnea, twin to Madison, brother to Charlotte

Charles Dillon Byrne—brother to Kyan, cousin to Brendan and Jesse, second husband to Linnea

Charles Patrick Byrne (deceased)—father to Dillon and Kyan, uncle to Brendan and Jesse

Charlotte Kyann Byrne—daughter of Kyan (deceased) and Linnea, sister to Xander and Madison

Chester—Bo's Australian Shepherd

Chloe Elizabeth Bennett Kerrigan Nolan—wife to Jesse and Taylor

Colleen Byrne Nolan O'Malley—mother to Jesse, sister to Charley and Mo, aunt to Brendan, Dillon and Kyan, second wife to Tadhg

Connie "Cici"—Shelley's next-door neighbor

Courtney—Kit's ex-wife

Curtis "CJ" James—Venery's (former) manager

Cynthia Robertson—mother to Bo

Danielle Peters—photographer, wife to Monica

Danny Damiani—Chloe's high school classmate and former boyfriend

Declan Byrne (deceased)—father to Charley, Mo & Colleen, grandfather to Brendan, Dillon, Jesse, and Kyan

Declan James Murray—son of Brendan and Katie

Andrew "Drew" Copeland—Katie's dad

Ed—Bo's driver on tour

Elliott Peters—son of Danielle and Monica

Ellen McCready (deceased)—Matt's grandmother

Emery Sage Robertson—daughter of Shelley Tompkins (deceased) and Bo, sister to Kai

Eric Brantley (deceased)—son to Hugh Brantley

Erin McCready (deceased)—Matt's mother

Gillian—former bartender at the Red Door

Gina Rossi—labor and delivery nurse, family owns Rossi's Pizza & Italian Bakery

Grace Martin (deceased)—mother to Linnea

Hailey—girl at warehouse accident

Hans Thurner—husband/Dominant to Brigitta, host/manager at Red Door

Hazel—Tommy's mother, waitress at diner in Crossfield

Hugh Brantley—real estate investor

Ireland Aislinn Kerrigan Nolan—2nd eldest child and daughter of Chloe, Jesse, and Taylor

James Murray (deceased)—father to Brendan, uncle to Dillon, Jesse, and Kyan

Pastor Jarrid Black (deceased)—father to Seth and Linnea

Jason—kitchen boy at Charley's

Jeffrey—boy at camp

Jenkins—construction/warehouse project manager

Jeremy Blythe—Ada's son, Jarrid's right hand in Crossfield

Jesse Thomas Nolan—cousin to Brendan, Dillon, and Kyan, husband to Chloe and Taylor

Jimmy Tascadero—friend of Bo's at age 14

Jonathan Reynolds (deceased)—childhood best friend to Seth

Jonathan "Kade" Black—son of Kodiak and Kelly

Kai Forrest Robertson—son of Bo and Ava, brother to Emery

Kara Matthews—third eldest sister to Kelly, aunt to Katie and Kevin

Katelyn "Katie" Copeland Murray—wife to Brendan, niece to Kelly, sister to Kevin, barista at Sugar Beanie's/college student

Kelly Matthews Black—wife to Kodiak, aunt to Katie and Kevin, owner of Sugar Beanie's

Kelsey Miller—girlfriend (former) to Dillon

Kevin Copeland—younger brother to Katie, nephew to Kelly

Kim Matthews—second eldest sister to Kelly, aunt to Katie and Kevin

Christopher "Kit" King—bassist of Venery

Seth "Kodiak" Black—son of Jarrid, half-brother to Linnea, husband to Kelly

Kristie Matthews Copeland—mother to Katie and Kevin, eldest sister to Kelly

Kyan Patrick Byrne (deceased)—brother to Dillon, first husband to Linnea, father to Charlotte, cousin to Brendan and Jesse

Kyle Donovan—Kelly's date to senior prom

Leah Brianne Murray—daughter of Brendan and Katie

Leena Patel Kerrigan—mother to Taylor

Leonardo "Leo" Hill—baker/co-owner of Sugar Beanie's

Paulina "Lina" Rossi—wife to Tony Rossi Jr.

Linnea Grace Martin Byrne—half-sister to Kodiak Black, widow to Kyan, wife to Dillon

Logan—nephew to Bo

Lon—Venery's driver on tour

London Elizabeth Kerrigan Nolan—third child and daughter of Chloe, Jesse, and Taylor

Luca Rossi—youngest Rossi brother, family owns Rossi's Pizza & Italian Bakery

Lucifer—friend of Brendan's, devil-masked member at the Red Door

Lyla Rose Rossi—infant daughter of Tony Jr. and Lina

Madison Margaret Grace Byrne—daughter of Dillon and Linnea, twin to Xander, sister to Charlotte

Mallory Rossi—daughter of Tony Jr. and Lina

Marcus—manager at Charley's

Mark McCready (deceased)—Matt's uncle, a firefighter killed in the line of duty

Matthew "Matt" McCready—rhythm guitarist of Venery

Michael Bennett—father to Chloe

Milo Veronin—Angelica's partner (also appears in Don't Speak)

Mitch Rollins—State Senator, member of the Red Door

Monica Peters—clinical psychologist, wife to Danielle

Margaret "Peggy" Byrne (deceased)—mother to Dillon and Kyan, aunt to Brendan and Jesse

Maureen "Mo" Byrne Murray (deceased)—mother to Brendan, sister to Charley and Colleen, aunt to Dillon, Jesse, and Kyan

Meaghan O'Malley (deceased)—first wife to Tadhg O'Malley

Murphy—Brendan's childhood friend, detective with the police department

Nick Rossi—second eldest Rossi brother, former classmate of Jesse, family owns Rossi's Pizza & Italian Bakery

Nina Rossi—daughter of Tony Jr. and Lina

Paul—rigger on Venery's tour

Payton Brantley—son to Eric and grandson to Hugh Brantley

Perry Harris—older brother to Ava, Minor League baseball player

Phil Beecham—Brendan's attorney

Rachel—girl at camp

Reverend "Daddy" John—camp director

Robert Robertson Sr.—father to Bo

Roberta Torres—obstetrician

Roman—Jesse's Bernese mountain dog

Rosemary Rossi—wife to Anthony Sr., mother to Tony, Nick, Matteo, Gina, and Luca. Owner of Rossi's Pizzeria & Italian Bakery

Rourke—alias of arrested priest and former Red Door member

Roy Francis Martin (deceased)—grandfather to Linnea

Ryan Sr.—husband to Allie, brother-in-law to Bo

Ryan Jr.—nephew to Bo

Salina Dara (deceased)—former hostess at the Red Door

Sara Malinowski Rossi—wife to Nick Rossi

Savannah Mason—college student from Denver, server at the Red Door (also appears in The Third Son)

Sean O'Malley—brother to Tadhg O'Malley, stepfather to Siona Dawson

Shelley Tompkins (deceased)—mother to Emery, groupie who instigated "baby mama drama"

Siona Dawson (pronounced Show-na)—receptionist at O'Malley Ink Emporium, step-niece to Tadhg O'Malley

Sloan Michaels—lead vocalist/lyricist of Venery

Stacy—former girlfriend to Kelly Matthews

Tadhg O'Malley (pronounced Tige)—Colleen's 2nd husband

Tammy—hospice nurse

Taylor Chandan Kerrigan—husband to Chloe and Jesse, lead guitarist of Venery

Matteo "Teo" Rossi—third eldest Rossi brother, family owns Rossi's Pizza & Italian Bakery

Thomas Nolan (deceased)—father to Jesse

Timo—Chloe's Bernese mountain dog (Roman's son)

Tommy—classmate of Linnea's, cook at diner in Crossfield

Anthony "Tony" Rossi—eldest Rossi Brother, classmate of Brendan and the Venery boys, family owns Rossi's Pizza & Italian Bakery

Vanessa Parisi—Journalist with Revolver

Vinny Passarelli—Gina's ex-boyfriend

William Arthur Kerrigan—father to Taylor